MW00941235

MIDNIGHT BLUES

BOOK FOUR
THE GABE MCKENNA SERIES

ROBERT D. KIDERA

SUSPENSE PUBLISHING

MIDNIGHT BLUES
By
Robert D. Kidera

PAPERBACK EDITION
* * * * *
PUBLISHED BY:
Suspense Publishing

PUBLISHING HISTORY:
Suspense Publishing, Paperback and Digital Copy, October 2018

Cover Design: Shannon Raab
Cover Photographer: iStockphoto.com/Tryaging
Cover Photographer: Shutter Stock/Dmitri Ma

ISBN-13: 978-1723845062

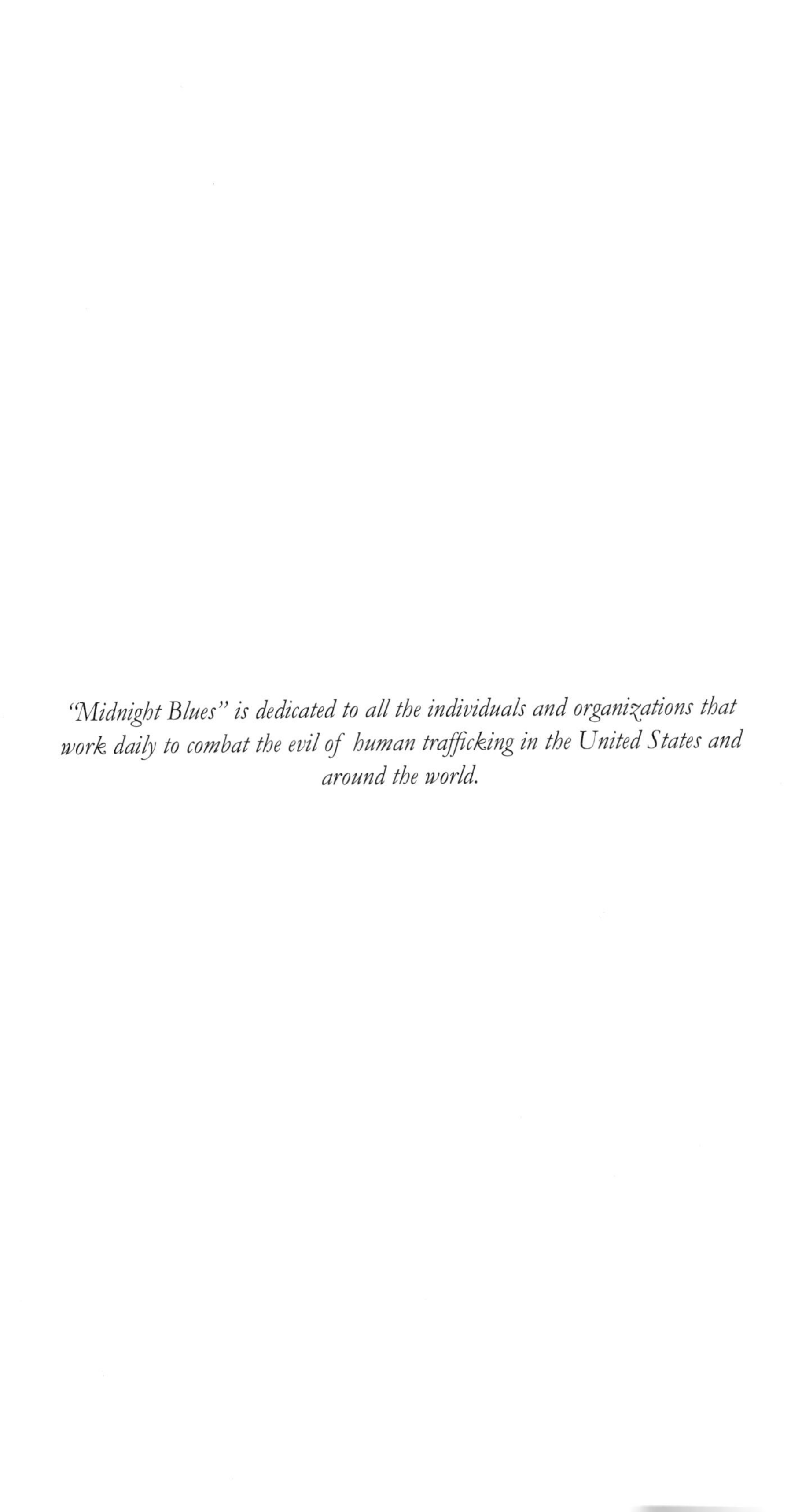

"Midnight Blues" is dedicated to all the individuals and organizations that work daily to combat the evil of human trafficking in the United States and around the world.

ACKNOWLEDGMENTS

To Annette Galvano, my wonderful wife, for her steadfast support and encouragement over all these years. She is my co-author in every sense and challenges me to hold myself and my writing to a higher standard.

To Susan Wrona Gall, my partner in crime and critique. Her generous gifts of time, her honest evaluation of my writing, and her many helpful suggestions are a constant source of inspiration.

Thank you, thank you, thank you.

PRAISE FOR THE *GABE MCKENNA* SERIES

" 'Midnight Blues' takes its readers on a remarkable journey filled with chilling evil, fiery valor, and heart-racing suspense. Author Robert Kidera writes with energy, passion and a beautiful appreciation for the power of language. At the end—which came too soon—I felt as though I had been holding my breath on a rollercoaster. Well done and highly recommended."

—**Anne Hillerman**, Author of the *Leaphorn, Chee, Manuelito Mysteries*

" 'Midnight Blues' grabs you by the collar in the first few sentences, and tosses you head first into Robert Kidera's wildest caper yet. The varied and distinctive characters who accompany protagonist Gabe McKenna on this trip are unforgettable. The dizzying pace will keep you turning pages into the wee hours."

—**Patricia Smith Wood**, Award-winning Author of the Albuquerque Based *Harrie McKinsey Mystery* Series

" 'Midnight Blues' is Robert Kidera's best *Gabe McKenna Mystery* to date. A page turner, as readers have come to expect from Kidera, it is also a sobering exploration of evil and the dangers of becoming infected by its methods. Thought provoking entertainment."

—**Dodici Azpadu**, Author of "Traces of a Woman"

"Kidera's characters and plot are constantly on the move. Talk about real suspense...just when you think you can take a minute to catch your breath, this book steals your breath away once more!"

—**Amy Lignor**, Author of the *Tallent & Lowery* Series

" 'Cut.Print.Kill.,' Robert Kidera's third *Gabe McKenna* novel is tight, smart, lightning fast-paced and filled with surprises. Hard to believe that Kidera could top the first two books in the series, including the Tony Hillerman award-winning 'Red Gold,' but he has!"

—**Paul D. Marks**, Shamus Award-winning Author of "White Heat"

"Robert Kidera mixes in a dash of Elmore Leonard with a pinch of Tony Hillerman and cooks up 'Get Lost,' an indulging, classy whodunit featuring an engaging cast of characters you'll look forward to visiting with again in future *Gabe McKenna* novels."

—**Alan Jacobson**, National Best-Selling Author of the FBI Profiler *Karen Vail* Series

"Robert Kidera is an absolute master of mystery! He grabs you with irresistible intrigue and fresh, seductive writing and refuses to let go while he pummels you with twist after delicious twist. I highly recommend this book and this writer!"

—**Darynda Jones**, *New York Times* Best-Selling Author

"The spirit of Raymond Chandler hovers over Robert D. Kidera's mystery writing. His gift for telling atmosphere and sharp dialogue and his continually surprising plotting make him an effortlessly skillful storyteller. His flawed but noble protagonist, Gabe McKenna, is a worthy modern successor to Chander's Philip Marlowe."

—**Joseph McBride**, Biographer of Frank Capra, John Ford, and Steven Spielberg

MIDNIGHT BLUES

ROBERT D. KIDERA

CHAPTER ONE

October 28th

What kind of person would harm a child? I gnawed on that question all one-hundred and thirty-eight miles on the interstate from Albuquerque to the edge of Gallup, New Mexico. A headache climbed aboard at milepost forty-two.

Deke Gagnon, my P.I. partner and a guy known as 'Onion' since our childhood days, squirmed in the passenger seat of my Land Cruiser. "Gabe, do we have to do this *tonight*?"

"Kidnappers don't wait."

"Maybe, but three a.m. and me have never been friends." A litany of his groans and carefully crafted grimaces filled the car.

Onion's not really that bad. In his own words, he's a man of many interests. Booze. Broads. Burgers.

He grabbed a flashlight out of the glove compartment, took the batteries out of its casing, put them back in, clicked it on and off, on and off. Then he leaned back in his seat.

A silent breeze blew sand and dust against our windshield. I turned on the washer and wipers to improve my view. No cars on the road, no stars in the sky, and nobody else around.

I crossed Old Route 66 in downtown Gallup and turned onto Vega Place. With half the streetlights burned out, and a cloud-covered, moonless sky above, we crept along at five miles per hour, straining to read the house numbers on a row of tired bungalows. No easy task on a night this dark.

New Mexico's newest private investigators, we were out on our first case—a frightened mother's phone call about her missing son.

Onion exhaled, his breath clouding the inside of my van. "You *sure* this is the right street?"

"Five-Twenty Vega. That's the address Estrella gave me."

"She cough up anything else?"

"Not much. Tears got in her way."

Onion rolled his window down and aimed the flashlight beam onto a dilapidated front porch. "That's it."

I eased into the driveway and cut the headlights. "Let's go."

We took some hesitant steps toward the front of the weathered cottage. Trumpet vines at the porch corners ran wild, engulfing the wooden posts. Their dragon-claw tentacles reached out, brushing my cheek, sap-sticky on my skin.

We climbed the steps and stood shoulder-to-shoulder before a wooden door that could have used paint. It had a circular etched-glass window and a rusted mail slot, like the front door in my childhood home. I nudged Onion aside. "Let me take the lead on this."

"Gabe, you're forgetting I'm the experienced P.I. here."

I sucked in a breath deep enough to hurt. "You didn't hear what I heard—a mother with her heart ripped out." I rang the doorbell and stepped back.

Nothing happened.

I rang again, and then a third time. Something clattered inside. The porch light flickered on. The door opened an inch, stuck for a moment, and then jolted open all the way with a high-pitched squeal.

"He's gone." Estrella Chissie's face showed pain times ten; her eyes were still small, lifeless and lost. But she'd had her broken tooth fixed, and her lips weren't battered blue as they were the first time we'd met.

I gave her my gentlest middle-of-the-night-tough-guy smile. "Hello, Estrella. We came as soon as you called. How can we help?"

She raised her hand like she was lifting an anchor. Then her body trembled, her eyes rolled out of sight behind her eyebrows, and she nosedived toward the floor. I caught her by one shoulder. She weighed less than my last dog.

"Lemme give you a hand." Onion grabbed Estrella's other shoulder and together we dragged her inside to a dimly-lit living room and laid her on an old brocade couch by the front window.

A second woman, no more than four-and-a-half feet tall, all curly brown hair and tan skin, burst into the room. "Estrella?" I heard a slight Hispanic accent, even in that single word.

I pointed to the front door. "She collapsed. We brought her inside."

"Thank you, señor." She knelt and stroked Estrella's cheeks. "It's all right, dear."

Onion and I stood there, fifth and sixth wheels, surrounded by a traffic jam of mismatched furniture that overwhelmed the room. The curtains were drawn, a single overhead light fought the darkness. The whole place smelled like a tomb.

Estrella gurgled, her shoulders shook. One at a time her eyes opened, and she blinked her way back to us. "I am sorry. I do not know what happened."

"Stay there, dear. Let me get you some water." The short woman glanced over her shoulder like she noticed me for the first time.

"I'm sorry. My name is Gabe McKenna. Perhaps Estrella's mentioned me. I helped her out of a jam a couple of months back. She called me earlier this evening."

"No..."

I looked to Onion for some guidance. He rubbed his nose. He checked the ceiling light. He shrugged. *Thanks, pal.*

Estrella motioned to me. I knelt next to her. She spoke in a whisper. "I'll be okay in a few minutes." She coughed some color into her cheeks. "Thank you for coming. Could you help me up?"

Onion and I propped her on the couch, then backed off and gave her space for the pain.

She pointed at the woman who'd returned and now stood across the room, a glass of water in her hand. "This is Luna. My sister-in-law. She lives with us." Estrella's shoulders slumped, like even that little effort had exhausted her. But she did accept the water from Luna and took a sip.

"Care for some coffee?" Luna looked my way and then at Onion.

We answered in unison. "Please."

"Is instant okay? It is all we have."

"That's fine." It had already been a long night and I had a three-hour drive back to Albuquerque ahead of me.

Luna smoothed her apron and flashed us our first smile of the night. She turned and scuttled down the hall with the quick, rocking gait of a small dog.

Estrella's hands never stopped clasping and grasping each other, like she was trying to wash off some stubborn stain. She draped herself at an angle across the couch. Bits of stuffing peeked out next to her knee. The sofa's dull, green fabric had worn away. An exposed spring nearly reached the floor beneath the nearest cushion.

She swallowed a couple of deep breaths and closed her eyes before speaking again. "He's gone…" Her voice was as quiet as an empty church, yet it held a startling note of acceptance I wasn't expecting.

"Tell us what happened. Why you called me. Leave nothing out." I looked at Onion. He had his spiral notebook and pencil in hand.

"Jay-Jay—"

"Your son, right?" I nodded to prod her along.

"Yes. Most people call him Jamie. I call him Jay-Jay. He's seven." She trembled and leaned forward. "Luna sent him to the pharmacy to pick up my medicine."

I nodded. "When was this?"

"Yesterday afternoon. An hour went by. I became worried. He's a good boy, you see. Then I get a phone call at three o'clock."

"A call from whom?"

She shrugged.

"Man or woman's voice?" I watched her eyes. The truth is in the eyes.

"A man. Mexican accent. Northern Mexico, *Norteño*. I know people from there. How they speak."

"What did this man say, exactly?"

"He has Jay-Jay. He wants money." She shifted around on the couch, the moisture in her eyes reflecting the overhead light. "Señor, I don't have any money. He demands ten thousand dollars." She stuck a finger under her glasses and wiped at the tears. "If I don't pay, he say I never see Jay-Jay again."

Onion scratched at his jaw. "Why would this man expect you to have that kind of dough?"

"I do not know, sir." She stared at the ceiling, watery eyes unblinking. Waiting.

I sat next to her on the couch. "Did you recognize this man's voice? Had you ever heard it before?"

She looked away. "No."

"Did he give you a deadline to come up with the money?"

"Twenty-four hours. He say twenty-four hours. By tonight."

She was staring at a clock above the fireplace when Luna returned with two cups of coffee, each set on a thin china plate. She served us like she'd apprenticed at a diner or two somewhere along the line.

The brew was too hot to drink right away. I rested my cup on a small table to my left. Onion placed his on the mantle.

The sister-in-law gasped. "Goodness sakes let me get you something for that." She hustled off toward the kitchen. I studied the silent, listless Estrella until Luna came back with a tan wooden folding table for Onion's cup. "There."

"Thank you, ma'am." A couple of weeks out west and he'd picked up a twang.

The coffee smelled like burned rubber, but I sipped at it anyway. "Okay, Estrella. You didn't recognize the man's voice. He gave you twenty-four hours to come up with ten grand. Did he say where to meet him?"

"I write this down. *Permiso por favor.*" She reached inside her shirtsleeve and pulled out a crumpled piece of paper, then read it in a soft monotone, "I must bring the money to Red Rock State Park at nine o'clock—that would be tonight. Thursday. Take the Church Rock Trail to a sandstone wall. The wall with foothold grooves in it. He say meet at the base of that wall and give him the money for Jay-Jay." She handed me her note.

Onion slipped his pencil into a shirt pocket. "So, you're supposed to meet up with a kidnapper in a remote area late at night?" He shook his head with some force. "Don't like it at all. More likely he'll kidnap *you* too."

I rubbed my forehead. The headache didn't budge. "I'm afraid he's right, Estrella. It's a sucker bet. I'm familiar with that area from my archeology days. Been there, though not since they made the improvements to the park. Let me check something." I pulled out my phone and Googled Red Rock State Park. "The park closes each weeknight at eight. How are you supposed to meet him at nine?"

"You're being lured, ma'am." Onion closed his notebook. "If all he wanted was money, there are much easier ways to get it."

Estrella's eyes glowed with a sudden fire. "I no care. I want my son back. I do whatever he say. I no care what happens to me." Luna sat at Estrella's side and wrapped an arm around her. She mewed and cooed. Estrella whimpered. Neither of them spoke.

Onion shrugged and put his coffee cup back on the serving table in front of him. He gave me a slight nod, like the next line was mine.

"Excuse us for a few minutes, would you? I need to speak with my partner." I motioned toward the door and Onion followed me outside. The porch light was still on. A couple of moths danced about our heads. A cricket chirped a sad lament from somewhere under the porch.

I pointed back toward the house. "What do you think?"

"The lady's holding back."

"She knows the man who called her."

Onion grunted in agreement. "Where's the husband?"

"I don't know. But I have an idea how we might find out. Police department back in Grants. That's where I took Estrella and her kid when I found them in the desert two months ago. Told the cops then I'd be glad to come back and make a statement, but they never asked for one. They must have tried to contact her old man."

"You think he could be involved in this?"

"I think I want to learn more about the guy." I stepped over to the front porch railing and looked at the sky. The clouds had blown away, along with any chance of rain. "What time you got?"

Onion still used the pocket watch his dad gave him at our high school graduation. "Three-thirty-two."

"Doesn't give us much time. Let me see that notebook for a second." He handed it to me. I scanned it and put a couple of thoughts together. "I have an idea. Back inside."

CHAPTER TWO

Estrella and Luna had taken places on either end of the couch by the time Onion and I walked back into the living room. Luna stood and picked up our coffee cups. "Would you like a refill?"

Onion cut me off. "No thanks, ma'am."

"None for me, either," I said. "Estrella, here's our plan. Onion and I will go with you to Red Rock. One of us will walk beside you, the other will follow behind, but off the trail, out of sight. For your protection you understand, just in case anything goes wrong."

"But the money—"

"We'll bring the money." I ignored a quiet choking sound from Onion. "But there's more going on here than you've told us, isn't there?"

Estrella drew back from my words and looked away. She didn't answer.

"You can't hold anything back and expect us to be able to help you."

"Señor McKenna—" Whatever she was about to say next didn't make it past her teeth.

Onion tried to open her up. "You sure he said ten thousand? Cash?"

"Yes. I have four hundred dollars in the bank. I can give you that much."

I waved away her offer. "Keep it. Think of this as a loan. When we catch this guy, we'll get it back." Onion's jaw had dropped so far, I thought he'd need both hands to lift it back in place. I silenced him with a shake of my head.

Estrella hesitated. "*Dios mío.* If you really want to. Thank you, señor. I swear you get every penny back. And your fee, of course. How much will that be?"

"We'll talk about that afterward. Right now, I want you to get some sleep. Onion and I will come back here this evening at six. Be ready. And dress warm, it gets pretty cold out at Red Rock. Pack some water. Hopefully by nine o'clock tonight, you and Jay-Jay will be together."

Her eyes lit at my suggestion. "How can I ever thank you?"

I raised a dismissive hand. "If you hear from the kidnapper between now and tonight at six, call us right away. You still have my card?"

She pointed above the fireplace. "On the mantel."

I studied her eyes once more. "Is there anything else you want to tell us? Anything?"

Color flooded her cheeks. She seemed to waver, then caught herself. "No, sir. I tell you everything I know."

I let her denial linger for a moment. "Then good night, Estrella." We exchanged an awkward hug.

Onion tipped the cowboy hat he wasn't wearing. "Ma'am."

The night felt darker now than when we'd arrived. I backed out of the driveway and headed for the interstate. I looked at my partner. "What's with all the *ma'am's*? You say it with your New York accent, you sound like the Midnight Cowboy."

Onion shrugged. "Trying to blend in, that's all. You got a problem with that?"

"No problem at all. What's your take on Estrella?"

He paused before speaking. "Not sure. I admit it. I'm more familiar with New Yorkers than the people out here. In the Big Apple, people are more up-front. Easier to read. Here though…tougher to get a handle on them. What is she? Navajo?"

No traffic coming toward us, so I turned on the high beams. "Couldn't say. She might be Apache. Mescalero. Chiricahua. From south of here. Her familiarity with the kidnapper's Northern Mexican accent makes me wonder."

"Does it really matter?"

I let that go. "We'll stop at Grants for some breakfast and so I can speak to the police. Find out what they know about Estrella's husband, okay?"

He stared out his window. Was that a quiet murmur of disapproval? It was. "Gabe—Ace—how the hell are we supposed to make money as P.I.'s with you risking ten grand on our first client? I hope you don't expect me to chip in. I'm living in Tap City."

"Keep your wallet closed. We'll do this on Tony Fredericks' dime."

"Fredericks? The producer of that movie you worked on? How does he figure?"

"Before he was killed, Fredericks sent me a check for fourteen thousand dollars, the amount I would have made if he hadn't shut down the film. Wrote me a note. Said he felt bad about all I'd gone through and wanted to help me out. There was a *thin* layer of decency to the man, hidden beneath his bullshit, bluster, and corruption."

"Yeah, Gabe, but ten grand—"

"Fredericks made most of that dough laundering drug cartel money. We may as well put it to good use."

"You got an actual plan for tonight?" He continued to look out his window.

"Sort of. First thing we do back in Albuquerque is call Sam Archuleta and pick his brain."

"A career cop? Trust me, he's gonna tell you to leave this one alone."

"Maybe, maybe not. Whatever he says, we're going to need climbing clothes, ropes, water, night vision goggles. And we'll go out to Red Rock Park fully armed."

Onion turned and framed the word 'NO' with his lips. "You know I swore off guns."

"I'll get you a knife."

He let out a long, slow breath. "Sometimes I can't figure you, Gabe."

"Too bad."

"You left four aces on the table."

"What are you talking about?" I checked the gas gauge. Quarter of a tank left.

"Back at our poker game. I saw the cards you dropped when Estrella called and asked us to drive the hell out here."

"We're private investigators, right? It's what we do."

"But four aces…you can't spit in the face of Lady Luck like that. She'll turn on you in a New York minute."

"So now you're an authority on luck? How many times you been married?"

"Three so far. Okay, I'll admit it, I've had significant difficulty with broads."

"Women."

"What?"

"The correct term is *women*."

"Yeah, right. You should talk. You haven't done much better, losing your wife to cancer, and then your girlfriend Nai'ya. And who's always been there for you?"

"You have. And I'm grateful." This was not the discussion I wanted to be having at four in the morning.

"But that *last* one you messed with. That actress…"

"Simone St. Cyr?"

"She had you by the—"

"Stop. She's the past. She's gone. And I turned against her, remember?"

"After she turned *you* into a pretzel. After all she did and all you missed—you're supposed to be a smart guy."

"Is that all?"

"No. The protection she got from the Feds to testify against that cartel—it pissed me off."

I slowed down. "Would you like to get out and walk?" I prefer to overcome my past mistakes by ignoring them.

"You need me to look out for you."

At times like this, there's only one way to change the drift of Onion's mouth. "What would you like for breakfast?"

He rested a hand on his stomach. "Anything that isn't moving."

My stomach was rumbling too. I pulled off at a truck stop west of Grants and we had a couple of cardiac-killer plates and black coffee. I topped off the Cruiser before driving to the police station on McBride Road. Almost six a.m. The day shift would soon be on.

I hadn't seen Cibola County Sheriff Stephen Velez in nearly two years. He looked pretty much the same, a bit more stoop-shouldered, a bit heavier, a few more wrinkles creasing his face. At least he still knew how to smile. "Professor McKenna, been a while. Listen, thanks for bringing in that woman and child two months ago. Sorry I missed you. My vacation."

"Yes. Estrella Chissie." I pointed toward Onion. "My associate from New York, Deke Gagnon. Can we talk somewhere?"

"Follow me, there's a break room down the hall. We can talk there." He opened a heavy metal door at the near end of the foyer and led the way. "You guys in some kind of business together?"

"Private detectives."

He tossed me one of those *you've-got-to-be-crazy* looks. "No shit? Haven't you seen enough suffering and pain by now?"

I returned a weak smile. "It's a living." We entered the break room—a couple of tables, four chairs per table, and dreary gray walls that might once have been white.

"Have a seat." Velez pointed to the metal folding chairs on the far side of the closest table. He sat across from us with the window at his back.

"We're on a case right now," I said. "We need anything you might have on the guy who beat up Ms. Chissie and her boy. By the time your men questioned them, I was back in Albuquerque. Never did get to hear the whole story."

"Sounds like what you're doing is a police matter, Professor."

"Estrella made it clear she wants private help. *Only*."

Onion nodded. "We need some background on the woman too, Officer."

Velez glanced at the ceiling before his eyes settled on us once more. "Why don't you ask her yourselves?"

I cut my friend off before he could crack wise. "We didn't want to dredge up bad memories. Thought maybe the police might have an informed opinion."

Velez sat back and folded his arms. "Or maybe you don't believe her story?"

I countered by placing both my hands on the table and leaning forward. "Sheriff Velez, we're trying to help a woman who came to us in trouble. We didn't come here to waste time or play games. Can you show us your file on Estrella Chissie? I'm assuming you questioned her and followed up on the matter. Did you ever track down her assailant?"

Velez's fingers *thunk-thunk-thunked* on the tabletop. He stood and walked over to a water cooler. It belched when he filled a paper cup and drank it down. He looked away and then straight at us. "What's the nature of this case you're working on?"

Onion cut me off. "The kid's disappeared. His mother asked us to look into it."

Velez checked his watch, sat back at the desk, and pressed a button on an outdated intercom. "Deputy Deleon, come to the break room. Bring the file on Estrella Chissie—that woman who was brought in beaten up seven, eight weeks ago. While I was away. Right, that one."

"Thank you, Sheriff."

His eyes narrowed. "I did read up on that case when I got back. I'm going the extra mile for you only because you're a friend of Sam Archuleta. Deleon conducted the investigation in my absence. He questioned the woman and her boy. Followed up to the extent our resources permitted. The case, such as it is, is still open."

Onion's eyebrows rose. "Her attacker is still at large?"

"I'll let Deleon fill you in." His mouth flashed a millisecond smile. The rest of his face froze. "If you'll excuse me." The office door opened, and Velez squeezed past an incoming deputy on his own way out.

"Victor Deleon." His handshake was firm enough and he looked at us in turn before sitting down. But he was younger than Velez. Smaller. Frail for a cop. His thin pencil mustache looked like it might have wandered onto his face in the middle of the night. He placed a yellow file folder on the table. "What is it you want to know?"

I reminded him I was the guy who'd found Estrella and her son and brought them to the hospital. I wasn't fishing for praise. I wasn't disappointed.

"My partner and I are P.I.'s from Albuquerque. We're here on a case that touches on the events covered in your file. We'd like to know what you can share from your investigation. It might help us in ours."

He eyed each of us in turn again, like the two of us overwhelmed him. "Very well. I was officer-in-charge. We questioned both Miss Chissie and her son—" he checked the top page of the report, "—James Jericho Chissie—the day after you brought them into the hospital. Neither was at all forthcoming, but we did uncover a couple of interesting details."

Onion popped out his note pad, "Such as…"

"She refused to press charges against the man who beat her."

I leaned forward again. "Did she at least identify him?"

"Yes, but only after a lot of coaxing. She gave us a name. Julio Cesar Cortana."

Onion looked up from his note-taking. "Cortana? With a C?"

The deputy nodded.

Onion took over. "Did you interview the woman we met at Miss Chissie's home in Gallup? First name Luna?"

Deleon closed the folder and pressed the fingertips of both hands together under his chin. "No. Her name never came up in our investigation."

I looked at my watch. "Anything else?"

"The name Cortana sounded familiar. We ran a search. The man has no criminal record. But there is a suspected operative in *Los Perros de la Muerte* with the same name. On the other hand, it *is* a common Hispanic surname. Might not be the same guy."

The hair on the back of my neck bristled when he mentioned the cartel that had recently moved into parts of New Mexico. I'd crossed swords with them only months before and barely escaped with my life. They knew me. They knew where I lived.

"Do you *think* it's the same guy?" I took in a long breath, held it, and leaned forward in my chair.

"We tried to press Estrella on that. She wouldn't budge. Clammed right up, wouldn't say a word. Draw your own conclusions."

I exhaled. "Is *Los Perros* active now in this area? Or in Gallup?"

"We haven't noticed anything recently."

"How hard have you tried?"

He glared at me as his voice rose. "I try to help you and you insult me. You insult the Cibola County Sheriff's office—men who once saved your life, as I recall. You think we have unlimited funds and manpower?"

"Okay, I'm sorry. Didn't mean it the way it sounded. You have my apology." I waited a beat until he leaned back. "I realize law enforcement budgets are tight." I looked at Onion. "But so are ours. Cooperation saves time and money."

"For your information, we *did* look into *Los Perros* and Cortana, and for a good while. As I said, we found nothing. And nobody came forward."

"You've noticed nothing that might be cartel-related?"

"No. Right now, our main focus is finding out why half a dozen young people have gone missing over the past month."

"Missing? From Grants?"

"One. The others were all from reservations and pueblos. Two Navajo, one Ramah Navajo, one from Acoma, and a Jicarilla Apache girl. Six, all told. Five female, one male. Most in their late teens or early twenties, but the missing boy is younger. Much younger."

Onion took this all down and closed his notebook. "Human trafficking?"

"It's a possibility. We've asked for help from the Feds. That takes time. We have our suspicions, but no hard evidence on which to proceed."

I stood. Onion took his cue and did the same. "Thank you, Deputy. Appreciate your help."

We shook hands. Onion and I found our way outside.

CHAPTER THREE

The sun glared over the Sandia Mountains and into my eyes on our approach to Albuquerque. We stopped at Charlie's Sporting Goods for a pair of used night vision goggles, an RF-V16 GPS tracker, and Micro SIM card. Onion added a case of bottled water and a large bag of trail mix. I visited my bank on Coors and noticed more than a few sideways glances when I asked to take out ten thousand dollars in fifties. We walked into our office at eleven-fifteen.

Onion recorded the serial numbers of all two hundred bills while I packed the Cruiser for our evening's assignment. Then I locked Onion's list in our safe and called Sam Archuleta, friend and retired APD Homicide Detective.

He sounded like he'd slept in. "What's up? Where'd you guys go after you left the poker game last night?"

"We're working. A missing child case in Gallup." I filled him in on the details. He already knew about Estrella and her son from my first encounter with them. I gave him the dope on this new crisis.

He grunted into the phone. "Don't swallow everything the lady tells you. She's probably too upset to be reliable. You touch base with law enforcement?"

"Spoke with your buddy Sheriff Velez and another deputy in Grants. We also checked the Cibola County police file from the time I brought Estrella and her son to the hospital. Officer Deleon is wondering if there might be a connection to a series of abductions over the past couple of weeks. All except one are reservation kids—mostly young adults."

"All these disappearances from the same area?"

"No, actually. The missing are from a bunch of different pueblos, the Navajo and Jicarilla reservations. And one local from Grants."

"That's bad."

"Of course it is."

"No. I mean if the abductions were from a smaller area, you'd probably be dealing with local crime. The statewide area suggests it could be cartel-related human trafficking. They're getting involved in New Mexico now."

My stomach objected to Sam's mention of the cartel. "We have to take that chance. Estrella's going to make the payoff tonight at Red Rock Park. Onion and I are going with her."

Sam groaned. "Don't do that, Gabe. Stay away from there. Too isolated. You'll be walking into a trap."

"We'll be armed."

"So will he, cowboy."

I plowed on. "Do me a favor? You still have your connections with the DEA Task Force?"

There was a pause. "I'm not currently working on anything for them, but yeah, what do you need?"

"Have them run a trace on a guy named Julio Cesar Cortana. Possible link to *Los Perros*."

"Them again."

"Yeah."

Five seconds passed. "Sam? You still there?"

"Put this one aside, Gabe."

"It's our first case."

"And you don't want it to be your last." He cleared his throat. "This woman—Estrella—how much do you know about her?"

"What I gathered from my earlier encounter with her, plus what we learned last night."

"You trust her enough to risk your lives on this?"

"Don't be melodramatic."

"Gabe, cases like this don't end well. Let me put it to you this way—you buy her story?"

Onion was trying on the night vision goggles. I walked away toward the window. "We don't think she's lying, but she hasn't told us everything, either."

"You sure this kid is actually missing?"

"Well..." I hesitated at the thought. "Now that you mention it, all we have to go on is her word. And her sister-in-law's."

"How does *she* figure into this?"

"Estrella's living at her sister-in-law's place in Gallup. Gal named Luna. She didn't give us her last name."

I heard the sound of a match being struck. "Gabe, maybe this thing isn't about her kid at all. Maybe it's about you."

"What the hell are you talking about?"

"If this has anything to do with *Los Perros*—"

"You're reaching."

"Listen to me. Cartels play for keeps. Sooner or later, they settle their scores. They remember you from that film work we did. They got you connected with Simone St. Cyr, with her son Tristan and the rest of the people on that movie."

I bit my lower lip. "Maybe."

"Yeah, and maybe you're a *loose end* to them."

I felt like a fighter being peppered with jabs by a quicker opponent. "To be honest, the thought did cross my mind. But I couldn't be that important to them."

"You don't have to be important. You just have to piss them off."

"Guess I qualify on that count." I checked the wall clock. "Okay. I'll be careful. Promise. But find out everything you can about Cortana through the DEA, okay? Onion and I will be in town for another hour. Then we're off to Gallup."

"Leave it alone, Gabe. I'm telling you..."

"What kind of private investigators only take risk-free cases?"

"Live ones."

I ignored that. "Call me on my cell if it's later than four-fifteen, okay? See ya."

Onion looked at me through the goggle lenses. "What did Sam say?"

I put the phone in my pocket, took the goggles from Onion, and fit them on my head. "He doesn't like it."

"Sam never likes anything. Shoulda retired sooner, if you ask me." He looked around the office and twitched. "So...how we gonna do this?"

"You walk with Estrella along Church Rock Trail while I flank you in the dark, maybe thirty feet off to the left, along the rock wall. I'll be armed and close enough to step in if the kidnapper tries anything."

"Might work." Onion hadn't oozed such enthusiasm since facing the broccoli and Brussel sprouts at our local Golden Corral.

I put the goggles down on the desk, then unlocked our filing cabinet and took out a leather gym bag that once belonged to my father. The zipper caught at first, so I added a drop of WD-40 to loosen it. "Hand me that tracker, will you?"

Onion brought the GPS device and SIM card over to the desk.

"Now the money."

"You sure about this?"

"I'm not running a charity here. The cops will need to know where the abductor is once we get the kid back." I took a pocket knife out of my drawer and made a two-inch-long slit in the bag's cardboard bottom. The RF-V16 fit snugly below it, with only a small bump visible. I pointed to the filing cabinet. "Third drawer down, there's a roll of double-sided tape."

Onion fished around for a bit, then came up with the tape and tossed it to me.

I cut a short section and placed it on the underside of the incision I'd already made in the bottom of the bag. "The device will record the bag's location every ten minutes. It kicks into sleep mode in between, so it's virtually undetectable."

"I know, Gabe. Used one of those back in Manhattan to trail a runaway husband. Damn thing was useless. The buildings blocked its signal."

I laughed. "You can count all the tall buildings at Red Rock Park while we're waiting to make the exchange."

"Those rock cliffs made of papier-mâché?"

He had a point. "Well...keep your fingers crossed." I didn't like the look I was getting. "Hey, it's better than doing nothing. Better than trying to follow them in the dark."

Onion scowled while we counted and banded ten packs of

fifty-dollar bills, twenty bills to a pack. Ten thousand dollars. My ten thousand dollars. The zipper shut without a snag.

I glanced at my friend who looked like he'd slept in his clothes. "You need to go home and get some sleep? Or change into something warmer?"

"Nah, I'll catch a quick nap here on the couch. Maybe go down the street later and grab a burger. Maybe two."

Onion's boots and brown flannel shirt were fine, but my loafers and dress pants needed to go. "I have to swing by my place. Change. Feed the cat. Where do you want to meet up?"

"I'll hang at Blake's. Should I get you something to go?"

"Okay. Lot-a-Burger, seasoned fries, large Coke. I'll pick you up at four." I checked the wall clock again. "Hour and a half."

CHAPTER FOUR

It's a five-minute drive from our office to my house in the North Valley. I left extra food and water for my cat, Otis, in case things became complicated. I changed into hiking boots, light-weight flannel and jeans, grabbed my .38 Detective Special from the library desk, loaded the chambers, and slipped a box of extra shells into a pocket of my leather jacket. The Land Cruiser was equipped with an emergency kit in the back, along with rope, a Coleman lantern and portable stove. We were good to go.

I found Onion sitting on a bench outside Blake's, chatting up a dark-haired twentyish woman in a short print mini-dress. Two youngsters clung to her legs. I pulled up alongside and rolled the window down. "Ready?"

He slipped the woman one of our business cards and hopped into the front seat. He raised a finger. "Before you ask, I was drumming up potential business. That poor lady has a world of troubles."

"Right."

The news of all the missing rez kids—and Sam's speculation—had me on edge. Around five-fifteen, Onion and I drove west past Laguna Pueblo. I almost turned off at the exit out of habit, wondering how my on-again/off-again daughter Angelina Turner—now going by her Native name, Payoqona—and her son Matty were doing. I'd stop in and visit them on my way back.

Orange-red sandstone of the Entrada Rock Formation shadowed us to the north. A couple of freight trains crawled along parallel to the highway; one heading east, one west. My stomach tightened the closer we came to Estrella's. Onion said nothing for the final hour of the drive.

We hit Gallup at five-fifty, missing what passes for rush hour. Ten degrees warmer than the Albuquerque we'd left behind, the temperature would drop twenty-five or thirty degrees after sunset.

Estrella's driveway was empty. The house looked as dark and uninviting as it had at three-thirty that morning.

Onion knocked twice. I called out. "Estrella? It's Gabe McKenna and Deke Gagnon. Open up."

The blinds on the far side of the door's etched-glass window parted a crack. A chain grated its way along the back of the door. A deadbolt clicked. The door screeched again as it opened. Estrella's face looked out at me, her eyes blinking against the light of the setting sun.

"Come in." She opened the door and stepped back.

"Be right with you." I turned to Onion and lowered my voice. "Wait here and keep an eye out. Just in case."

"Right."

Estrella was standing by her dining room table when I walked inside. She made a motion toward the couch. "Will you sit down?" She sagged into a nearby chair and leaned against its back. After inhaling a great, slow breath, she exhaled in a rush. Her hands fumbled with an apron covering her dingy, short-sleeved cotton dress.

I pointed to her bare arms. "You're going to need something warmer tonight."

"I will take a sweater." Her voice sounded like it came from another room.

I spread out a map of Red Rock Park on the ottoman between us, turning it around so she could read it. Her hands clasped the apron, twisting it so hard I expected to hear it scream.

"You sure you're up for this?" I waited for an answer.

Her back stiffened. A sudden spark of defiance flashed across her face. "I want my son back."

The clock on the living room mantle chimed six-fifteen. We

needed to hide inside Red Rock Park before the entrance gate closed at eight.

I patted down the edges of the map until it lay flat in front of her. "Our plan is to enter the park by seven-thirty and drive east along Church Rock Trail. That's here." I traced the route with my finger. "I've been to this place before. The roads might be a bit different now, but the rocks haven't moved."

My joke drifted right past her. She stared at the map in silence.

"Church Rock Trail is three or four miles long. We can drive most of it, but we'll have to get out and walk the last mile or so. You'll carry my gym bag with the money inside it. Onion will walk beside you to make sure you're safe. I'll follow off to the side. I'll be wearing night vision goggles and I'll be armed. Onion will help you make the exchange. Are you okay with that?"

She looked up at me, her lips drawn tight. She shook her head and then her finger. "The man told me to come alone."

"Onion won't interfere. He's just there to protect you. He's done this kind of thing lots of times before."

"Well…"

"We have to look out for your safety and that of your son."

Her shoulders rose and fell. "If you say so, señor."

"Just don't hand over the gym bag until Jay-Jay is safely in your hands. Then turn and walk away as fast as you can. Don't look back. Onion will hold his ground until you're a safe distance away. And I'll have you covered from my hiding place. Go straight back to my Cruiser."

Her eyes narrowed. "What if he doesn't let Jay-Jay go?"

"That's why you need us with you. To see that nothing does go wrong. I'll move in if he gives me a signal. Speak in a loud voice. That way I can hear what's going on."

"I will. When must we leave?"

I checked my watch. "Right now. My Cruiser's outside. You sit in the passenger seat."

Estrella turned out the lights and locked the front door behind us, but left the porch light on. After checking her purse, she walked down the front steps at my side.

I pointed back at the overhead light. "Is that for Luna? I kind of thought she'd be here tonight."

Estrella shook her head. "No. She is away."

I wondered where, but didn't ask. Just another unanswered question.

CHAPTER FIVE

We piled into the Land Cruiser, Estrella holding the gym bag on her lap, Onion in back with all our gear. With the sun dying in the west, I backtracked east on the Interstate with my lights on, turning into Red Rock Park at seven twenty-five. I nodded to the entrance guard. "Good evening, sir."

"Park closes in half an hour."

"I know. Just want to show my friends the sunset view from here. We'll take the back way out."

He walked around the Cruiser, peering through the windows. Three adults. No booze. He waved us through and I drove past the main parking lot, still heading east. I glanced at the GPS on my dash, continuing past ancient red rock formations and an untamed, primitive terrain of scrub, sand, and dry riverbeds. Enough light remained to make out the silhouettes of three rock spires in the distance. Our destination was the rock wall just in front of them.

We drove within a mile of the spires before a two-foot wide rift in the trail prevented me from driving any farther. I climbed out and walked ahead, a flashlight in my hand. The rift was six feet deep in front of me, and at least a three-foot depression as far as I could see in both directions. At another time, I might have chanced it on a dare, but not tonight, not with so much at stake. Ten feet of red boulder off to my left would be enough cover to hide the Cruiser. I pulled off the trail and parked behind the boulder, then turned up my collar at the night chill and opened the back door to get my gear.

Estrella remained seated until Onion opened her door and offered his hand. He steadied her when she slipped and dropped the gym bag onto the sand. He picked it up and rested it atop the front hood. "We better check and make sure the tracking device is still working."

Estrella gasped, and her eyes widened. "What is that? *Dios mio*, what are you doing?"

"Relax," I said. "The kidnapper won't find out until long after you and Jay-Jay are safe. It will help the police track him down. And return my money."

She shook her head and backed away from me. "*No quiero eso.* The man, he say no tricks. No cops."

Onion laid a hand on her forearm. "It's the best way. Your son isn't the only person who's been abducted. There are at least six others. They'll need to be rescued too."

Estrella seemed to consider that, then gave a grudging nod and stared at the ground. I checked my .38 one last time, pocketed the gun, and grabbed a flashlight from the Cruiser. Onion handed me the night vision goggles. We helped Estrella across the trail fissure and walked toward the sandstone wall. Just like Jay-Jay's abductor had demanded.

Another hundred yards in and Onion and I grabbed Estrella, preventing her from stumbling into another chasm that cut across the trail. Only half as wide as the first one, it was bordered only by sandy ground, a few scattered rocks, and the growing darkness. No stars above us with all the night sky's clouds, so I aimed my flashlight into the fissure. Too deep to see bottom.

"What do we do?" Estrella switched her hands on the gym bag.

"We have to cross it." I handed Onion my goggles and flashlight, took a short running start and leaped to the other side.

Onion tossed my gear across, and then the gym bag. He nudged Estrella to the fissure's edge and spoke softly to her. "Don't look down." She let out the whimper of a frightened kitten. Onion responded in a forceful tone. "Stretch out your hand. When I count to three, you have to push off as hard as you can toward the professor. Can you do that?"

"I'll try."

I stretched my hand out toward hers.

Onion flexed his knees and braced himself. "One...two...three."

He pushed. I pulled. Estrella made an awkward jump. I heaved back, my hand crushing hers like a vice, and fell onto the sand. Her body landed full force on top of me. I groaned and struggled to regain the use of my lungs. But she was safely across.

Onion made his leap over the crevice and the three of us huddled on the ground, darkness gathering around us. I pulled out my cellphone and logged into the mapping platform for the GPS. Our coordinates popped up a second later.

We edged forward, hand-in-hand-in-hand, Onion and I bracketing the frightened mother. She mumbled something in Spanish, perhaps a prayer. The rock wall grew larger as we closed in, at least thirty feet high, much taller than it had appeared from the Cruiser. Onion and Estrella pressed themselves against the wall while I stood ten feet away and donned the night vision goggles.

The wind carried a faint sound of laughing children in the distance that I found reassuring. Then the blare of a car horn was answered by another. I checked my watch and handed the flashlight over to Onion, I didn't need it now. "Eight-fifteen. You ready?"

He took the light and aimed it at his feet. "Guess so." He grabbed Estrella by her left arm. "Stay right by my side. And don't hand over the gym bag until I say so."

Her voice was little more than a whisper. "Okay."

I pointed off to the left. "We're early, so we may have to wait a while. I'll pull off about twenty-five or thirty feet where the wall swings away. I'll hug the edge and keep you in my sights."

"And if anything happens, you'll come flying like the Rough Riders. Yeah, I know." Onion's lack of enthusiasm gave me a start. He rubbed his jaw. "If we're dealing with a pro, he'll get here early too. Better take our places now."

I moved into the darkness. The goggles painted the landscape a nightmarish green. A headache was building on the right side of my skull. Another migraine. Thirty feet along, I pressed against the edge of the rock wall, adjusted the goggles, and took out my gun. Onion and Estrella stood side-by-side in front of the three rock spires, their backs toward me.

Ten minutes passed. Then a faint glow of two lights shone to the north, bouncing in rhythm. They grew brighter, revealing the silhouettes of three people. Two adults on either side of a child. A gust of cold wind stung my face.

CHAPTER SIX

I pressed my back against the rock wall, adjusting the focus on my goggles. Onion and Estrella remained about thirty-five feet away now. He spoke into her ear. She hugged the gym bag against her chest and moved behind him.

The three people on the trail stopped about twenty feet short of them. The taller man wore a large cowboy hat. A dark patch stained his left cheek, but I couldn't make out any other features. He motioned for the other man and boy to stay put. I didn't see a gun, but his right hand remained inside the pocket of his coat. He walked ahead like he owned the land.

I strained to hear, surprised when Estrella spoke first. Her voice sounded strong, but then I had asked her to speak loud and clear. "Julio. I knew it was you."

Julio Cesar Cortana.

He took a gun out of his coat pocket. "I told you to come alone."

Onion raised his hands. "I'm just a friend. Estrella didn't know the way here. So, I drove her."

"Shut up." He pointed the gun at the gym bag. "Ten grand?"

Estrella extended the bag toward the man, but Onion caught her arm. "In exchange for the boy."

The man whirled his gun on Onion and held it there. "You take chances, don't you?"

"Only when I have to."

I edged out from the rock wall. The .38 felt heavy in my hand. As long as the three of them remained this close together, my gun was useless. I hadn't figured on that.

Julio called back to his accomplice. "Bring the boy up here."

"His name is Jay-Jay," Estrella said. "He is our son. Have you forgotten?"

He tilted his head back and stared at the sky. More of his face became visible. The darkness on the left side of his face looked like an eye patch. "Bitch." He pistol-whipped Estrella's cheek. Her head twisted to the left. She groaned and sagged to the ground, the gym bag dropping from her hand. Onion lunged at the man. Cortana stepped back and shoved Onion down. Cortana pointed his gun at the fallen Estrella and fired. His second shot kept Onion on the ground.

"Stop!" I ran out, and with Onion and Estrella now laying prone, I risked two warning shots above Cortana's head.

He slouched down, but only to pick up the gym bag. My shots had done nothing. He ran back toward the boy who was still in the grasp of the second man. I ran out farther from the wall, dropped to one knee to steady myself, and got off a third round. Cortana's accomplice groaned but managed to stay on his feet. He, too, pulled out a gun and shot blindly in my direction. I hugged the ground, a bullet buzzing over my head. By the time I got back on my feet, Cortana and the other man had put twenty feet more between us. Jay-Jay struggled to free himself, but they dragged him along with them. They disappeared into the dark, shooting back at me every few seconds. My gun was again useless. I couldn't see the boy and didn't want to risk hitting him by mistake.

"Mom! Mom!" In the dim light, I caught the silhouette of Jay-Jay, still struggling to escape. Then his screaming stopped. They were gone.

CHAPTER SEVEN

Onion moaned. "Did you get them?"

"No. You hit bad?"

"My shoulder, I think. In the back, right side. I stayed down so he'd think I was gone. How's the woman?"

Estrella lay face-down on the sand. I knelt and checked the side of her neck for a pulse. Nothing. When I turned her over and closed her eyes, some wetness rubbed off on my fingers. A prayer seemed right, so I did the best I could, looking up to the sky. A westbound airplane glided overhead, its lights blinking in time with the pounding in my chest. "She's dead."

"Gabe." Onion collapsed onto his back and groaned.

"Hang on, Deke. We're gonna get you to a hospital."

"Call an ambulance. Then go after those bastards. I'll be okay." Blood from Onion's bullet wound had seeped into the sand, creating a dark circle beneath his shoulder.

"Not a chance. I'm taking care of you first."

"They'll get away—" He winced, closed his eyes and whispered, "Stop them, Gabe. The guy who shot me had a patch on his left eye."

"Don't worry. In this darkness—on these dirt roads—they can't make more than fifteen, twenty miles in an hour." Maybe that was true, maybe not. But it sounded good enough that Onion nodded, seemingly assured. I squeezed his hand. "Be right back."

The night vision goggles were clogged with sand. I shook them out and placed them back over my eyes. I'd stored a box of flares and a first-aid kit in the rear of the Land Cruiser. The bleeding in Onion's shoulder needed immediate attention. I stumbled as fast as I could back up the trail and grabbed the kit.

Onion had lost consciousness by the time I returned. I unrolled a gauze bandage and pressed it against his wound. He didn't move but let out a groan when I shifted him to dress his back. I placed a ring of flares around the crime scene and lit them before taking out my phone.

My 911 call got routed to the Gallup Police Department. The old man who answered talked through a yawn. "Where are you?"

"At the base of Pyramid Rock, northern edge of Red Rock Park."

"What are you doing out there at this hour?"

Jeezus. "I have a dead woman, a man with a severe gunshot wound in his shoulder, and two men fleeing north with an abducted boy."

"Stay where you are. The McKinley County Sheriff and an EMT crew will be there in twenty minutes. I'll call the medical investigator at his home."

"I've placed some flares all around. I hoped the park guard might see them, but I guess he's gone. But what about the kid? Can you go after him?"

"We'll issue a Code Red emergency message right away. Give me all the details you can."

"He's seven. Name is Jay-Jay Chissie. Straight, dark hair. About four feet tall. Thin. His abductors are both male. One goes by the name of Julio Cesar Cortana. He's maybe forty, heavy set. Has on a black or dark blue hoodie and jeans. Patch covering his left eye."

"And the second guy?"

"The other guy—actually, I didn't get a good look at him. But he was shorter than Cortana. Dark clothing, I think. They're armed. Cortana shot and killed the woman and injured my partner."

"Partner?"

"We're P.I.'s from Albuquerque. We'd arranged a ransom exchange for the boy. It all went bad."

Silence on the other end of the line.

"Listen, Mac, my buddy's bleeding here. Can we get some help?"

"It's on the way. Stay put."

I hung up and checked Onion's wound again. I felt his pulse. Steady, but weak. His face had an uneven, yellowish hue, but that could have been the light from the flares. I waited. Twenty minutes, the man said.

Twenty minutes to watch my friend ebb away. Twenty minutes to study the face of a poor, dead woman I'd twice tried to help. Twenty minutes to reflect on how thoroughly, completely, and utterly I'd fucked this thing up.

CHAPTER EIGHT

The flares sizzled around me; a ring of fire. No other sound. No sign of help. The tracking app on my cell indicated the gym bag and my money were less than a mile away, moving off at a snail's pace. If the killers had a car nearby, they hadn't reached it yet.

A McKinley County Sheriff's car arrived first, speeding in from the east. A deputy stepped out, gun in hand, leaving the lights of his squad car shining on the two bodies at my feet.

I stood and raised my hands. "Is an ambulance coming?"

The officer glanced at Onion and Estrella before approaching me. "You the one who called this in?"

"Gabriel McKenna. Private Investigator." I extended my hand.

He ignored the overture. "EMT will be here soon. What the hell happened?"

In a hundred or so well-chosen words, I covered the essentials.

The officer shook his head through most of my explanation. "You should have called in the law before coming out here."

A siren broke the awkward silence following his comment. An EMT vehicle was approaching.

"Stay here," the officer said.

I stayed.

The sheriff's deputy hurried to the first white-clad EMT worker, a rail-thin six-footer with a tribal braid. Their conversation lasted all of ten seconds before a second EMT crew member joined them.

He ran back to the ambulance while the other two examined Onion and Estrella.

I tried to be helpful. "The woman's dead. My friend has a single bullet wound in his right shoulder. I attempted to stop the bleeding. Think I at least slowed it."

The braided EMT man called the Gallup Indian Medical Center. "We're coming in with an injured man. Prepare surgery for a bullet removal. Call in an anesthesiologist. You'll need to transfuse him, too…half an hour…right."

I turned to the deputy. "Can I go with him?"

"No. Once the medical investigator arrives, you're going to the station and making a full statement. Then, if everything goes your way, you can meet him at the hospital."

"But the killers are getting away—"

"Let the law handle them. Something you should have done in the first place."

"So you've said."

He looked me up and down. "You cold?"

I was and told him so. He let me wait in his police car. Even turned the heater on for me.

Time crawls in the back of a squad car. My only encouragement came from the thumbs-up sign Onion flashed me when they loaded him into the emergency vehicle and sped off to the hospital.

Another hour passed before the medical investigator arrived, all six and a half feet of him, sniffing the air like a trained hound. Deputy Clark came over to get me. The three of us conferred over Estrella's lifeless body.

"Doctor Freyling," Clark said, "this is Gabriel McKenna. He witnessed the killing."

The doctor squinted at me through a pair of Coke-bottle lenses. "How far away were you when the shooting took place?"

"About thirty feet back." I turned and pointed in the direction of Pyramid Rock. "I was wearing night vision goggles, so I had a pretty clear look at it all."

Freyling's eyebrows rose when I mentioned the goggles. He opened his mouth as if to speak, then closed it and looked at the deputy.

"Ransom payoff gone bad," Clark said. "Dead woman was the mother. Her son is still held by the kidnappers." He knelt next to the body and reached toward Estrella's face.

"Please. Don't touch the body." Freyling unlatched a black bag he carried in his left hand. "I'll take over. You'll have my report by noon tomorrow."

"Anything else you need, Doctor?" Clark rose to his feet and stretched out his back.

"No. I've spoken with Sheriff Maestas. He'll be along directly with an ambulance to transport the dead woman back to my office. I'll start a post-mortem right away. If any tests are needed, we'll have to ship her back to Albuquerque."

Deputy Clark turned to me. "Okay, McKenna, back to headquarters. You parked nearby?"

"About a mile back toward the park entrance. There's a chasm in the trail I didn't risk crossing."

"What kind of car?"

"Toyota Land Cruiser. Metallic red."

"Okay. Meet you at the park entrance. No tricks."

"Twenty minutes." I gathered my goggles and picked up the flashlight Onion had dropped in the sand. Its beam guided me along the trail, over the cuts, and back to the Cruiser.

I tossed the gear inside and broke open a fresh bottle of water. I let my first swig slosh around a bit before spitting it and half a mouthful of sand onto the ground. Clouds owned the sky now, not a star in sight. Thunder rumbled in the distance off to the west. Another darker-than-normal night.

Deputy Clark stood by his car at the park entrance. I pulled in behind him and rolled the window down when he approached the Cruiser.

"Follow me into town. The McKinley County Sheriff's office is on Nezhoni Avenue. We'll need your formal statement, but then you should be free to go for the time being. Lucky for you, stupidity isn't a crime in this county." He returned to his car and edged out onto the road.

"Thanks a lot, Officer," I called after him, then muttered to myself. "Idiot."

We stayed on Old Route 66 where it parallels I-40 all the way across the Gallup city line. I saw only two other cars, and they were traveling in the opposite direction. Anyone who had any sense was heading somewhere else.

At a stoplight on the edge of Gallup, I felt the road tremble beneath me. The overhead traffic light was swaying on its cable when I drove through the intersection. Yellow-green light flared up in the western sky ahead of me. Then a shock wave rattled my vehicle, causing me to swerve perilously close to the guard rail on my right. Deputy Clark kept right on driving. So did I.

A few minutes later, Clark turned on his flashers and siren. I accelerated at first, just to keep pace with him, until he swerved to the right-hand curb and jumped out of his vehicle. I slowed and swung in behind him, shifted into Park, and rolled my window down again.

A powerful odor of bleach hit me hard. I looked ahead. The yellow-green light seemed brighter, more intense. Sirens sounded from all directions. "What's going on?"

"Goddamn freight train derailment right in the center of town. They're saying it's a chlorine gas leak. The whole downtown area is being evacuated. All personnel were called to the scene. I can't take you to the sheriff's office. Public safety first."

"What should I do?"

"Right now? Stay away from the spill. Give me your card and contact number. I'll be in touch when it's safe for you to come in and give your statement."

I tugged a business card out of my wallet and passed it through the open window. "Will do. What about my friend?"

Clark thought for a bit. "Your friend's going to be part of a crowd at the medical center once they get the influx of sick and injured. You might go and keep an eye out."

"Got it. I'll wait for your call. Thanks." I pulled away from the curb and sped toward the hospital.

The closer I got to downtown Gallup, the more surreal the scene became. The low-hanging clouds that had moved in earlier glowed a fluorescent green. A foggy mist clung to the ground. Flashing lights gave a nightmarish quality to it all. My eyes stung and now my throat burned. I closed the window and shut all the vents.

A police roadblock stopped me at Boardman Drive. A burly cop with flashers in both hands tried to swing me left. He shouted something I couldn't hear. Whatever it was, my windows were staying shut.

Then a burst of light blinded me. A second flash followed a moment later. Two thunderclaps and a blast of rushing air buffeted the Cruiser. The force lifted the cop with the flashers off his feet. He landed ten feet away on the right-hand shoulder.

The guy needed help. I opened my door.

"No! No!" A man wearing a reflective vest emerged from the darkness. "Get back in your car." He fumbled with a gas mask, trying to get it on with one hand and direct me with the other.

A loud, shrill bank of far-off sirens, like the civil defense alarms I remembered from my childhood, filled the air. They made it impossible to hear anything else.

I clambered back into the Cruiser and sped south on Boardman Drive. I was doing at least sixty, but an ambulance hurtled past me in the northbound lane. I accelerated to keep pace, hoping he would lead me to the hospital and to Onion.

Six other ambulances clogged the hospital's emergency entrance. A fire truck pulled into the line, a team of volunteers stumbling off, staggering to the emergency entrance with rags over their mouths. The last guy off had bandages over his eyes as well. His buddies dragged him inside.

I drove over the curb and came to a stop on the grass as close to the entrance as I could get.

Somewhere inside the hospital, Onion had a bullet in his arm. As far as I could see in every direction, Gallup was ablaze with poison, its people frightened, wounded, maybe even dead. Off to the east, two men dragged a young girl into the darkness, away from the motionless body of a woman on the sidewalk.

The Land of Enchantment had become a world of hurt.

CHAPTER NINE

All kinds of vehicles—from motorcycles to fire trucks—jammed the traffic circle in front of the Gallup Indian Medical Center. A pair of helicopters hovered overhead. The wind still blew from the north, still spreading the angry yellow-green cloud that had turned this sea of humanity into a coughing, pushing, terrified mob.

I jumped from the Cruiser and joined a throng of people pushing their way through the emergency room entrance. Squeezing in sideways, I left a trail of "excuse me...pardon me" in my wake. A ceiling-mounted television monitor at the far end of the room broadcast CNN's live coverage of the "Gallup Tragedy," as this mess had now been christened.

You couldn't hear the TV, but the scrolling subtitles spelled out the details. Sixteen people confirmed dead...hundreds more in peril from a chlorine gas spill...New Mexico Governor declares state of emergency...roads closed except to emergency vehicles...first responders from a four-state area heading to Gallup...

Holy shit. I said my second quick prayer of the night, hoping Onion had received medical attention before this deluge. A sign on the wall above me read "Nursing Station" with an arrow pointing down a corridor to my right. Maybe somebody there would know.

The entrance door to the corridor was blocked by a three-hundred-pound guard who looked like he knew his way around a good bar fight. He stood, arms folded, scanning the desperate crowd.

A sudden surge shoved an elderly Native woman against a wall. The guard moved a couple of feet in her direction. "Take it easy, everybody. Calm down." He pushed his way through the mob.

I seized the moment. Pressing my shoulder against a metal bar on the closed door, I opened it far enough to slide inside. It clicked shut behind me.

Twenty feet down the hall, a hive of activity swarmed about the nurses' main desk. I was halfway there when the guard barged into the corridor. "Stop." I turned. His stubby hand went to his belt. Gun? Radio? It didn't matter.

I shouted at him. "There's a witness to a killing in one of the rooms down here. Deputy Clark sent me to see him." I made a quick, feeble attempt to open the left side of my jacket, as if a badge was pinned inside.

Fists pounded against the door behind the massive guard. Somebody screamed in the lobby. He waved me on.

I ran to the main desk. Nurses and medical staff were entering and leaving the area in a discordant frenzy. Two nurses sat behind the desk, talking on their phones, punching in different lines and talking some more. Neither looked up at me, so I pounded on the counter.

The nurse closest to me lost patience with the person on the other end of her phone. "No." She shook her head. "You'll have to route them elsewhere. We have less than one hundred beds here and three times that many people already needing emergency care. Try Rehoboth or Presbyterian Clinics. I'm sorry." She hung up and slumped in her chair. I cleared my throat as loud as I could. She looked up and glowered. "What do you want?"

"My name is Gabriel McKenna. I'm a detective looking for a patient named Gagnon. Came in with a bullet wound in his shoulder. Loss of blood. Deputy Clark of the County Sheriff's office sent me over."

"Can't you see what's happening?" She pressed her cheeks with her hands now, like she was trying to squeeze away a migraine of her own.

"If he's able to move, I can get him out of here. Free up a bed for somebody else. Is he in any condition for that?"

She spotted a man in a white lab coat coming up the hall from some other wing of the facility. "Doctor Walker." The nurse stood and bustled over to him. They talked. He glanced at me over his glasses. I tossed him a somber wave and nodded.

Doctor Walker report to surgery. Stat. He looked up at the speaker, said something to the nurse, and disappeared the way he'd come.

I shot the nurse a questioning glance. She motioned me to follow her across the station area, down a corridor, and through a door marked "Recovery."

"Mr. Gagnon's wound was treated and cleaned. The bullet was removed."

"I hope you saved it. That's evidence in an attempted murder."

"Of course we did. He's been given a pain-killer. He's weak and groggy. We didn't have time to finish treating him before this hell broke loose." She stopped walking and frowned at me. "You're not taking him to jail, are you? He's in no condition for that."

"No, ma'am. Mr. Gagnon was the victim of the shooting. I'll see he gets home safe and sound. Do you have a wheelchair, by any chance?"

"He was sitting in one when I saw him. Don't ask him to walk. Under normal circumstances, we'd be reluctant to release him as he is. Obviously, we're in an emergency."

I nodded. "Terrible thing…I'll see to it personally that this man gets the best of care."

She turned, I followed. Onion slumped in a wheelchair at the far end of the corridor.

"Let me speak to him. That is, if you don't mind."

"I have to get back to my post. You'll have to sign him out."

"Not a problem. Thank you for everything." I waited until she'd disappeared before kneeling beside Onion's chair.

His eyes were shut. I couldn't tell if he even knew I was there. I jostled his good shoulder. "Onion? You okay?"

"Huh?" He lifted his eyes, but they stared straight ahead. "I'm thirsty."

"There's water out in my car. We have to get you out of here."

"Gabe?" He twisted his head. "What the hell is going on? Where'd all these people come from?"

"Horrible train wreck downtown. Poison gas leak. They declared a state of emergency. You don't want to stay here, trust me."

"I'm not good for much right now."

"You don't have to be. You'll be better off any place but here. Can you sign yourself out?"

"Watch me."

CHAPTER TEN

I cajoled Onion's wheelchair through the crowd, trying not to run over people or furniture. The signing-out process took almost an hour with all the confusion. Truth be told, I could have just wheeled Onion out to the Cruiser and nobody would have noticed. But we'd need the cops on our side when things went down, so I played it by the book.

As I struggled with the passenger door, a dark-haired teenager offered to help get Onion into the back of my vehicle. He even lowered the back seat, inflated my camping mattress, returned the wheelchair to the hospital, and turned down my offer of a twenty for his help. At the worst of times, you often meet the best of people.

I adjusted the rearview mirror. The most I could see were Onion's feet. "You okay back there?"

"Been better. The mattress helps some." He coughed, then settled into the darkness.

I exited the parking lot and headed back to Vega Street. The dashboard clock said it was two-thirty, more than three hours before sunrise.

"Where we heading, Gabe?"

"I want to drive past Estrella's. If the cops aren't there yet, I'm going inside."

Silence came from the back seat until Onion let out a sigh. "Risky business. What are you gonna say if they arrive and find you there?"

"You're not going to let them find me."

He let out a rasping cascade of coughs. "What the hell am I supposed to do? I can't move. Barely staying awake back here."

"Hold on." I turned onto Vega Street and crept past Estrella's house. Dark. No cops visible. No crime scene tape, no sign hers was any different from the dozen other bungalows. I did a U-turn and parked across the street.

I switched off the engine and tossed the keys into the back seat. They made a soft landing somewhere on Onion.

He grunted. "Why you giving me these? I can't drive."

"You're going to listen for the cops."

"I can't sit up. How do you expect me to see them?"

"You don't have to see them, just listen for them. See that button with the red horn on it? If you hear the cops, press the button. The horn will warn me to get the hell out."

"Great. Just great. So, the cops come over to the car and see me laying here with the alarm in my hand, a bullet wound in my shoulder, and a shit-eating grin on my face?"

"Tell them the party got out of hand. Anything. By then, I'll have left the house through the back door. Don't worry. I'll take it from there."

"Your track record on this caper doesn't inspire much confidence."

"You'd rather they arrest me for breaking and entering?"

"No. I'd rather go back to Albuquerque and forget the whole thing."

"Every minute we sit here, that poor kid gets more lost. Deke, I'm not letting go of this. If you're in too much hurt or feel disinclined, I'll drop you at a motel and have somebody come out and take you home."

"Nah, that was my pain talking. Just get in and out fast, okay?"

I took the flashlight and popped out of the car, closing the driver's door without a sound. Each of my steps echoed down the block. The same damn cricket moaned from beneath the front porch.

The porch light was out. The front door was unlocked.

I could have sworn Estrella had left the light on and locked the door on our way out. Had someone gotten back to the house before me? I paused at the door, aiming the flash at the porch floor before switching it on. The door screeched, of course. I opened it just enough, then entered with my gun drawn. The living room looked the same. Nothing unusual in the kitchen or dining room.

I edged down the hall to the master bedroom. The bed was made. A half-filled water glass sat on a bedside table. On the dresser, a school portrait of Jay-Jay smiled back at me. Next to it, a family photo. Estrella, Jay-Jay, and Cortana, sporting the patch on his left eye. I grabbed both pictures and swung the flashlight to the far side of the room.

A bookshelf filled the space between the windows. Romance novels, most of them in Spanish. An album with more photos. No time to look through it now. I grabbed it. The wastebasket stood empty. Clothes neatly hung in the closet. I moved on.

The second bedroom must have been Jay-Jay's. I didn't expect to find much there. I wasn't disappointed. The kid collected baseball cards, another reason to bring him back unharmed.

One final bedroom. A woman's dress lay crumpled atop a blue and white bedspread. Same dress Luna was wearing yesterday. No other clothes in the closet. Nothing in the dresser drawers. The lady vanished…

A crumpled piece of paper lay on the floor beside her bed. I smoothed it out on the dresser. The printed message was brief:

MEET US AT MIDNIGHT—J

I checked my watch. We were almost six hours late.

CHAPTER ELEVEN

I handed Onion the album through the Cruiser's back window. "When it gets lighter, page through those other photos. See if you can find a better picture of the guy who shot you."

"I was about to take a nap, man. What else did you find?"

I climbed in and passed the note from "J" over the seat back. "This. What do you think? I found it in Luna's room. She's gone."

Onion read the note and took a second. "Not surprising. I thought there was something fishy about that lady."

"She could be running away from the killers."

"Or toward them. What time you got?"

I didn't have to check my watch. "Five minutes after six."

"Those bastards have too much of a head start. What options do we have left?" Onion repositioned himself, groaning in pain. "Damn." He sucked in a couple of quick breaths.

I took out my map of New Mexico and laid it flat against the steering wheel, glancing back and forth, trying to align it with the reading I was getting from my GPS app. "The gym bag is about forty miles away."

"Only forty miles? They don't seem in much of a hurry."

"Maybe one of my shots hit Cortana or the other guy. Maybe they're having car trouble. They're moving across Navajo land. Maybe they got stopped. Could be a lot of reasons." I took a closer look at my phone. "They're moving east."

"What's to the east?"

"Chaco Canyon, but that's forty, fifty miles north of us. They're on Indian Land Route 9, the one that runs south of Chaco. I've been along there a couple of times. Can't go more than ten or fifteen miles an hour. Not in the dark. They'll be coming up on Whitehorse soon."

"Whitehorse? That a city?"

"A Navajo Chapter House. Meeting place. Been there too, about twenty-five years ago."

"I'm sure they all remember you."

"If they don't, you'll let me know. Settle down, we've got hours of rough road ahead. You up for this?"

"Yeah…yeah." Onion's voice came from the bottom of his lungs.

I drove east on Vega, then north on Boardman until we reached the roadblock on Old Route 66. I motioned to the cops we wanted to turn right, away from the downtown melee. They waved us through.

Morning sun would soon be hitting my eyes. I whipped out my Ray-Bans and hooked them on the front pocket of my shirt. "Sky will be brightening in half an hour. Feel strong enough to go through those photos? Maybe find Julio Cesar Cortana?"

Another guttural response. Taking a bullet hadn't improved my partner's disposition.

The fuel gauge read a quarter of a tank, again. I stopped at a Valero gas station, topped off, grabbed a couple bags of chips, two wrapped sandwiches with some kind of brownish meat, and two more bottles of water to add to the case Onion had bought. Before getting back on the road, I reloaded the empty chambers of my .38.

I checked my cellphone GPS one more time. The gym bag, Jay-Jay, and his abductors hadn't moved much, if at all. I turned off Old Route 66 and pulled onto I-40 heading east. This made the route longer, but with better road we'd move faster.

One hour later, I exited at Thoreau and headed north. We passed into an orange and sand-colored world, Navajo Country, a sometimes-hostile land, now under clearing sky. And the morning sun. Always, the damned sun. Go out unprotected even at this time of day, and you can almost feel your skin wrinkle.

We crossed the Continental Divide at Satan Pass Canyon. No cars for miles, lonely country here. A white Piper Matrix, just like the plane my brother-in-law flies, passed overhead. It banked in the distance and disappeared over a sandstone mesa off to our right.

"Got him." Onion sounded interested again.

"Cortana?"

"Yeah. Two photos. A family portrait of him with Estrella and the kid. The other is him in an army uniform. Mexican, I think."

"Pull those out of the album. Let me see." He handed the photos over the seat. Cortana, all right. Jay-Jay looked about three or four in the first picture. "Cortana's had that eye patch for several years. But that uniform isn't Mexican."

"How can you tell?"

"They have green and red stripes on either side of their flag insignia. His badge has blue stripes top and bottom. El Salvador, that'd be my guess."

"How do you know all that?"

"You're forgetting I spent part of my Army years in Latin America."

"Right. Where'd you put those sandwiches?"

"Sure you're strong enough to eat one?"

"You're kidding, right?"

"In the cooler. Should be there on top."

Onion rustled around, then cursed when the Cruiser bottomed out in one of the potholes dotting the back road.

"Jeez. What is this shit?" Onion's first bite was not going down well.

"Roast beef, maybe? Best I could do."

"You got anything stronger than water to wash it down?"

"Sorry. Get some rest."

He clammed up the twenty miles to Crownpoint. I veered northeast onto Navajo Service Route 9. The sun blazed down on us now, rippling the blacktop with rising waves of heat. I looked in the rearview mirror. "Hand me a water, okay?"

Some mumbling followed before Onion's hand passed a Dasani bottle over the front seat. "We getting close? It's been hours."

"No, it hasn't. And we've got some ways to go yet."

"You have a garbage bag?"

"Hand it to me." He might have complained about the sandwich, but the crumpling wrapper told me he'd eaten every bit of it. I stashed the wrapper in the plastic bag that hung from my dashboard ashtray.

"Seriously, Gabe. I don't know if I can stay awake any more. Maybe it's the meds they gave me. How much farther?"

"Let me pull off and check." I eased onto the right shoulder, cut the engine, and rolled the window down. A couple of scattered buildings stood off in the distance, well beyond the fence that ran along the south side of the two-lane road. Another red rock mesa to the north. Nothing else, just us and the sun.

The GPS showed they hadn't moved since my last check. They were straight ahead and less than ten miles away. Why had they stopped? I swallowed hard. Maybe they'd found the tracking device. If they tossed it, we'd be high and dry, with no Plan B.

CHAPTER TWELVE

Two miles from Jay-Jay.

I hadn't heard from Onion in too long. "You okay back there?"

"I'm trying to think of some way I can help you once we catch up with those guys. You got any bright ideas?"

"Can you sit up?" I adjusted the rearview mirror to see him better.

"I'll try. But not 'til we stop." He turned his head toward the sound of a small plane landing nearby.

"I need a second pair of eyes."

"Yeah. Sure." He didn't sound convinced. Not a bit.

The blacktop turned into a gravel road near the top of a ridge a quarter mile ahead. I wanted a look at what lay beyond the rim before we drove on. Fifty feet from the top, I pulled the Cruiser to a stop.

Onion's head popped into view. "What's going on?"

I pointed up the road. "Going up there on foot to see what's ahead. I should be back in a minute. Try to prop yourself up while I'm gone."

Onion struggled to raise his body off the mattress. "Be careful."

Grabbing a pair of binoculars from the glove compartment, I opened my door, the motor still running. The air outside had to be thirty degrees hotter. A crummy little breeze gave no relief. I reached the top of the ridge and crouched, shielding my eyes from the sun.

An airfield stretched along the western side of the road. One tiny blockhouse with peeling paint on its walls, one landing strip with weeds growing through cracks in its asphalt. The half-mile runway was plenty long enough for the Piper Matrix, N4408, that circled overhead and came in straight and low at its far end. The plane touched down and taxied to a halt well short of the brush at the near end of the runway.

Parked a hundred feet from the runway, Cortana and his assistant dragged Jay-Jay from their van and toward the aircraft. A gust of wind carried the boy's screams to my ears.

I ran back to the Cruiser. "We're going in. Hang on."

"Gabe?"

"Jay-Jay's alive. They're trying to put him on a plane. This may be our only chance." I checked my .38 before flooring the accelerator. The Cruiser screamed across the gravel, over the rise and down the hill. "Grab something back there and hang on."

"Grab something? Shit, Gabe, you're gonna get us killed."

I drove straight for the plane, hoping to keep it from taking off. Seventy miles per hour. A closed gate blocked the airfield entrance. I plowed through. The impact veered me off course, onto loose sand, rocks and through a patch of scattered pinon pines. Wrenching the wheel in the direction of the skid, I corrected enough to get out of the rough.

They'd spotted us.

Keeping one hand close to his body, the short man grabbed Jay-Jay and dragged him toward the plane. A pair of arms hoisted the boy aboard. The pilot jumped back into the cockpit. I didn't dare ram the plane now, so I angled away from the aircraft toward the Chevy van.

Cortana crouched behind a front fender, his gun hand extended across the hood. A chain of bullets whizzed past us, one striking the passenger window. It left a cobwebbed crack, but the glass held. Cortana and his accomplice ran back and jumped back inside the Suburban. A rush of smoke poured out from their van's exhaust pipe.

I braced myself for impact. "Hold on again. We're gonna crash."

"Jeez..." Onion disappeared behind the seat.

I again swerved onto the sand, hoping to cut them off. A four-foot chamisa shrub crunched under my wheels. The Cruiser *thunked*, then shuddered. Sparks shot out from beneath the hood. We jolted to a stop.

"Damn." I popped open my door. A gray metal power box I hadn't seen lay scattered in pieces behind us.

Onion hollered from the back seat. "Incoming! Three o'clock."

An old-fashioned motorcycle with sidecar barreled down the incline from the main road. Its bright red paint glistened in the sun. The driver wore goggles, a leather helmet, and a too-long scarf that fluttered behind his head. The person in the sidecar looked no bigger than a child. That didn't keep him from firing a Thompson submachine gun perched on the rim of the sidecar. At least, he tried to fire it. The bucking and swaying of the motorcycle bounced the gun left, right, up, down. The recoil flung the gunner back, time and again.

I hit the seat. Bullets were flying everywhere around the Cruiser. "Stay down, Onion!"

He didn't respond. I raised my head and peered over the dash.

The gunner's final burst trailed off at an angle into the empty sky. The motorcycle swung toward us. Then it, too, died in the sand twenty feet away.

A sudden roar lifted me onto my elbows. The Piper Matrix was speeding down the runway. It lifted off and banked to the east. The short man in the motorcycle's sidecar swung his submachine gun toward the plane and fired off a hail of bullets. They missed.

Cortana and his partner sped off toward the ridge. They mocked me with their car horn and disappeared. Everything went silent, except for the sound of the plane receding in the distance above us.

Onion's head popped above the seatback. "You okay?"

"I'm not shot or anything, but we're one-hundred percent screwed."

"Hold it right there, fella." The rail-thin goggled man from the cycle approached my passenger door. His pistol rested in a holster tethered to his right leg. A young man no more than three feet tall trailed behind him. The old man stopped. His hand went to the gun. "Who are you?"

"My name's Gabriel McKenna. Private Investigator from Albuquerque."

"Anybody hurt?"

"My partner's in the back of the van. He's got a bullet wound in his arm."

"I didn't see it happen."

"Not now. Last night. By the guys who just got away."

"Then you're not one of them? That's good." He fingered the crack in our windshield and peered inside the Cruiser. A mop of black hair swung along beside him, just over the bottom window rim, the barrel of the little man's Thompson sticking up a few inches higher. The man looked down at his companion. "It's okay, Alto." Then his steel gaze returned to me. "Don't mean to bust your chops, but you boys coulda been killed."

I pushed against the driver's door. It stuck for a second, then gave way. I checked Onion. "Stay inside." The sun burned like fire now. A sudden wind blasted my face with sand. "Where'd you guys come from?"

"Over the hill." The tall man took off the goggles. A lifetime of high-desert sun had left so many lines and creases on his face I wondered how he managed to shave. "Let me take a gander at that buggy of yours. Pop the hood, flyboy."

I reached in and pulled the hood release latch. The old man nearly disappeared head-first into the engine chamber.

Mr. Machine Gun walked up beside us and stood on his toes to see. He barely reached the old man's waist. "What you see, boss?"

A voice emerged from deep among the wires and hoses. "Fuel line snapped clean. We can rig a temporary patch, but this'll have to go back to the house."

"Wait a second," I looked down at the dwarf by my side. "We've got to follow those guys. We can't stay here."

The old man straightened and shook his head. "Son, it's like this. You can stand here, holler all you want, and let me fix your fuel line. Or, you can get to a phone, try to get a tow truck to come out here from Crownpoint, Milan, or maybe Cuba. If you're lucky, somebody'll come around day after tomorrow." He wiped his brow on his sleeve. "Don't make no never-mind to me."

The old guy was right. I raised my hand to ward off any other wisdom this relic might feel like hurling my way. "How far you figure we can go with a patch job?"

"Bupkis. You'd end up stuck someplace even more nowhere than this." His head plunged a second time beneath the Cruiser's popped-up hood. It reemerged ten seconds later. His eyes, however, remained focused inside the engine compartment. "Shorty."

"I'm right here."

"Get some duct tape out of your sidecar. Couple of clamps, if you got 'em."

His assistant ran to their cycle and returned with a roll of tape. "No clamps. Sorry."

The old man took the tape and paused to cough his lungs out before returning to work.

I looked down at the diminutive man next to me. Sweat dribbled down from beneath his headscarf. "Who are you guys? How come you showed up here when you did?"

"I'm Alto Valorgrande. Most people, they call me Shorty. Those who like to talk more call me The Dwarf. I no mind neither one."

"The old guy?" I pointed to the front of the Cruiser.

"Boss? Phil Friganza. Lives a mile or so from here. Been here forever, as long as I remember. We're neighbors. I help him out with stuff he can't do no more."

"He's ancient."

"Ninety-three."

"No kidding?" I watched from a respectful distance while the old man fidgeted with wires, hoses, and belts. "Not too sociable, is he? Where'd you meet him?"

Alto shifted the Thompson to his right shoulder. "Phil and me, we meet ten years ago. I decided to run away from a Mexican circus. Got tired of being used. Most people look at me and figure, 'There goes a dwarf,' call me names, expect me to amuse them. So, I come to New Mexico. Just bumming around. Then I run into Phil. He looks at me and sees a person. That doesn't happen to me much. So, we get along okay."

"Why the submachine gun?"

"Phil and I been watching these guys for months. Every couple of days, same thing. A plane arrives, they drag some poor people into it and disappear. Sometimes a kid, even. Like today."

"You been to the cops?"

Alto dismissed my question with his hand. "Phil don't talk to nobody and police don't believe me. So, we're dealing with it our own way. They got to be stopped." He looked at me, at the Cruiser, and then at Onion in the back seat. "What are *you* guys doing out here?"

"The same." I told him about our busted ransom plan, the shooting death of Estrella, Onion's wound, and the disaster in Gallup. I mentioned the tracking signal we'd been following.

His eyebrows rose. "That kind of thing interests the boss."

"Yeah?"

"Phil always loves mechanical stuff. He can fix anything. He'll have your wheels back on the road faster than any garage could."

"He's got an unusual way of talking."

"Yeah, well you get used to it. His head's stuck back in the old days. Forties. Says he was a POW in World War II and I believe him. Joined up at sixteen. Shipped out to the Philippines. Spent three years on a prison ship. Kinda screwed with his head, *comprende*? But he's a decent old guy."

Friganza appeared by our side. "I'm no better than the next." He gave me a hard stare. "I jerry-rigged a patch to your fuel line, young man. Keep it in grandma gear and you should make it back to my place." He coughed again, hard and long, until his face turned red. "Give us a few minutes to get the Indian up and running. Then follow me. It's about a mile. You okay with that?"

"Yes. Thank you."

I crawled into the Cruiser, brought Onion up to date, and waited for the post-war Indian Chief motorcycle to start. Alto hugged the Thompson to his chest like a newly found puppy while they sped up the gravel drive. Onion and I crept after them at fifteen miles per hour.

CHAPTER THIRTEEN

It wasn't easy keeping the motorcycle within sight. I rolled my side window down, hoping to hear the roar of their engine, but the midday heat forced me to close it and pump up the A/C. A mile or so later, an abandoned gas station loomed on the left side of the road. A rusted gas pump sat beneath a faded sign: "*SIGNAL – The Goes Farther Gasoline.*"

By the time we reached the station, Friganza stood by the front entrance, under the open door to a single service bay. Alto leaned against a low-slung Coca-Cola machine—its red paint faded pink by too many days in the sun—one of those machines that opened from the top and gave you six and one-half ounces of ice-cold relief for a dime. Once upon a time.

I rolled the driver's window down again and poked my head out. "Help me get my friend into the shade?"

Friganza pointed behind him, toward the station's open front door. "Put him inside. There's a cot and a small fan." Alto walked over to us and opened the back door on the passenger side.

"This is my business partner. Call him Onion." We helped him into the station.

The interior reflected the station's aged exterior. A couple of incandescent lights hung overhead. Two six-by-three metal cabinets, with dials, metered displays, and vents emitted a low hum on the far side of the room. On their sides, small metal plates read: *Property of the United States Navy.* Transmitters, World War II vintage.

All around, wires connected something to something else, or disappeared into the walls or through the ceiling tiles. Shelves loaded with tubes, small boxes, spools of string, wire, and metal lined each inside wall. Two cigar boxes on a metal desk overflowed with vacuum tubes. Most of all, the place was filled with tools, everywhere, all shapes, sizes, and purposes. Everything ship-shape. Everything at least fifty years old.

"Gabe." Onion rasped a long breath. "I'm dry. Open a water, okay?"

"Here." Friganza pointed to a wineskin bag hanging on a nearby wall. "There's water in there. Sterilized this morning." He picked up a coffee mug and filled it halfway. "Don't spill." He handed it to Onion and hung the bag back on its hook.

Onion drank it down, took a deep breath, and collapsed against the cot. "I gotta rest."

I took the mug from his hand. "Don't worry. That's your job now."

The rest of us walked outside to the open service bay. I moved closer to the old man. "May I call you Phil?"

"Sure. *Forties Phil.* That's how I'm known from Crownpoint to Pueblo Pintada. 'There goes Forties Phil' they say. They have no idea who I am."

His coughing made me pause a moment. "You from around here?"

"Tierra Amarilla. North of here a piece. Up by Chama. Left there on the tenth of September in Forty-One. Sixteen years old. You could see trouble was coming. Thought I'd make a difference." He turned and spat dark phlegm on the ground. "Got shipped out and arrived in Manila Bay on December Sixth." His watering eyes fixed on mine. "How's that for timing?"

This guy was living history. "Did you see action right away?"

"Hah." Friganza turned away and spoke while walking to my Cruiser. I followed. "Not for long. Wouldn't call it action, exactly. I was with Wainright's Seventy-First. The Japs overran us near Lingayan Gulf sixteen days later. Bunch of us were kids like me. Some regular Army and Navy old timers. Some Filipinos." He took a large, oily handkerchief from his back pocket and mopped his brow. "Spent the next thirty-two months as a Japanese POW."

I did the math. "Then you must have been freed in September of Forty-Four? You caught a break there."

He spat on the ground a second time. "Caught a break? I was on a Japanese prison ship, you get that? Me and eight-hundred other guys. A rust bucket called the *Shino Maru.* What we caught were a couple of torpedoes from an American submarine. *USS Paddle.* Friendly fire, for God's sake. Hundreds of us died that day. I made it to shore. Don't ask me how, I don't remember."

"I'm sorry, I didn't realize."

"Neither did the rest of the world. Not for a long time. Big-wigs hushed it up. A bunch of villagers found me and two of my buddies washed up on the beach. Took us to their homes and fed us. They had a radio. Navy came by and picked us up. Ten weeks later, I was stateside."

"What a life story. You were a survivor." I didn't know what else to say.

"Not all of me survived." He walked away about ten feet and stopped with his back turned. He didn't move or speak for more than a minute. His shoulders shook all the while. Then he cleared his throat and walked back. "Most of me died over there, you get that? I come home in December of Forty-Four. My Christmas present. Fuck. Too many things had changed. Dad died the year before. My brothers and sister looked at me screwy. The town wasn't the same. Neither were the people…neither was I." He glared at me. "Why the hell did you bring all of this stuff up?"

I wanted to say I hadn't. I swallowed my words instead.

"They sent me home. Only it wasn't home any more. So…I left." He took a long look over at my Cruiser. "Drive that heap into the bay. Line it up over the opening there." He pointed to a service hole about six feet deep between two metal wheel guides above and on either side of it. "Don't screw things up."

The old man's story knocked around inside me as I walked back to the Cruiser. After three attempts, I got the motor chugging and pulled into the bay. Forties Phil dropped into the service hole, carrying a length of rubber hose he must have gotten while I moved my vehicle.

"Alto." His voice lifted from inside the hole.

The dwarf appeared. He looked at me. "Your friend Mr. Onion is asleep."

Friganza's voice crackled with impatience. "Go get me a couple of clamps. And a clean rag."

"Sure thing, Phil." Alto scurried back into the main room, returning with the items in less than a minute.

I squatted down and gazed into the hole beneath the Cruiser. "I truly appreciate this, sir."

"Don't call me sir. Don't patronize me."

"I didn't mean it that way. Sorry." If there was a way to get along with this guy, I hadn't found it yet.

"Look, I'm sorry, son." His voice softened a bit. "Ever since the war, I can't be with people. Can't take them. Just can't. Nobody understands what we went through. Shorty—." He handed a cut-off piece of rubber hose to Alto. "I found this gas station abandoned the year after I got back. Fixed it up. Been here seventy years…more."

"Have you been living off the grid that long?"

"Off the grid? What grid? Weren't any grid around here back then. Anyway, I've done okay."

"What did you do for a living?"

He shook his head and looked at me the way a parent confronts a foolish child. "Do for a living? I *lived.* That's what I did. Every blasted minute of every blasted day. Do for a living…" His voice trailed off.

Alto motioned me away from the service bay and out into the sun. He'd been listening in. Now he was whispering. "The old man, when he gets like this, you can't tell him nothing." He shrugged, then braced a hand against the antique gas pump.

"Alto, where are you?" Phil's voice was distilled impatience.

The little man walked back to the service bay and bent down next to the Cruiser.

"One of these clamps is no good. Get me another. And get me a knuckle buster, too."

"Okay, boss." Alto hustled back inside the station and returned with another clamp and a crescent wrench. "Here you go."

Five minutes later, Forties Phil Friganza crawled out of the service hole, dusted off his clothes, and stretched his back. "Done."

"Thanks," I said. "How much?"

He took out a pocket watch. "Almost four o'clock. You guys stay for dinner and we'll discuss terms."

I tried once more to be solicitous. "I was worried about you down there. With that gas line and all..."

Five seconds of ninety-three-year-old silence followed. "Son, I hope you were paying attention. Next time, you go down there and fix the damn thing yourself."

"I just meant—"

"I'll thank you to bug off and let me be."

CHAPTER FOURTEEN

In some parts of rural New Mexico, you feel lost even when you know where you are.

I sat in the Cruiser with the motor running to test Friganza's fuel line fix. The air conditioning and radio were on. The toll from the Gallup chemical spill now stood at twenty-three dead, more than five hundred hospitalized. First responders from around the Southwest continued to assist and relieve local personnel.

My tracking software reported Cortana and his accomplice moving again, heading northeast on Route 9 just this side of Pueblo Pintado. Unfolding my New Mexico state map, I calculated their escape route. The road they were on swung southeast past the trading post, then on to Cuba, a small town I knew well.

A wizened hand rapped against my window. "Chow time. Bring the map."

I nodded to Phil, pocketed my phone, folded the map, and breathed in one more lungful of cool air before turning off the A/C. When I closed the door behind me, the old man thrust a flat plastic package into my free hand.

"Enjoy your grub."

I glanced at the package's label: *Meal, Ready-to-Eat, Individual. Do Not Rough Handle When Frozen.*

I groaned. "You've got to be kidding. MRE rations?"

Friganza cast a dismissive eye at me. "You allergic to exothermic heat?"

"No. But I had more than my fill of this crap in the Army. In Grenada."

Friganza's face lit up. The process looked painful. "You a vet? Why didn't you say so?" He pointed to the plastic bag. "I gave you the meat chunks in beans with tomato sauce, but if you don't like that, you can have meatballs in marinara. Come on." He turned and walked back to the filling station's main room.

I examined the bag as I followed him, wondering what manner of animal had to die to make this meal possible.

Phil must have noticed the expression on my face. "I've got others, too. The chili and macaroni's damn tasty."

Onion had his packet open on the cot. Pain and fear colored his voice. "Where the hell do you find this stuff?" For the first time in our long acquaintance, he displayed a lack of enthusiasm while in the presence of food.

Phil sat down on a folding chair. "I know this guy who runs a survivalist warehouse outside of Nageezi. Go there twice a year. Take some of the surplus and stuff that's past its expiration date off his hands." He checked Onion and then me. "You guys know how to heat up those packs?"

Onion shook his head. "I've never been that far away from civilization."

Before Phil could go off on another rant, I took over. "Here," I opened the top of my pack. "You pour in some water, close her up, and wait. Ten minutes. That gives you time to review the milestones of your life, ask forgiveness from those you've wronged, and try to muster enough courage to go on."

Onion fumbled open his bagged dinner with the hand of his one good arm. "Don't we still have some potato chips back in the Cruiser?"

Friganza's back stiffened. He glowered at my friend. "*Fried* food? It angers up the blood. Stay away from that stuff."

"Here, let's look at the map," I said, unfolding it on the room's only counter top. "My tracking device—"

"Your *what*?" Friganza moved in for a closer look. "Damn. Look at that. You got a signaling device hidden in their car?"

"Sewed into the bottom of the bag with the ransom money."

Phil did a jig step and slapped my back. "First smart thing you've done today."

I ignored his remark. "Question is, once they get past Pueblo Pintado, which direction will they go?"

Alto spoke up. "Only one road goes anywhere past that point, right boss?" He popped something resembling a Cheez-It into his mouth and looked at the old man.

"He's right," Friganza said. "And I know a short cut that'll slice the distance between us in half. As long as they don't try to drive on at night."

I didn't recall inviting these two guys to join us, but what the hell. They knew the country. I studied the read-out on my phone and checked it against the map. "Looks like they're at Pueblo Pintado right now. They've stopped again. Haven't moved in the last ten minutes anyway."

"The chase has just begun!" Friganza felt inside his dinner bag. "Should be just about done. Eat up, troops. We ship out in the morning." He tapped the gun at his thigh. "Locked and loaded."

I took the plastic spoon from my dinner kit and scooped up some of my meat chunks and beans. It sat there in my mouth, daring me to swallow. My taste buds sent shock waves across my tongue all the way to the back of my throat. I gagged.

Alto looked up from his feed bag. "Don't like it? Here, try mine." He held his bag out to me. "Beanie-weenies."

"No thanks, I'm fine." After dinner, the moist towelettes were a nice touch.

CHAPTER FIFTEEN

I beat the sun out of bed the next morning. To be more precise, I bolted from the back of the Cruiser when the first grating notes of Phil Friganza's interpretation of *Reveille* abused my ear drums. It was 5 a.m.

"Phil, a little mercy." I tried to stretch the pain from my back. "We're awake, for God's sake."

He tucked a beat-up brass bugle under his arm. "We ship out in thirty minutes. Alto's making breakfast and coffee." He turned away, one cough following another.

"I better check on Onion. See what he's up for."

My partner against crime emerged from the filling station. "I'm up and hungry as hell. My arm feels a little better. It's gone from excruciating to merely painful. I got a couple of painkillers they gave me just in case it gets worse."

Alto poked his head around the corner of my Cruiser. "How you guys like your powdered eggs?"

"Fresh," I said.

Phil shook his head side to side. "You boys need to show some gumption. From what I've seen, those killers could take you six ways from Sunday."

Onion's face soured as he approached. "Thanks for the sunrise sermonette, Phil." He shot me a desperate look. "You still got that second sandwich in the Cruiser?"

I shook my head. "Ate it around 1 a.m. Have some eggs."

Onion shuffled around to Alto's makeshift campfire. That left me alone with the old man. "You said something about a short cut last night, Phil."

"I did. Fetch me the map."

I opened the driver's door, pulled the map from the glove compartment, and handed it to him.

He spread it out on the hood. "Cortana's at Pueblo Pintado?"

"That's what the tracking device said last night. Same thing this morning. Must have stayed the night."

"The only paved road out of there is Navajo Route 9. Runs north of Chaco Mesa, then southeast to Torreon. Then it swings north to Johnson Trading Post, and on to Cuba. It's the only way out of these badlands."

"I can see that."

"But what those guys probably can't see is there's a dirt road runs along the southern edge of the mesa. Route 7004. Cuts twenty miles off the route to Torreon." He ran his finger along some empty space on the map.

"Can you make it on your motorcycle?"

"Thunderation! How the hell would I know about it if I hadn't driven it myself?" Phil's voice receded into an unbroken stream of invectives. His ancient hands folded the map and stuffed it into my gut. "Go eat your eggs. Be ready to go in fifteen minutes."

We left in fourteen minutes, but not before Alto tossed a dozen ration bags into the back of the Cruiser.

Phil, Alto, and their 1946 Indian Chief cycle led the way. I had to follow some ways back to give their dust a chance to settle. I thought about my rubber fuel line every couple of minutes but kept the A/C on anyway.

We drove through a forbidding land of orange-topped mesas and dry-wash arroyos. The sun burned off a morning haze. We continued on as the temperature rose beneath a clear blue sky.

Sure enough, just beyond Whitehorse, Phil and Alto waved us off to the right at a bleached road sign for Route 7004. The country ahead looked drier, rougher, more desolate than any we'd traveled. I half expected to see a jagged little sign warning: *I'd Turn Back If I*

Were You.

Onion hadn't lodged a single complaint since we left the filling station. Not a sound.

I glanced in the mirror. "You okay, pal? There's water in the cooler if you need it."

His voice sounded weary. Resigned to Fate. "I'm fine. Just watching a pair of vultures. They seem to be following us."

"Relax. Those are turkey vultures. Probably after your potato chips."

The road was still dirt, but level and dry. The motorcycle and sidecar in front of us pulled away, kicking up dust and small stones. I accelerated to forty miles per hour. Phil Friganza knew no fear.

"Brain," Onion used the nickname he'd called me since grammar school. "I've been thinking."

"Always a good thing."

"This is not a good day to die. Not a good place, neither."

"Relax. It's all that bad food. It's gotten to your brain."

"It's more than that, Gabe. Ever had a premonition? I gotta strong feeling this is not going to end well." Not the usual Deke Gagnon bluster I'd known over the years.

"Then it's up to us to see that doesn't happen. We can do this."

"Yeah…"

Just before seven a.m. we crossed the Sandoval County Line. Barbed wire fencing ran along both sides of the road. Somebody actually lived out here. Twenty miles to our south, Cerro Cuate Peak caught the morning sun, dominating the landscape all the way to Cabezon.

Ten minutes later, I followed Phil's lead and pulled up to the only store in Torreon. Its lopsided porch offered a bit of shade to lost travelers.

I hopped out of the Cruiser before Phil or Alto could extricate themselves from their motorcycle and opened the back door on my driver's side. Onion propped up on his elbow.

"You have those two pictures of Cortana?"

Onion fumbled inside his jacket. "Here."

I leaned down and took them. "Stay put. Stay low."

Before walking into the store, I took a pair of twenties from my wallet and offered them to Phil. "I'm going to ask around inside. Can you fill up the tanks?"

"I'll do it for you, boss. You rest." Alto hopped out and around to the pump. "It says you have to pay inside."

"Then come on with me." I took the twenties back from Phil and led the way through the front door. The establishment offered us our choice of cigarettes, convenience store munchies, and sundries for the modern nomad. A large hand-written sign by the cash register instructed us to: *Pay Here for Gasoline.*

Two middle-aged men—one in denim, the other wearing brown overalls—stood on either side of the counter talking and laughing. They went silent when we approached. Both looked down at Alto and then resumed their laughter.

The guy in overalls spoke in my direction. "Better tell your friend to climb out of that hole if he wants service around here." He smirked at Mr. Blue Jeans.

I stared them down for a couple of seconds, not moving an inch. "Watch what you say. He's got a submachine gun back at his motorcycle." Then I made like it was a joke and the four of us ended up laughing. "Can one of you guys help him with the pump?"

The man in overalls nodded. "Sure." He looked down at Alto. "Let's go, Big Fella." They left together.

I took Cortana's photos out of my jacket pocket and leaned against the counter. "Can I ask you something?"

The guy in jeans looked at my hand and hesitated for a beat. "Guess so, mister. What do you want to know?"

I slid the photos across the counter. "Seen this guy?"

He didn't have to look more than a second. "Yeah, he stopped in here no more than half an hour ago."

My heart pounded. "What did he want?"

"Gas. Same as you and your friend." His face scrunched up like he was figuring out how much he wanted to say. "There was another guy with him. Had a gauze wrap on his left hand. You could see blood through it." His eyes narrowed. "What's going on?"

"Did either of them say anything? Ask for anything else?"

"This guy did." He pointed to the picture of Cortana in his Army uniform. "He asked if this was the way to Cuba and how far it was.

I told him yes, that it was about twenty miles up the road. Told him to go straight past Johnson Trading Post and on from there. I just wanted them out of here."

"Thanks."

"What did they do?"

"Kidnapping. Extortion. Cold-blooded murder."

I left him with his mouth open and roamed the two food aisles for Onion, picking out three bags of chips, a quart of Mountain Dew, and several Slim Jims. For Phil and Alto, I picked up two packs of red chile elk jerky. I took a ginger ale out of the refrigerator case for myself. When I placed them all on the counter, my eyes caught sight of the *Gallup Examiner* on a nearby newspaper rack.

I picked up the top copy—yesterday's edition—and paged through the news section. Lots of details about the "Gallup Tragedy" and the latest bullshit from Washington, D.C., but not a word on the murder of Estrella Chissie.

The guy in overalls burst through the front door, breathless. "You're not going to believe this. That little guy *does* have—"

I cut him off. "How much for the gas?"

"Thirty-one seventy-six."

I left both twenties on the counter and added a ten. "Keep the change."

CHAPTER SIXTEEN

Onion, Phil, Alto and I held a conference by the gas pump, plotting our moves against Cortana. With Jay-Jay gone, we'd have to take greater chances.

My tracker said they were now twelve miles ahead of us, two miles out of Cuba, moving along Route 197. "They don't seem to be in any hurry, just moving slow and steady." I showed the screen to Onion.

He checked the read-out. "Maybe they're getting overconfident?"

Phil shook off that possibility. "They're being methodical like before."

"Lemme go in first." Alto smiled and patted his Thompson. "Smallest target with the biggest gun."

I shook my head. "Maybe we need to see what the deal is when we catch up with them."

Onion mumbled his approval, Phil and Alto nodded, but tension radiated among us. I looked at the clock on the outdoor wall of the convenience store. It must have been broken. High noon.

"Let's go." Phil motioned to Alto. They mounted the cycle and took the lead once again.

I pointed to my cellphone in Onion's hand. "Can you handle the tracking?"

He mumbled yes. We took off but hadn't gone more than a mile when he spoke up. "They've stopped. Somewhere in Cuba. Middle of town. Ten miles away."

A plane buzzed overhead, crossing our path west to east. It was the white Piper Matrix, N4408N. "Keep an eye on that plane," I said. "It's the one that took Jay-Jay."

Onion slid closer to the window and struggled to an elbow. "Dammit. The plane just disappeared over that mesa off to our right."

"We'll check for a local airport when we get into town. The tracker show any movement from Cortana?"

"Nope. They're in the same place."

Eight miles later, Cortana still hadn't moved. I hit the horn, motioned Phil off to the side of the road, and pulled up behind him.

He remained seated. "Fuel line trouble again?"

"No. But Cortana's been stopped for more than ten minutes. Two miles away."

"So?" Phil slid his goggles up on his forehead and glanced around. Alto checked the sight on his Thompson.

"Hold on." I took my cellphone from Onion and checked Google Maps, trying to match it against the tracking data. "They've turned off onto Route 550. Looks like they're at a drive-in. Let me zoom closer." I adjusted the screen. "Louie's Burgers. Probably grabbing an early lunch."

"Perfect time to surprise them," Onion said.

"Let's play it careful. Phil, you and Alto hang back. Let us drive up first. Your cycle is too distinctive. They'll spot it right away. Onion, you slouch down so it looks like I'm driving alone. Neither of them has seen me up close."

Phil spat on the ground. "We were on to these guys first. You can't keep us out of this fight."

"For God's sake, I'm not trying to. Give me a minute to make contact. Then you pull up and box their Suburban in with your cycle. Think you'll be able to recognize it?"

"Don't flip your wig, son. I've seen it a lot more than you have."

I took a deep breath. "Right."

Phil revved his engine. Alto climbed back aboard, and they followed my Cruiser toward town. Onion slouched down and monitored the tracker. Eleven-fifteen a.m.

"I've been to Cuba a couple of times before—more than twenty years ago."

"You were everywhere twenty years ago. So what?"

"I know where that drive-in is. Place had a different name back then. Talk me in."

Onion leaned over the seat. "Will do."

I merged onto Route 550 and stayed with it past the Rio Puerco Bridge. "Got to be coming up soon."

"On your right. Five hundred feet ahead."

I slowed to fifteen miles per hour. A red and white sign announced: *Louie's Burgers – The Biggest Thrill Since Your Grill.* The parking lot was half full, mostly pickup trucks. I didn't see Cortana's Suburban anywhere. "You sure you're reading that display right?"

"Brain, I was using devices like this before you were teaching school. It says the signal is straight ahead. Less than fifty feet."

I pulled into the lot and took the empty space closest to the road. "Give me that thing. And stay here. Make sure Phil and Alto don't interfere." I reached over the back of the seat, took my phone from Onion, checked the read-out on the GPS, and stepped out into blinding midday sunlight.

"Leave the door open, Gabe."

I did, then scanned the lot. No Suburban. A lonely-looking woman with wavy red hair sat off to my left at the only picnic table offering any shade. Her eyes followed me when I walked forward. The tracking signal said I was standing right next to the device. There was nothing around.

Except an overflowing garbage can.

"Shit!" I turned off the app and stuck my hand through the can's swinging lid. Flies buzzed around my head. A wasp emerged from the bin and crawled up my arm. I shook it off, pocketed my phone, and pried the lid off the garbage can with both hands. My stomach knotted up when I peered inside.

Onion, Phil, and Alto hurried to my side. Alto lowered his submachine gun toward the ground and moved in closest.

I tossed aside crumpled bags, dirty napkins, sticky soda cups, and cardboard trays. There it was—halfway down the can—my gym bag. I felt around inside it. Cortana had ripped the duct tape enough to expose the tracker. Before that, he'd removed every single bill of my ten thousand dollars. I pocketed the tracking device and tossed the bag back into the bin, too pissed to pick up the garbage around my feet.

"Hey, you," a female voice called out. The woman who'd been watching me pointed to the garbage on the ground. "Don't leave that mess there."

Phil gave her the finger. She stood up from the picnic table and stomped in our direction.

"Uh-oh," Alto said.

I looked at him. "Maybe you better take that weapon back to Phil's cycle."

Before he could leave, the woman reached us. Her shirt was as red as her hair. As red as her face. "You bright boys get a thrill tossing garbage around?"

I raised a hand in protest. "Easy there."

She got right in my face. "Don't talk down to me, mister." Then *her* finger appeared. "I'm standing right here until you clean this mess up." She did, too, until every bit of garbage had found its former home. She stomped around the bin. "That's better."

Phil started another coughing fit. A bad one.

The woman looked at his goggled head like he'd dropped in from another planet.

"Go sit down, Phil," I said. "There's an empty table over there." I pointed to my right. He and Alto walked off together.

The woman turned to me. "What the hell is going on?" Her dark eyes had a deep, piercing quality. Small green daggers.

"We're looking for a couple of guys."

"Well you won't find them inside a garbage can." She fumbled the second button on her shirt closed.

"I'm sorry. I should introduce myself." I held out a hand. "Gabriel McKenna. I'm a professor of pre-Columbian North American History. Retired."

She passed on the handshake, backed up a step, and looked me up and down. "Dr. Gabriel J. McKenna? Author of *Mystery of the Anisazi*?"

I think my eyes lit up. "Yes, as a matter of fact. I'm that guy."

"We used your text in one of my beginner archeology classes at Bryn Mawr."

"I hope you found it helpful."

"Not really. I found it boring, rather shallow. Lacking in insight."

"Don't hold back."

She cracked what I believe was her smile. It didn't last long enough to be sure. "You asked me a question. I gave you a straight answer. I never lie."

"Refreshing."

"Now, if you'll excuse me, I have things to do." She turned and walked back to whatever she'd been doing before we arrived and upset her world.

Onion appeared at my shoulder and let out a low whistle. "Some dame." He caught himself before I could say anything. "Let's eat. Then we can figure out what our options are."

"Assuming we still have any," I said. We passed Phil and Alto on our way to the front door of Louie's Burgers. "You coming inside?"

"No. We're staying out here." Phil laid his goggles on the table and wiped his brow on a sleeve.

"Suit yourself," Onion said. "More food for us."

The two of us walked into the eatery. Nobody in line. An adenoidal teenage boy in a red and white striped shirt and thick glasses stared at us from behind the counter. "What'll it be?" He turned away and sneezed into his elbow.

Onion stared at the menu on the wall. "Fucking three-fifty for a hotdog?"

I ignored my friend. "Green chili cheeseburger, small fries, medium Coke."

Onion cleared his throat. His voice sounded stronger than at any time since Gallup. "I'll have three of each. And a large Coke."

I pointed at the sling on his left arm. "You gonna need help carrying?"

"Nah." He smiled at the young man. "Can you bring the food over there?" He nodded to one of the many empty tables.

"Sure. For an extra twenty-five cents." He pushed his glasses up to the bridge of his nose.

Onion fished around in his pocket for a quarter and tossed it on the counter. "I think I'll stay here inside where it's air conditioned."

"Lunch is on me." I took out my wallet and did the math in my head. I gave the kid twenty-six dollars. He gave me another blank look. "What?" I said. "You owe me thirty-seven cents—" I looked at his name tag. "Gerald. We'll be over there." I pointed to the table where Onion sat rubbing his bandaged arm and flexing his fingers.

He fished my change out of the register. "Coming right up."

I slid in opposite my friend, peered at him, and swatted away as many flies as I could. "So, what do we do now?"

"Eat. Then we look to see if there's an airfield nearby." Onion rubbed both of his chins. "Assuming that Piper we saw was the same one that picked up the kid, it's our only connection."

"We don't even know if it landed," I said.

"No, and if it did, we don't know where. There's also no way of telling which direction Cortana might have driven. If we're lucky, he went to meet the plane." Onion cast a worried look toward the kitchen.

"That makes sense." I felt a surge of energy and drummed my fingers on the table. "Eat fast. Maybe bring a couple of those burgers with you in the Cruiser."

"Gabe. Calm down. We gotta ask around. Find the airfield first, if it even exists. One thing I'm pretty sure of."

"What?"

"If it *is* the same plane, it's not likely the kid's still in it. They took him away yesterday. Probably dropped him somewhere. Came back for whatever else they needed to do." He turned again toward the counter. "Where's my order?"

"How can you be so sure?"

Onion shook his head. "I can't. It just makes sense. If you're kidnapping kids, you drop them off where nobody can find them. You don't fly them around the countryside. Too risky. Too noisy."

"Okay, we start asking around. There used to be a tourist information center, back up the road where we merged onto 550."

"Good place to start." He licked his lips. "Here comes our food."

Gerald set an overloaded tray between us and left. More flies swarmed our table. They must have been as hungry as Onion.

I unwrapped my burger, then quickly bundled it back up. "I can't eat like this. Going outside where I have a fighting chance." I grabbed a couple of salt packets on my way to the door.

Onion called after me, "Go ahead. Meet you later." I don't think he even noticed the flies.

CHAPTER SEVENTEEN

I shoved Louie's front door open and approached Phil and Alto. They sat next to each other at a picnic table, waiting for their MRE ration bags to heat up. Phil glanced up and pointed at the food I was holding. "How can you eat that slop?"

I shrugged and walked past them to the table in the shade, where Miss Congeniality multitasked, scribbling in a notebook and muttering to herself. I don't know why I returned to her table; maybe I hadn't suffered enough. Maybe I just needed to get away from Phil.

She looked up for a moment and then went back to writing in her notebook.

"Mind if I sit here?" I pointed to the far corner of the bench across from her.

She studied my face the way a doctor analyzes an x-ray. "Free country." No hint of emotion.

I sat down, unwrapped my burger and took a bite, hoping to taste something. It didn't happen. I took a salt packet and tore it open.

The woman grimaced. "Crystals of death."

"You review food in addition to textbooks?" I added a second packet. *So there, lady.*

The corners of her mouth rose like they wanted to smile. Or it might have been gas. "You still teaching?"

I swallowed. "No. My friend inside and I are private investigators. We work out of Albuquerque."

"Interesting career arc. How does one go from being a college professor to a private investigator searching through garbage in Shangri-La?"

"Fair question." I put my burger down on its wrapper. "Do you want the short version or the long?"

She glanced at her watch. "Short."

"After my wife died—"

"Stop right there. It's none of my business. I didn't mean to pry. I'm sorry." A pause followed, so I filled it by popping a couple of limp fries into my mouth. She cleared her throat. "Seriously, how did you end up here?" She looked over at Phil and Alto. "And where the hell did you pick up *those* guys?"

I gave her the condensed version of the past two days. With each detail, her demeanor mellowed.

"The old fellow there interests me. I've always been drawn to antiquities."

Her eyes studied me a second time. Maybe I was sitting in a petri dish or something.

I shifted my body forward. "So, how did you like Bryn Mawr? I attended a couple of conferences there back in the Middle Ages."

"It was okay. I went on to the University of Chicago for my grad work. Met some *real* scholars there."

I let that dig pass. "Would it be impertinent to ask your name and what brought *you* to this back of beyond?"

She glanced at the table top and then raised her eyes. "I've been rude." She extended her hand and I got her best shake. "Dr. Naomi Costic. I am—or rather I *was*—working on a research grant from UNM. I received an e-mail this morning. An *e-mail*, would you believe that?"

"I'm not following—"

"They cancelled my grant. Just like that. UNM is cutting back, or so they say. Backed out of my publishing arrangement with UNM Press, too. Cutbacks, my ass."

"Sometimes academia sucks. I'm sorry."

She gave me her odd look again. "I do believe you are. It's just—I mean, you work so hard, give years of your life…"

I backed away a bit, so as not to invade her space. "What are you going to do? You have family?"

Her eyes moistened. "Not much. My mother was institutionalized when I was three years old. Never saw her after that. I was raised by my dad."

"Is he still back east?"

"For the long haul. Wilton, Connecticut. White Haven Cemetery, section four, row sixteen, plot twelve. Shall I open a vein for you?"

I looked away. "I'm sorry again." *Way to go, Gabe.*

"Looks like we've both reached the end of the road today. Your guys got away, my work has been terminated. Do you drink?"

"Please don't go there."

"Understood."

I wrapped the last bit of my burger in its paper. The remaining Coke tingled its way down my throat. "I don't like to admit defeat. A vestige of my boxing days."

She sat upright. "Your *boxing* days? That's the first surprising thing you've said."

"Some fighter I am. My client is dead, her son is gone, my partner's arm is shot up, and they got away with ten grand of my own money. And all I have left to go on is this." I took out the piece of paper from Estrella's floor and tossed it on the table.

She un-crumpled the note. "*Meet us at Midnight—J.*" She looked up at me. "What does that mean?"

"Who knows? That note's two days old. It was our only lead. But what good's knowing when, if you don't know where, or why?"

Naomi said nothing. She read the note a second time. Her attention seemed to drift off for a moment. "I wonder..."

I watched Phil and Alto pick up their trash and drop it in the garbage bin. The dynamic duo marched over, the old man squinting in the sunlight, his face looking as furrowed as a newly-plowed field.

Instead of coming to my side of the table, Phil walked around and stood next to Naomi, staring down at her. "Hey, sugar. You rationed?"

She shot me a pleading look. Her voice held alarm. "What's he talking about?"

"You just got a cornball come-on from a by-gone era. I think."

Her face soured. She leaned back, distancing herself from the old man. "Tell me, Phil—whatever your name is—were you ever married?"

His shoulders slumped. He shook his head. "Never met the right woman." Then he perked up and winked at Naomi. "Hubba, Hubba…"

I stepped in before things could descend any lower. "Ms. Costic, what was it you were about to say a minute ago?"

"About what?"

"About that." I pointed to the crumpled note on the table in front of her.

"I was just wondering…it's probably nothing."

"Tell us."

She unwrapped the note once more. "The project I've been working on is a study of New Mexico ghost towns, their history, how they were shaped and then destroyed by the precious metals market and the railroads."

"I'm not tracking."

She pointed at the note. "What if that is referring to a *place* and not a time?" She looked at me. When I didn't react right away, she pressed on. "One of the ghost towns I documented in my study was a place called Midnight. There's not much left of it now, but back in the 1890s it was a small but operational community."

"I remember that place." Phil sat down within cringing distance.

I waved off his remark. "You can't be *that* old, Friganza."

Phil banged the table. "Don't tell me, son. I heard about Midnight from my mother, may she rest in peace. She was born near there, in a place called Anchor. Not much more than a mining tent camp, it was. North of Red River."

Naomi's jaw dropped. "He's right. Midnight and Anchor were no more than a couple of miles from each other."

"I'll be damned." I turned the note over in my hands. "How far away is this Midnight?"

"Hundred miles," Phil said. "Give or take twenty."

Naomi checked her notebook. "I visited the ruins of Midnight and Anchor eighteen months ago. Lots of lousy road between here and there, especially the closer you get. Too bad you don't have a plane."

My ears perked up when she suggested flying into Midnight. "It's a long shot. On the other hand, what do we have to lose?"

"We'll need gas," Alto said. "Might not be easy to find along the way."

Naomi reached across the table and touched my hand, the one that held the note. "Mind if I go with you part of the way? I'll lead you on the main route to Midnight, as far as the Coyote Forest Service Station. Got a friend there I need to see. I don't feel much like going back to UNM."

"Don't see why not." I glanced at Phil. "If you can stand us."

"I know how to handle myself. Even with the Old Ranger there."

Onion rambled up to the table, a white bag swinging from his sling-supported left hand, a large soda grasped in his right. "I picked up a couple extra burgers for later." He looked at the lot of us. "What's going on here?"

I jumped up. "Get in the Cruiser. First, we're going to find that airfield, if it exists. Then we're gonna drive to Midnight."

Onion checked his watch. "Maybe I should go back and get some fries."

CHAPTER EIGHTEEN

Before getting into the Cruiser, I told Phil, Alto, and Naomi that the Visitors' Center back on Highway 550 might have information on nearby landing strips.

Alto jumped into the Indian's sidecar. "What are we waiting for? Let's go."

I led the caravan, bringing Onion up to speed on Naomi and her suggestion that Estrella's note might refer to a place named Midnight.

He sat in the passenger seat, a good sign. "I don't see any other hot leads staring us in the face. Might as well give it a try."

"Means a couple more days with Phil. Can you handle that?"

"Sure. If I don't have to eat that food of his." He stuffed the paper bag with his extra burgers into the console between us.

The Visitors' Center had an *Open* sign and an empty parking lot. Onion pushed against his door. "I'll get this." He stepped onto the gravel, ambled to the front door, and disappeared inside.

I climbed out and walked over to the other two vehicles. "You guys mind waiting while I make a call?" Nobody objected, so I moved over to the shade of an aspen tree and called Sam Archuleta. "It's Gabe."

"Where the hell are you?"

"Cuba."

"Laying a wreath on Castro's grave?"

"Cuba, New Mexico. A small town in Northern Sandoval County, just west—"

"I know where it is. What are you doing there?"

"Everything you told me not to do."

"Big surprise. And now you call because you're either in trouble or want a favor. Which is it?"

I paused. "Both. Look, if you're too busy, I can…"

Silence.

I cleared my throat. "You're *not* too busy, are you?"

"I'm in the garage. I think they call it 'puttering.' "

"Good. Listen, this is important, or I wouldn't bother you."

Archuleta sighed into the phone, a touch of melodrama I let pass. "What is it this time?"

"Info on a private plane. Piper Matrix. N4408N. Find out who owns it. If it's filed IFR flight plans during the past few days or anytime recently when the weather was bad. Can you do that?"

"N4408N. I'll find out what I can."

"ASAP?"

"Naturally."

"By the way, Sam, how are you?"

"Nice of you to ask. I'm fine. How's your client?"

I swallowed hard. "She's dead."

"Shit, no."

"Shit, yes. And Onion took a bullet in his left shoulder. I'm out ten grand—"

"I'm so glad you took my advice."

"I know, I know. We got caught up in that mess in Gallup—"

"Jeez. Onion holding up okay?"

"As long as I supply enough burgers. The Gallup cops and state police are so swamped with the chlorine gas spill, we're pretty much dealing with this on our own."

"That's what I was afraid of. I'll get on that info and call you back."

"Thanks, Sam."

"Gabe—"

"What?"

"Have a nice day." Sam cut me off.

Onion was halfway across the lot, waving a piece of paper at me. "Got it."

"Nearby?"

"Five miles north. Place called La Jara. Lady said there's a sign to it and a turn-off from Route 96. You can see it from the highway."

"Great. Climb in." I walked over to the others. "We're going to make a short stop at an airstrip near La Jara. See what we can find out. Follow us, but better you stay in your vehicles until we're done. Should take us no more than five or ten minutes."

Naomi frowned at the be-goggled Phil. "Can I come with you when you ask your questions? I know this area. I've been driving around this part of New Mexico for three years. The smaller and older the town, the more likely I'll know where it is and the fastest way to get there."

Phil spoke next. "What about us? We were in this thing first, you know." Alto nodded.

"Okay. But be careful. We don't know what to expect."

Phil suffered another coughing fit.

I couldn't take him in with us, we might need the element of surprise. But I didn't want to start another argument now. "I need somebody experienced to stay with the vehicles when we get there. Be our lookout, Phil. What do you say?"

"Roger."

The drive took less than ten minutes. Bright morning sky had given way to light gray clouds. Wind had picked up. Not a single car on the highway.

A road sign off to my left read: *La Jara Airport – Private.* The gate was closed. A white Piper Matrix lifted off from the far end of the runway and headed east over a nearby mesa.

I hit the brakes and scanned the area before moving over to the gate. No lock. I lifted the metal crosspiece and walked it clear of the gravel roadway. Then I hurried back to the Cruiser, signaling all except Phil to follow me inside.

A silver Toyota sat outside a twenty-foot square, single story masonry building. One small window faced the parking lot. The blinds were drawn. A windsock ruffled on the roof.

I crept over and peered around the edge. Two private planes were moored side-by-side, their wheels blocked, fifty feet from the hard-packed runway. Nobody in sight. I retraced my steps and rapped against the front metal door. Onion and Naomi moved in close behind me.

"Who is it?" Male voice. Gruff. Unfriendly. Faint Spanish accent.

"I'm a private investigator from Albuquerque. Have a few questions."

The door opened until its chain latch caught. One dark eye peered at me and blinked with a nervous tic. "I'm busy. Go away."

I drew the .38 from my jacket and kicked the door hard with my right leg. It gave way. The man tumbled into the dark interior, banging against the side of a desk. He fell to his knees. I pushed my way inside and grabbed him by his collar. "Get up."

"Okay, mister. Don't shoot." The man, maybe fifty years old, thick around the middle and bald on top, struggled to his feet and raised his hands. "I'm not armed. We got no money here. What do you want?"

"N4408N. Whose plane is it? Where does it come from and where does it usually go?"

"Okay, okay. That's Mister Madison's plane. Let me check the flight logs." He pointed to a three-ring binder on top of the desk.

"Do that."

"I'll find out all you want to know from there. Just take it easy, mister."

I stepped back, lowering my gun while he sat behind the desk. He opened the binder wide. A split second later, his right hand came up from below the desk with a revolver. His round, fat face grinned at us. "Put your gun on my desk. Nice and slow."

I slid my gun onto the desk and raised my hands. Naomi lifted hers without being told. Onion lifted his good arm. The man motioned us to stand side-by-side.

"Some fucking nerve you got, coming in here like that." He glared at me. "You'll pay for the door too."

He dialed a single number on his cellphone. Speed dial. "Get out here right away. I got a bunch of people thought they'd come in and muscle me around. Fifteen? Right." He hung up and smiled a second time. It didn't last.

I felt something brush against my left leg. My eyes caught a flash of gunmetal gray. Alto jumped in front of me. "Put the gun down, señor. Show respect to your guests." He fired off a couple of rounds from his Thompson into the ceiling. One bullet clanged against the overhead light, ricocheted off the desk, and hit a filing cabinet against the far wall. The man dropped his revolver onto the desk.

I flinched at the shots, then caught myself. "Say hello to my little friend." My turn to smile. "And slide that log book over here right now." I grabbed it as soon as it was within reach, then handed it to Naomi. "Take this back to the Cruiser. Onion, get his phone." I glanced around the office. A nylon cord held the blinds in place. I ripped it off. "Hands behind you." I tightened until his skin bulged over the cord.

Onion peered out through the broken door. "Better get moving."

"Right." I motioned Alto to go ahead of me and glanced around the office one final time. A Rolodex sat on top of a cabinet to my left. I grabbed it on my way out.

CHAPTER NINETEEN

Naomi bounded into her car and led us on the road toward Midnight. "The only road," she insisted. I gave her my cell number and made Alto put his Thompson in the back of the Cruiser. No time for itchy fingers now. We headed north on Route 96, maintaining random distances between us, so it wouldn't look like we were traveling together.

Five miles out, a police car screamed past us going south, siren blaring away, its right front fender bashed in like it had been in a recent accident. My cell rang. I expected Naomi. It was Sam Archuleta.

"Got something for you."

"That was fast."

"N4408N has been registered for the past five years to a Paul Angel. U.S. citizen. Lives in Vail, Colorado when he's not wintering in Cabos San Lucas or skiing in Gstaad, Switzerland."

"In the resort business?"

"No details on that yet. I'll keep checking."

"Nice work. Any record of his using an alias, like Madison?"

"Did not come across that. No criminal record, if that sort of thing matters to you."

"One more favor to ask."

"Let me start my meter."

"I need a listing of all Sandoval County law enforcement personnel. Local cops too. Cuba. State Police in the area. Then Rio

Arriba County—"

"Gabe, I can only do so much. Why do you need all these names?"

"Just a hunch."

"I gotta have more than that. I'm not gonna stick my nose into a hornets' nest based on your hunches."

"I have to be sure that any uniformed personnel we encounter won't shoot us."

"Jeez, Gabe. A little beyond paranoid, wouldn't you say? I'll go this far. You give me a guy's name, I'll check him out. Okay? But I'm not going fishing for you."

Naomi had slowed down. I got a buzz that another call was coming in. "Okay. Gotta run. Naomi's on the line. I'll call you tonight."

"Do I get to ask any questions?"

"Sorry, Sam. Of course."

"Who's Naomi?"

"Oh. She's this college professor—"

"Don't say another word. Bye."

I tapped on the second call.

"Naomi, don't worry about that cop. It'll take him a while to get to the airport. And he might not connect us with it."

"I didn't call about that. Once we get around these San Pedro Mountains, the road turns due east. That's where the ranger station is, just before Coyote. I get off there."

"Understood."

"They had a bad wildfire in Ojitos Canyon a month ago. Might not be one-hundred percent contained yet. They could still be stopping vehicles and warning drivers of the fire risk. Or maybe driving restrictions are still in force. Just wanted you to be ready."

"Think we should pull off before we reach the station and bring Phil and Alto in on this?"

"Not a bad idea. I'll look for a siding."

I glanced across at Onion, who'd been silent through both of my calls. "You want to chip in here?"

"You took some big chances back at the airport, Brain."

"Get ready to take some more."

"What if that guy at the airfield was legit? By my count, we're guilty of breaking and entering, assault with a deadly weapon, and theft. Did I miss anything?"

"I spoke rather harshly to the man..."

"Be serious, Gabe."

I filled Onion in on what Sam had told me. "We're dealing with something more than murder, kidnapping, and theft. Something much bigger. I can feel it."

"Is that what you're gonna tell the cop if he puts two and two together at the airport and comes after us?"

"After I check his badge."

Five miles later, Naomi pulled off at a spacious scenic overlook. We all followed. A sudden downpour drenched me when I stepped out of the Cruiser. Rain dribbled down Phil's forehead when he wiped his goggles.

I looked at Alto, who'd taken out a yellow poncho and was doing up the buttons. "You guys going to be okay in this weather, or should we wait it out?"

Phil wrapped an oversized scarf around his neck and adjusted his leather helmet. "We'll be okay as long as there's no thunder or lightning. Alto goes off when that happens."

Good thing the submachine gun was secure in the back of my Cruiser. "I'll tell Naomi to go slow. There's a ranger station up ahead. She knows the guy who's stationed there. We'll stop and rest a while."

Phil gave me a thumbs-up. "Alto filled me in on what happened back at the airfield. You are one rootin'-tootin'-son-of-a-gun."

"Yeah, well. Thanks for that. Rendezvous at the ranger station."

"Check." He gunned the Indian Chief until mud shot out from its rear tire.

I walked over to Naomi's car and sat in the passenger seat.

She looked out the window at Phil. "How's the old guy doing?"

"Appears to be having the time of his life. Better slow it down from here to the station, though. And if it starts to thunder, call me." Her quizzical look prompted my explanation. "Alto freaks at the sound."

"Figures."

"He'll be okay. What's the name of your friend at the ranger station?"

A wistful look came over her face. "Jed Stanley. Why do you ask?"

I shrugged. "Just curious. Can we make it to Midnight by the end of the day?"

"Not likely, it's a hundred miles as the crow flies, but the road is twice that. Your driving time will be about five or six more hours. I'd be worried about pushing Phil too hard."

"Agreed." I traced what I knew of the route in my mind. "I have friends on Santa Clara Pueblo. Know where that is?"

"Of course."

"If we can get there by sundown, they'll put us up."

"A girl in every port, eh?"

"Hardly." I hoped what I told her was true. I hadn't seen any of Nai'ya's relatives in the three months since her funeral. "Let's get to the ranger station."

Naomi pulled out first and kept to about twenty-five miles per hour. Wind blew the rain on a diagonal across our path. I checked Phil in my rearview mirror every ten seconds.

CHAPTER TWENTY

The rain stopped as abruptly as it had begun. Naomi skirted the northern slopes of the San Pedro Mountains toward the Rio Chama River Canyon. We trailed behind. Cerro Pedernal dominated the landscape to my right, rising five thousand feet toward the sun. I'd been there when they scattered Georgia O'Keefe's ashes atop that mesa, when she became one with her art.

Naomi's horn interrupted my memories. She motioned us to turn right toward a sand-colored adobe and wood structure. Coyote Ranger Station looked brand new, its walls, wood trim, and roof showing little evidence of weathering. Two benches flanked a large glass window and a metal door.

A shiny U.S. Forest Service SUV sat at the left end of the parking lot. Despite the recent downpour, a wooden sign warned of extreme fire danger.

Naomi stepped from her car, then reached back inside and honked her horn again. "Jed? Jed Stanley? It's Naomi. Come on out." Nothing happened. She walked onto the concrete front porch and rapped against the door. "Anybody in there?"

By now, we stood in a group behind her. Phil tottered from one end of the porch to the other. "Any water around?" He tried to peer into the window, then shouted to no one and everyone. "What's buzzin', cousin?"

A man appeared around the western edge of the building. Rail-thin and a couple inches short of six feet, he wore the gray short-sleeved shirt and green khaki pants of a forest ranger. His too-big cream-colored hat sat precariously atop his head, like an angel food cake balancing on a fence post.

"Who are you? Whaddya want?" His hand went to his belt. No gun, club, or even a radio. Curious.

Naomi moved away from the window. "We're looking for Jed Stanley. He's the ranger here."

"Who?" The man pulled out a bandana and wiped sweat from his neck. "Oh, him. He ain't here no more. Hauled ass about a week ago."

"Why did he leave? Where did he go?" Naomi's voice held a cup of concern with some teaspoons of hurt.

The man scratched the back of his neck. "Beats me, lady. Only been here three days."

Her words picked up speed. Her face lost ground. "Did he leave a forwarding address?"

"I couldn't say. You might try contacting state ranger headquarters."

I stepped in. "And where would that be?"

He looked at me and took a step back. "I—uh—I'd have to look it up for you."

"Your name is?" I checked the name tag on his shirt pocket. "Gerald Parra?"

He hesitated. "Yeah…"

Onion tapped my forearm. He wanted in on this. "Gerald, where were you stationed before they sent you here?"

"What do you mean?" Beads of sweat broke out on the man's forehead.

"I mean, where did you work before coming to Coyote?" He didn't give the man a chance to respond. "Come on. That's not a difficult question."

Parra shrugged. "I'm new to this. My first job."

"You don't say?" I moved in close enough to grab his front teeth. "Whatcha been doing the past ten years or so?"

He held his hands palms-up in front of his chest. "Please…I don't want no trouble. Not this soon."

"What do you mean, 'not this soon'?" I grabbed his shirt collar and brought him up close to my face. "Answer my question. The past ten years—what were you doing?"

His eyes moistened. "Time." He looked away. "I was doing time."

It was Naomi's turn to pile on. "Where? What for?"

It felt like he'd crumble if I let go, so I squeezed his collar even tighter.

"Leavenworth."

"The Hot House?" Onion's brows raced one another to the top of his forehead. "A federal offender?"

"No." Parra shook his head. "I got transferred there from the New Mexico State Pen. Ten years ago last week."

I took out my small notebook and a pen. Important information, this. "What were you in for?"

"I robbed a bank."

Onion stepped forward. "You're lying—"

"I swear."

"Only two reasons a con gets transferred from state to federal custody," Onion's voice was slow and firm. "Either what you did was so serious the state didn't want anything to do with you, or you crossed somebody and figured you'd be killed in prison unless they moved you out of state. Which was it?"

"Okay, okay." Parra was beat. I let go of his collar.

He pulled his shirt back into shape and brushed back his thin, black hair. Sweat glistened on his forearms. "There was this gang thing down in Albuquerque. Big-time drugs. I ratted in exchange for reduced time. My lawyer convinced the judge I wouldn't last in Santa Fe. He got me the transfer." He gulped for air. "I swear."

Onion stared him down. "This lawyer have a name?"

"Pelfrey. Oscar Pelfrey. Something like that."

"Erskine?" I said. "Erskine Pelfrey III?"

"That's the guy. Looked like a weirdo. But he saved my life. Got me out of hell."

I shook my head in wonder. "No shit." I looked around at my colleagues. Phil and Alto had backed off and were checking out the surrounding area. "If Pelfrey got you a break, we're going to respect that. But only if you cooperate, you understand?"

"Sure. Anything."

I took two photos from my jacket pocket. First, the one of Jay-

Jay, his mom and dad. "Ever seen this kid? Might have stopped by here recently?"

He studied the picture, then shook his head, "No."

I handed him the shot of Cortana in uniform. "Him?"

Parra took the photo and brought it closer to his face. His eyes widened. His head shook. "Nope. Never seen him either."

I grabbed his collar with even more force than before. "Look again."

"He'll kill me."

"And we've got a submachine gun in the back of my Cruiser that will leave your body parts all over this porch. Where do you know him from?"

"Name's Cortana. Mr. Cortana. He got me this job."

"He hired you?" I glanced at Onion, who looked as surprised as I felt.

"Not exactly. He came to Leavenworth last week. He works for Second Chances."

"What's that?" I said.

"It's an outfit that helps ex-cons find work. Gets them back on their feet. Cortana is one of their reps."

"When was the last time you saw him?"

Parra looked away. I squeezed his collar. Had to do it twice. "About an hour ago."

I looked at Onion and Naomi, then back to Parra. "Why did he stop here?"

"I dunno…to check up on me. I dunno."

"In a white Suburban?"

"No. A black car. Nice car. An Infinity, I think."

"Was he alone?"

Parra paused, then flinched. "There was one other guy in the car with him."

"Tell us about this other guy."

"Zig. That's all I know about him—his name is Zig. He didn't get out of the car."

Onion took out the map he'd picked up at the Cuba Information Center. "Show us which way they went."

Parra's hands shook when he spread the map on the hood of

Naomi's car. He twisted it halfway around and oriented himself. "This way." He pointed to Route 96, sliding his finger toward the east.

It all figured. The way to Midnight.

CHAPTER TWENTY-ONE

Phil ambled over to me. "I'm going to need gas soon. Can do another forty, fifty miles on what I got left. That's all."

"There's a station in Abiquiu," Naomi said. "That's twenty-five miles up the road." She turned to me. "I'll drive behind them and make sure nothing happens. We can meet up in front of St. Thomas Church. You'll be less noticeable there than if you hang around the filling station." Her eyes narrowed with worry. "Guess I can't stay here." She pulled onto the road, following a short distance behind Phil's motorcycle.

Onion sat next to me, studying my map with great intent. I hoped he understood what was going on better than I did. "Before we start, one question for you, Deke."

He folded the map. "Shoot."

"How does somebody get the power to hire replacement forest rangers? Shouldn't that come from Santa Fe?"

He nodded. "Or beyond. Forest Service is part of the federal government. Department of Agriculture. I'm thinking the same thing. Second Chances, or whoever is behind it, has connections. Knows where the strings are and how to pull them."

"We need to take Cortana alive."

"Exactly right." He reached into the console between our seats. "Burger?"

I shook him off and pulled out onto Route 96, checking my own fuel gauge. "I need a different kind of gas."

"Something else I'm wondering about," he said. "Jed Stanley. Did he go quiet-like? Or did he leave under duress?"

I checked the rearview mirror. "A better question—is he still alive?"

"That's occurred to Naomi too. You see how upset she was when she drove off?" He folded the burger in its wrapper and returned it to the bag without taking a bite.

We topped off at the only service station in Abiquiu and met our comrades in front of St. Thomas' Catholic Church. All except for Phil, who was nowhere in sight.

I popped out of the Cruiser. "Where's the old man?"

Naomi pointed to the front door. "Inside. He didn't say anything, just turned and walked in."

"Hmmm." I looked at Onion. "Stay here with Naomi and Alto."

"And do what, Brain?"

I thought a moment. "How about you check that Rolodex I lifted back at the airfield? See if any names jump out at you."

"Like what?"

"Start with the A's, like Paul Angel…then anybody last name of Madison…Zig…any names connected to the Forest Service. Jed Stanley. Second Chances." I looked at Naomi. "Use your judgment. Be back in a minute."

The church door resisted my efforts to open it. Damn thing was close to a foot thick, aged, carved in a primitive style. I slid inside, allowing my eyes to adjust to the dim colored light that filtered through stained glass on the western wall.

Phil knelt up front to the right of the altar. A statue of the Virgin Mary towered above him. Candles burned on a silver rack in front of the statue, giving his silhouette an unearthly, golden edge.

I crept up behind him. He didn't move. Resisting the urge to tap his shoulder, I stood there and listened to his quiet, murmured prayers. His thin shoulders quivered. His head bobbed to their rhythm. The hands clasped in front of his face trembled.

I whispered, "Phil? You okay?"

His murmuring stopped, and he took a deep breath without

turning around. A coughing fit shook him so hard I was afraid he'd fall over, so I grabbed his shoulder and steadied him.

When he did turn, the colored light caught the tears in his eyes. "Ease up, son. I'm feeling a little cock-eyed, that's all."

"Anything I can do?"

"Not right now. It's just…back during the war…me and my pals—the other POWs—we learned how to pray. I mean *really* pray. For each other. We made a vow back then. No matter what happened or where we ended up, anytime we were in a church, we'd say some prayers for the rest of the guys, most of all for the ones who didn't make it." He looked at me and blinked the tears from his eyes. "Today is my first time in a church in all the years since then."

I let his words linger. I considered the handful of times I'd bothered to pray as an adult. I thought maybe this old guy wasn't so crazy after all. I put an arm around his shoulder and we walked back outside to join the others.

CHAPTER TWENTY-TWO

Before we took off east on Route 84, I phoned Nai'ya's cousin Estefan on Santa Clara Pueblo. His phone rang on, before a click and a recorded message interrupted my call: *The number you are trying to reach is no longer in service.* I swallowed hard. Estefan's home had been firebombed when he tried to help me find my daughter, Angelina, less than a year ago. I paid to rebuild it. Where was he now?

The day was dying and we needed a safe place to spend the night. Hoping Estefan and his wife had just ditched their landline, I called Information and asked for a new number. They didn't have one.

Sheriff Pedro Naranjo, Santa Clara's Chief of Security wasn't a friend, but if there was a way to reach Nai'ya's family, he'd know. He hated me but loved the check I'd given the pueblo the year before to repair damage from the Las Conchas wildfire.

"McKenna?" His voice bellowed like always. "What the hell now? I thought I was rid of you."

"I'm trying to reach Estefan Garry. His phone seems to be disconnected. It's important I speak to him."

"Then I'd suggest you drive to Washington State. He and his wife packed up and moved to Coeur d'Alene Rez two weeks ago. She was born there. They're starting over."

"I don't blame him."

"So long, cowboy."

Love you too.

I hung up and glanced at Phil, who was fidgeting with his goggles. He coughed up some phlegm and spat it on the ground. "What was that about?"

"I was trying to snag a place for us to stay tonight, but it fell through. Anybody got any suggestions?"

"I do," Naomi said. "Drive to Española. The rooms at the Casino del Norté are reasonable." She made a rather sour face at Phil and Alto. "And judging from the clientele last time I was there, you should fit right in. I'll stay the night and leave for Albuquerque in the morning after I get you on your way."

"Sounds like a gas." Phil straddled his bike, ready to go. "Never been to a casino. Think they'll have dancing girls?"

"If we're lucky, no." I turned to Onion. "Check the map. How many miles from here?"

Naomi didn't give him the chance. "Thirty-five. But an hour's drive over some rough mountain road."

I checked my watch. "That should get us there in time for dinner. Phil—stay away from the slots, okay?"

"Duck soup, Professor. I don't have any money."

I should have known. "Tonight's on me—the meal and the rooms."

Naomi shook her head. "I'll pay for my own room, thanks."

"Okay. Suit yourself. Let's go." I turned away and walked back to my Cruiser.

An uneventful hour later, we trooped into Española, a modest town of ten thousand mostly modest people. Naomi rolled her window down and motioned us toward a glaring neon sign above a half-acre parking lot:

CASINO del NORTÉ — *FOOD-SLOTS-POKER-FUN!*
One Million Dollars in Winnings per Month!

Smart money knew most of those monthly winnings went back to the house. A red-lit scrolling ribbon off to the side flashed a second message:

Annual Halloween Ball—October 31—9 p.m. to 1 a.m. $500.00 prize for best costume.

A small ocean of trucks—from F-150s up to eighteen-wheelers—filled the lot. Some of the larger diesels sat with their motors running.

Resting alone in the shade of a cottonwood tree, a semi with shining white sides and no lettering or logo had parked diagonally. Blue light leaked out from a thin opening in a side door. As we drove past, I caught cheesy Vegas lounge music seeping through its cracks. Two men stood in front. Business suits. Bulges under their arms. Scowls.

We parked about twenty feet away, side-by-side, under a metal light pole.

Naomi got out of her car first and waited for the rest of us. "Follow me." She marched toward a garish, green neon archway heralding the front of the casino.

Phil stretched out a day's worth of stiffness before he followed. I waited. "You okay? That was a lot of riding you did."

"McKenna, I've been through worse things than you can imagine. You look after yourself. I'll be fine."

By the time Phil and I stood rag-tag behind her, Naomi was conversing with the front desk clerk. She turned to me as soon as she had her room number. "I'm going to get a few things from my car. Meet you back here at six-thirty, okay?"

"Sounds like a plan." I took her place in front of the desk clerk while she hurried out the door. My turn at bat. "I'd like two doubles."

Without looking up, the clerk cleared his throat. "Would you like to upgrade those to suites?"

I glanced back at Phil and Alto. I checked Onion. "I don't think that will be necessary." I handed him my credit card. When he swiped it through a rectangular machine, a light on top of it glowed red and let out an irritating buzz. The clerk handed it back to me before writing room numbers on a couple of paper folders. Phil peeked over my shoulder. The clerk handed me a pair of key cards for each room. I distributed the first two to Phil and Alto. I gave one of mine to Onion and slipped the second into my shirt pocket.

Phil turned the plastic card over in his hand. "What's this for?"

"I'll show you," I motioned toward the elevator with my head. "Follow me."

We rode to the third floor. Our rooms were next to each other, down the hallway to the right. Outside Room 315, I asked Phil for his card. "Watch this." I pressed it against a black circular pad on the door. When the light turned green, I pushed down on the lever and held the door open.

"Dang." A smiling Phil took the card from me and slid a finger along its magnetic strip.

Alto pushed past us. "I get the bed by the window." He bounded on top of the queen-sized bed farthest from the door.

Onion had already gone into Room 317. I spotted a digital clock between the two beds. Ten-after-five. "Let's meet down in the lobby. Fifty minutes to freshen up before we eat."

"Might get some shut-eye." Phil tottered over to his bed and sat down. In the fading sunlight pouring through the window, he looked every one of his ninety-three years.

I left and moved next door. Same décor, same furniture, same picture of Billy the Kid on the wall. I felt rejuvenated after a hot shower. Onion spent the time on his bed, channel-surfing his way to disappointment, or so his face suggested.

I dragged a comb through my wet hair. "What's the matter?"

He pushed with even greater vigor on the remote buttons. "No adult channels."

"Life sucks." I didn't like putting the same shirt back on, but I had no choice. "You need to use the john before we go downstairs?"

"Yeah." He groaned his way across the carpet.

I picked up the remote and found KOAT, the ABC affiliate out of Albuquerque. The six o'clock local news was just ending:

Updating our top story, the body of thirty-five-year-old Jedediah Stanley was discovered in the Carson National Forest north of the village of Taos Junction today. Stanley, a Forest Service Ranger, had been missing for more than a week. Stanley worked at the Coyote Ranger Station in Rio Arriba County. State Police would not speculate what might have brought him over to Taos County, nearly fifty miles from his post. An autopsy will be performed tomorrow to determine the cause of death.

I sagged onto my bed and tried to figure out how to break this news to Naomi.

Onion and I met the others in the main lobby at precisely six-thirty.

Phil looked a few years younger, if not any more fashionable. He and Alto turned left and right, like a dance team loosening up. "Too many people in this place," the old man said.

I sniffed the air and rubbed my nose. Phil smelled like overripe fruit.

"Dang, McKenna, that room of ours is *swell.* You got your own shower in there, with little bars of soap, even tiny bottles of toilet water. It may not be lilac vegetal, but it's *pret-ty-good-stuff.* Here, have a whiff." He leaned in closer to me.

"Lilac vegetal?" An image of my grandfather in his later years flashed through my mind.

"*Yessir.* It's all I ever use. Last bottle ran dry about thirty years ago."

"Amazing." I scanned the lobby. "Where's Naomi?"

"She's not down yet," Alto said. "You want we should go and get a table for dinner? They got two places you can eat here, the Chuck-Wagon Diner and Casa del Norté Restaurant."

Onion held up a finger to me. "Perhaps we try the diner tonight, whaddya say, Gabe?"

"Right. You go in with the boys. I'll check on Naomi. Call her cell. Maybe she fell asleep."

Phil's face lit up. "I'll save her a seat next to mine."

"You do that." I stayed in the lobby and placed the call. Nobody answered. I tried again.

Naomi spoke in a whisper, "Who is it?"

"It's Gabe. Are you okay?"

Several seconds passed before she spoke. "He's dead."

"I know. May I come up?"

"Okay…room three-two-five." The phone clicked.

I knocked on her door. After ten seconds, the latch turned and the door opened. Tears were streaming down Naomi's face. She spun away and walked back to her bed, sitting on its edge. She buried her face in her hands and didn't look up.

"You and Jed Stanley…good friends?" I walked across the room to a small sink, unwrapped a glass from its paper, and filled it with water.

"Yes. I hoped we might be something more. Eventually." She

fell back on the bed. "What the hell, I was probably dreaming. But this..." A sigh struggled its way out of her lungs. She rubbed her eyes and sniffled twice. "Jed was a good guy. Not many of them around anymore."

"I'm so sorry, Naomi. Here." I offered the glass, but she waved it off. "Do you want me to have some food sent up to your room?"

"No." She struggled to her feet, straightened her skirt, tousled her hair. "I'll come down. Just don't make me sit next to Phil. I don't think I could handle that tonight."

"You don't have to do anything. If you want to split, we'll understand. I think the rest of us can find our way to Midnight."

Her back stiffened. "Not a chance. You know as well as I do, whoever killed Jed is part of this thing. They have to pay. I'm coming with you and don't say I can't."

I wasn't sure that was a good idea, but Naomi might be better off with us than on her own right now. "Okay, come with us. We'll all pull together. And they *will* pay."

Her reddened gaze followed me to the window. I felt it on the back of my neck when I peered down into the parking lot. A white semi with the single word *Navajo* streaked across its side pulled out of the lot in a swirl of dust.

"We'd better go down now. The boys will be waiting." I turned.

"Gabe, has anyone ever mentioned there's a sadness about you?"

I didn't need anyone to tell me that. Not before. Not now. I walked over to the door and glanced back, "Coming?"

Naomi settled back down on the bed. "Where does *your* pain come from?"

My stomach grumbled. I kept my hold on the doorknob. *A burger—yes—a burger with a side of fries.*

"I don't handle loss well." Naomi's melancholy touched me from across the room. "I never got over Mom's mental collapse...or her death. Is that what happened to you? Did you lose somebody you loved?"

I thought of Angelina. Would my daughter carry her scars as long as this woman on the bed? I held the conversation off with a hand. "Some other time."

She wouldn't let go. "What was her name?"

I took a deep breath. "Which one? Let's go."

"You've lost more than one?"

"Her name was Nai'ya." I made a point of turning the door knob. "My favorite color is blue and my favorite food is pizza, okay?"

"Nai'ya. That's a lovely name. Native?"

I nodded, then tried to stare her down. Her eyes were off somewhere else.

"Were the two of you together a long time?"

I let go of the door. My hands dropped. "Less than two years."

She lay there and fixed her gaze on me like I was some kind of ancient map. Then her eyes widened with an irritating look of anticipation. "Surely, you must have found someone long before middle age."

I reached for the door again and gripped the knob until pain shot down to my fingers. "I did. *Her* name was Holly. We were married for more than twenty years."

"Happily?"

"Of course…she died less than three years ago…ovarian cancer. I'll send you a copy of my memoir when I get it written." Dear God. *My shoes needed a good polishing.*

"I'm sorry." She rolled away and lay with her face toward the window. "How did you cope with a loss like that?"

"I visited her grave every day for more than a year."

"That help?"

"No." I stepped toward the bed.

She turned halfway toward me and lay on her back now, staring at the ceiling. "Me, I suppose I'd have stayed drunk most of the time."

"I tried that too. It was never more than a short walk to the nearest bar. The road back was longer."

"I know. My first years at college, I spent every weekend about thirty or forty swallows ahead of Capistrano."

"You too?" I tried to smile, but her obvious pain stopped me. I made a motion with my hand, like I was raising a glass. "Still?"

She sat up. Her eyes took on a little bit of life. "Seventeen years of sobriety. Before that, it got so bad, my dad forced me into Hazeldon Betty Ford. The one and only time he did something good for me." She slid her legs off the bed and stood.

I gave her a thumbs-up. "Impressive. I managed a year off the sauce, once. Sobriety didn't seem to make the world any better."

"No, I don't think it does. It *can* change the way you respond to it." Naomi walked past me to the door and turned the knob herself. She had a nice walk, and I caught a dirty blonde tint in her hair I hadn't noticed before.

An elevator ride later, Naomi and I strolled into the diner. The head waitress came over. "We're meeting some friends," I said. "One is an old man with dirty-gray hair, the other—" I lowered my right hand below my waist.

"Please follow me." She grabbed a couple of menus and led us to a dark corner table, the kind of place they hide eccentrics.

I pulled out the chair next to Onion and helped Naomi to her seat. Phil's face turned sour, but I gave him one right back. "I'll sit next to you, pal. You guys ordered yet?"

"No." Onion held up a menu. "We were waiting for you."

"Before we start…Phil, Alto, you have a right to know. Jed Stanley's body was discovered today. Halfway between here and Midnight. He and Naomi were…friends." I looked straight at Phil, "So, go easy."

He nodded and buried himself in the menu. A few seconds later his head bobbed up, his eyes bright. He pointed to an inside page. "They got shit on a shingle here. Side of peas, too. This place cooks with gas!"

Alto pressed into the table. "What's that, señor?"

I left Phil to his happy thoughts and explained. "Creamed chipped beef on toast. Historic favorite of servicemen everywhere. Ate all I ever wanted during my first week of boot camp."

Alto frowned. "Think I'll have the enchilada platter."

"Smart move." I looked at Onion. "Burger, right?"

"Of course."

"What about the two you still have out in the Cruiser?"

"Breakfast."

That thought took some time shaking its way down my spine. I leaned toward Naomi.

"I'm not hungry, Gabe. Maybe a salad. Ice tea with lemon."

The menu was one of those four-page laminated fold-outs. Eggs ten different ways. Salad choices as long as your arm, each one no doubt bulging with croutons. Chopped meats *de jour*. Ribs I wouldn't touch. Mexican specials. Seafood, after a journey of a thousand miles. I thought again of Onion's two burgers congealing in the Cruiser. "Chicken strips and fries." My attempt to sound enthused crashed and burned.

The waitress came back and we ordered. Phil gazed everywhere, from the wallpaper to the ceiling tiles, carpeting, even the salt and pepper shakers. An old kid in a big city.

The sound system poured out elevator music. An instrumental version of *My Way*, the one Sinatra song I can't stand. I rearranged my silverware, grabbed a napkin, and rubbed a streak of grease from my knife. "Naomi, you want us to stick around? Try to check with the cops who found Jed's body? Find out what they have?"

"No." Naomi drew some kind of design on the table with her index finger. "We need to get to Midnight as soon as we can."

"I agree." Phil's voice became a clarion call to action, "Up at dawn. On to Midnight!"

Onion held up a cautionary finger. "I have a couple questions. What the hell do we do when we get there? Do we look for Cortana and that other guy? Or for somebody bigger?"

"Like to take Cortana first, if we can," I said. "Squeeze him hard for whatever he knows."

"Do we trust the Red River cops? Should we go to them first?" Onion looked around the table.

Gone were Naomi's grief and introspection I'd seen back in her room. "I say no. Not after what happened to Jed." Her gaze landed on each of us in turn. "The way I see it, the people behind this have money, contacts, and influence."

"She's right," I said. "We can't trust anyone but ourselves. The earliest we go to the cops will be after we nail Cortana."

Our meals arrived. Nobody wanted coffee afterward. Even Onion passed on dessert. The whole world was changing.

CHAPTER TWENTY-THREE

Back in our room, I took a hot, relaxing bath while Onion caught the end of a basketball game. When he opted for a much-needed shower, I checked the Weather Channel to see what we'd be facing in the morning. My fingers fumbled with my cellphone when the damn thing rang. No Caller ID.

"Dad?" It was Angelina.

"Honey? Where are you calling from?"

"A pay phone down in Paguate. Matty's disappeared. We've looked everywhere but can't find him." Her words turned into a stream of tears.

My heart pounded. My own grandson was missing. "When was the last time you saw him?"

"This morning. When he got on the school bus." The line crackled. Angelina and I have often had trouble maintaining a good connection.

"You call the school? Did he show up there?"

"Yes. But he and a friend of his never returned from lunch. I didn't learn about it until the school sent a guard out to the house. I'm working from home today."

This was not good. "Have you called the state police?"

"No. I don't trust them. I called Laguna Pueblo Law Enforcement."

"And?"

Her crying drowned out whatever she said.

"Angelina, I can't understand you. Take a deep breath. Speak slowly. Are the Laguna Police actively searching for them?"

"Yes. A patrol sergeant and someone from the Criminal Investigations Bureau came out about four o'clock. A bunch of other officers did interviews at the school. They've put out an Amber Alert."

My stomach bottomed out. I slumped onto the bed. "Any progress?"

"No."

Onion barreled out of the bathroom, his body wrapped in a towel, his wounded arm supported by his blood-stained sling. "Something going on?"

I held up a hand to silence him. "Try not to panic. They might have gone on a hike. They're boys, after all. Might have gotten lost. Lots of things could have happened." I had to give her hope, even while mine was slipping away.

"Can you come here?"

Shit. My mind churned over the decision. "Yes…I'll come as soon as I can. But I can't right now. Maybe day after tomorrow?"

Her voice held an edge of betrayal to it. "Why not *now*?"

"I'm on a job up in Española. We're trying to find a lost boy up here too. Look, here's what I can do. I'll call C.J. and have him come out, okay? He can report to me and I'll be there as fast as I can. I'm so sorry I can't leave right this minute."

"What if Matty's dead?" Her voice dissolved in loud, wailing tears.

I held the phone away. *Why couldn't I come up with something better?* "Angelina, Matty needs you to be strong right now. Let the Laguna Police do their thing. C.J. will be there tomorrow. I'll keep in touch with him and you both."

A lifetime seemed to pass before she responded. "Well…okay. But get here as soon as you can, Dad. I can't believe this is happening."

"You have my word. The minute I'm free, I'm on my way. I love you so much. You have to be strong."

"I'll try." She sounded a world away. "Bye."

I smashed my cellphone into my pillow. My face followed.

Onion jumped back. "Jeez, Gabe, what's the matter?"

"Matty's disappeared from Laguna Pueblo. Sometime earlier

today. He and a friend went missing from school after lunch."

"Oh, shit."

"And Angelina was pleading with me to come and help, and I can't leave here right now. I need to call C.J. and cash in a favor."

The hour was late for a phone call, but I didn't care. Unfortunately, C.J.'s wife Charmaine answered.

"Gabe, do you know what time it is?"

"I'm truly sorry. I have an emergency."

There was a long pause. I bit my cheek and waited. "Exactly what kind of emergency?"

"Charmaine, my daughter called. My grandson Matty has disappeared. I'm two hundred miles away. I was hoping C.J. might—"

"Hold on, he's right here."

"S'up, Champ?"

"I need to ask you a huge favor."

"Shoot."

I filled him in on the situation. He interrupted before I finished.

"What's her address? I'll leave first thing in the morning. Even if it means closing the restaurant tomorrow."

"God bless you both." I gave him Angelina's home and business addresses. "Call me as soon as you learn anything, okay? Onion and I are in the middle of a huge shitstorm on this case. It'll be a day or two at least before I can get away."

"Don't worry, Champ. You'll hear from me as soon as I have anything to report. With you all the way."

"I can always count on you. Do me another favor if you can."

"What's that?"

"Give Charmaine a big kiss for me."

"I was planning on doing a whole lot more before you called."

We hung up on that note. Thank God for C.J.

CHAPTER TWENTY-FOUR

Thunder and lightning woke me around three-thirty. I listened for rain but didn't hear any. One of those New Mexican *virga* storms, where the drops evaporate before they reach the ground. I turned over and dreamed I was at a ball game back in old Yankee Stadium. Knot-Hole Day. In the bottom of the sixth, all the children disappeared.

Onion and I walked into the diner at seven a.m., half an hour before we'd all agreed to meet. Only four people in the restaurant, an elderly couple sitting by the empty salad bar, some guy buried behind a newspaper, and Naomi, at the far end of the room gazing out the window, sipping coffee and taking in the morning haze. A green khaki coat hung from her shoulders.

I felt a jab in my ribs. "That Naomi's not a bad looker, don't you think?"

"She's not your type, Onion."

"Whaddya mean?" There was a pause. "You trying to run me off?"

I looked away. "I'm not in the market. Not now. Nai'ya left me empty and confused."

"Same way she found you, Brain."

The strong smell of overripe cologne caused me to turn, just as a hand slapped my shoulder. "Care if I join in on this heart-to-heart?"

I let Phil finish another coughing fit before asking the obvious question. "Where's Alto?"

"Slept in. He was watching one of those cowboy channels all night. He's a big fan of this tall geezer with a skinny little cigar. Guy needs to get rid of his blanket and get a regular jacket, if you ask me. Anyway, I shook him awake before I left."

"Good."

The old man's eyes searched the room and settled on Naomi. "There she is." He took off in her direction, Onion and I following in his wake, ready to limit any damage. He cranked himself down into the chair at her side and leaned her way. "How you feeling this morning?"

"Better, thanks."

Phil looked at the empty space between her knife and fork. "Nothing to eat?"

"Still not hungry."

"Want me to get you something for the road? Might be a while before we stop again."

"Thanks, I'll manage." She signaled a nearby waitress with a coffee carafe in her hand. "Refill?" Once her cup was again full, Naomi nodded and retreated to her thoughts.

"Boys?" The dark-haired waitress rested the pot of coffee on the table and pulled an order pad from her apron pocket.

Onion rubbed his left shoulder, winced, and ordered first. "Steak and eggs. Coffee. Side of hash browns. Large orange juice." Eating his way out of pain.

Phil examined the menu, flipping it over and back. "Can you make *Waffles de Luxe*? With apple butter?"

"Never heard of it." The waitress scratched at her hip and looked out the window.

I stepped in again. "How about waffles with whipped cream and strawberries for my friend? I'll have some Canadian bacon and a western omelet."

"Coffee all around?" She filled my cup before I could answer. We were all getting coffee.

Alto bounded to the table and dragged up a nearby chair. "Breakfast burrito."

The waitress smiled for the first time. "You got it, kid."

A couple of minutes later, I lifted my coffee for an early morning toast. "Here's to a successful day."

Naomi pulled several pieces of paper from the inside pocket of her jacket and handed them out. "I couldn't sleep last night, so I wrote out directions for everybody. Also, a rendezvous location in Red River. In case we get separated."

I glanced at Onion, whose eyebrows were as high as my own. "Good work."

Naomi continued, "Midnight is ten miles north of downtown Red River. Figured we'd stop and work out the best way to proceed from there. If there's been rain, the gravel road up the mountain could be a problem." Her eyes narrowed. "Who knows? They might even have gotten their first snowfall by now."

Phil's face lit up in admiration. "Isn't she a firecracker?" Mercifully, our waitress plopped a plate of waffles in front of him, along with a small container of syrup. "Look at all that whipped cream, Alto."

My omelet looked a bit scorched, but it tasted okay. Alto made quiet, purring sounds as his burrito steadily disappeared. Syrup oozed down Phil's chin. Onion's right hand became a blur. Naomi stared out the window.

CHAPTER TWENTY-FIVE

It was almost eight a.m. when our party marched out of the diner into the lobby.

"Gabe, look." Onion grabbed my arm and pulled my ear closer to his mouth. "It's Cortana. He's talking to the desk clerk."

"Everybody move out of sight. Quick." I strolled up behind our prey like I was the next in line and did a bit of eavesdropping.

"Will you be checking out now, Mr. Cortana?" The clerk punched something into his computer.

"No, Charles. They want me to stay on for another day. Just wanted to make sure the same room is available."

"Of course. Will you be attending our big Halloween festival tonight?"

He let out a quiet laugh. "Maybe. Got a morning paper?"

The clerk pulled a copy of the *Santa Fe New Mexican* from behind the counter and slid it across to Cortana. "Compliments of the house."

Walking back toward the others a second before Cortana turned, I pressed a finger against my lips to quiet Phil. "Upstairs. We have to change our plans." I glanced at the casino entrance. Cortana was walking down the front steps. "Hold on here for a minute."

Onion's gaze followed him all the way. "Where's he going?"

I held up a reassuring hand. "Wherever it is, he'll be back. He just extended his stay another night. Everybody up to my room. We have to figure this out." I fast-walked to the elevators and punched all the *Up* buttons. The door to my right opened first. Thirty seconds later, we piled out onto my floor and hustled down the corridor to my room.

Alto and Phil claimed the two beds. Onion sat at the desk. I walked to the window and opened the blinds. Naomi had the first question. "Okay, Gabe. What's our plan now?"

"With Cortana staying over, we don't have to rush on to Midnight. We can squeeze him right here."

"Good." Onion nodded. "How?"

CHAPTER TWENTY-SIX

A banner above the double-wide aluminum door swayed in the morning breeze: *The Halloween Store—Where Fantasy Comes to Life.*

"You serious about this, Gabe?" Onion struggled to keep pace with me. Naomi didn't bother. She inched out of my Land Cruiser like someone on her way to a root canal.

I called to her, "Come on, Professor."

She stopped and glared at me, hands on hips. "This is the dumbest thing I've ever heard. Why do we have to do this?"

"Cortana's staying over until tomorrow. If he goes to the Halloween festival, it's our best chance to get close to him."

Onion winced and adjusted his sling. "Just give me two minutes with the guy."

"We'll go to the festival tonight and mingle. See what we can learn. If he's there, and the chance presents itself, we lure Cortana outside and take him."

Naomi caught up with us. "How do you lure a killer outside?"

"I was hoping you'd help us figure that out."

"I want to get back at Cortana as much as you do, but this is too risky." She stared at me, perhaps expecting I'd waver.

I didn't. "Do it for Jed Stanley."

Her face turned as red as her hair one more time. "Okay, I'll give it half an hour. Then, Cortana or no Cortana, I'll be going back to my room to come up with a better plan."

Her words stung. "Fine. Thirty minutes. Then you go hang with Phil and Alto. Watch some westerns." I held the door and she stomped past me into the building.

The store, a barn-like structure with exposed steel ceiling beams, held row after row of costumes, organized by theme and size. The flickering fluorescent lights made me feel edgy.

A young woman wearing a blue and white checked gingham dress and a square, white apron approached. A small, stuffed dog peered at me from a wicker basket set in the crook of her forearm. I knew there'd be ruby slippers before I glanced at her feet. "May I help you, sir?" She curtsied.

"We're just looking, for now." I scanned the nearest aisle. Comic book heroes were big this year. "Do you have any fitting rooms?"

Dorothy pointed to somewhere over the rainbow. "Against that back wall."

"Great. Give my regards to Scarecrow."

She paused to think, got it, giggled, and moved on down the road. Naomi drifted down the aisle, her right hand brushing costumes she passed.

"Gabe," Onion pointed to his sling. "What the hell do I do about this? Cortana didn't just get a good look at my face. He also knows he shot me in my left shoulder."

I scratched the back of my neck. The rack to my right held dozens of super hero costumes. I picked out an adult-sized Captain America and stretched it across Onion's chest and stomach. "How about this one? You could hide the sling behind your shield."

He made a sound like he was coughing up a hairball. "Naaaah." Then his eyes came to life. "Elvis!"

I pointed to his waistline. "You'd have to be a mid-seventies Las Vegas version. And keep your shirt buttoned all the way up."

"I can rest my hand on a guitar and use its shoulder straps as my sling. Whaddya say?"

"Sure. Look around. I bet they have The King in stock."

"So, who you gonna be?"

I looked around and pondered the possibilities. "Thor."

"Have *you* looked in a mirror lately?"

"Wait, hear me out. If I'm Thor, I get to go in with a hammer in my hand, right? I'm sure the costume comes with a cardboard or plastic one. I'll substitute a real one."

"That's why we call you the Brain."

Ten minutes later, I stepped out of a fitting room, plastic hammer in hand. The King was waiting for me, bulging in unfortunate places. I pointed to the mass of fake rhinestones on his jumpsuit. "How much does it go for?"

"It says fifty-nine-fifty on the tag."

"Put it on my bill."

He struck his best karate pose despite the sling. "Thank you *vurry* much."

I scanned the nearby aisles. "Where's Naomi?"

"Right here." Her voice was no longer hard. More like soft, smoky syrup.

Onion and I turned. "Mother of Mercy," he said.

Naomi stood before us as Black Widow. "I figure if we have to go through with this nonsense, might as well let the real me come out."

I let out a slow breath. "Be careful with that front zipper."

We changed back into our civvies and I paid for the costumes. I drove to a second-hand music store to get Onion a beat-up acoustic guitar, then to a hardware store to buy a solid wooden mallet.

We arrived at the casino and met Phil and Alto in my room. Onion took orders for food. It was burgers and fries all around except for Naomi, who wanted another salad. He went down to get the food so I didn't have to pay room service. I turned to the others.

"We need to review our plans."

Alto raised his hand. "Can we eat as soon as Onion gets back? Wouldn't want anything to get cold."

"Listen up. You guys need to wait here in my room tonight. Naomi, Onion, and I are going to the Halloween festival. If we see Cortana, we'll try to draw him outside and jump him. Maybe bring him back up here, maybe take him to my Land Cruiser. In either case, we're going to try and take him alive. Then we'll drive somewhere isolated and squeeze him for information on Jay-Jay and the compound in Midnight."

Alto raised his hand and waved it now, like an eager student. "What if he don't show up?"

"Then we follow him when he leaves tomorrow. We have to stop him before he reaches Midnight. Find out all we can about whatever Angel's running there. We can't go in blind."

Phil struggled to get out of the room's only chair. "Everybody will be in costumes at this Halloween thing, right?"

I nodded.

"Then how you gonna tell which one is Cortana?"

"He has to wear his eye patch all the time. That's our key. Maybe he'll be dressed as a pirate. Captain Kidd, Jack Sparrow, somebody like that."

Phil nodded. "Right. Or he might be Hannibal, or James Joyce…" He turned to Naomi who was looking out the window. "You be careful, my dear."

I interrupted. "She will. We all will. Any other questions?"

Onion came back with lunch and the discussion died. I suggested naps all around and room service for dinner. Phil and Alto said they'd go watch more movies. Onion and Naomi opened the sliding glass door to our balcony and sat outside catching some rays. I pretended to sleep, but a rage grew inside of me as I imagined all the things I wanted to do to Julio Cesar Cortana.

CHAPTER TWENTY-SEVEN

An orange searchlight scanned the Halloween festival room while a rag-tag country and western combo did the best they could with Buck Owens' *Monsters' Holiday*. At that precise moment, Christmas music didn't seem so bad.

Naomi, Onion, and I snaked over to the main restaurant room someone had decorated as a sleazy haunted house.

The twenty-dollar admission fee gave me forty more reasons to be glad I'd convinced Phil and Alto to stay in my room. As long as the cowboy movies continued and the room service money I'd left them held out, they'd be fine.

Onion scoped out the dance floor. "This place is packed."

I made a quick study of the crowd. Looked like I was Thor Number Three, but mine was the only hammer that mattered. Naomi looked a world better as Black Widow than Onion did as the King of Rock and Roll. "How's that guitar sling holding up?"

"Shoulder hurts like hell, but the sling-thing couldn't be better. I might keep on using it after tonight."

"As long as you don't sing." Naomi stood on her toes to get a better view of the crowd.

I pointed to the front of her costume. "You lower that zipper any more, you'll get us mobbed."

She tossed her head and her hair followed. "Eat your heart out, Professor. Any sign of Cortana?"

"Not yet." I pointed into the distance. "You and Onion cover the far side of the room, I'll walk this one. Meet me in front of the bandstand." I moved to my left through a sea of lost souls. Not a single eye patch to be seen. The only other Thors I encountered had shoulder length hair that looked to be their own.

I reached the bandstand first and wished I hadn't. Listening to *The Monster Mash* played on a pedal steel guitar hurts you in so many ways. My next migraine was coming up fast along the rail.

After a few minutes, Onion pulled up, looking back over his shoulder and shaking his head.

I peered in the same direction. "What's wrong?"

"We found Cortana. He's here. And it doesn't look like he has any bodyguards."

"Great. What's the problem?"

"I was just about to tell Naomi to come right back here and let you know. Fool woman lowered her zipper a couple inches, walked over, and tossed her curves at Cortana. Ten seconds later, they're dancing."

"You think he might have recognized her?"

"I doubt Cortana's ever seen her. Besides, he wasn't looking at her face. What do we do now?"

I searched for the nearest exit and found it on the far wall, maybe thirty feet away. "Now we do a variation of the old badger game. Here." I handed my hammer to Onion. "Go through that exit door. Give me two minutes and I'll have Cortana outside. Hit him hard enough to buckle his knees, but not hard enough to cause brain damage, okay?"

He took Thor's hammer and waved it with his right hand before heading for the door. "Back of the neck just under his skull. I got this."

I retraced his path through the crowd. Halfway to the bandstand, I saw Captain Jack Sparrow and Black Widow in the center of the dance floor. I bulled my way toward them, came up behind Cortana and spun him around as hard as I could.

"What the hell are you doing, dancing with my wife?" I pressed in, face-to-face, chest-to-chest, giving him the kind of challenge he couldn't ignore.

He looked at Naomi. "Who does this *pendejo* think he is?"

"I'm Thor."

He spat a laugh at me. "And I am a bloody pirate. I dance with anybody I choose."

"You want to take this outside, beaner?" I figured Cortana would respond to an ethnic insult, if nothing else.

"You will regret this, gringo." He searched the room for the exit. Perfect.

"Let's go," I said, then glanced at Naomi. "I'll deal with you back in our room."

I barged my way to and through the side exit door, scowling all the way. "You're going to need a doctor before tonight is out." I didn't hold the door. That created enough separation for Onion to get a clear shot. Once outside, I swerved right so Cortana's back would be to him.

I squared off like I was daring him to take the first shot. Instead, he slipped a hand inside his pirate's coat. Somcthing metallic flashed in his hand.

"Now." Thor's hammer landed on the back of Cortana's neck with a soft, fleshy *thunk*. He dropped to his knees, a hand gun skidding along the ground.

I measured the distance between us and delivered a full force, right upper-cut that caught the bottom of his chin. His head snapped back. He was out before he hit the ground.

"We have to get him away from here—into the shadows." With Onion as my lookout, I dragged Cortana into the darkness.

Naomi stepped outside. "What's going on?" She peered into the night, one hand shading her eyes from the light above the exit door.

Onion showed her the hammer. "I nailed him. Gabe followed with his fist. He's out." He tucked Thor's hammer into his sling, bent over, and grabbed Cortana's gun. "Went down nice and smooth, thank God."

"Naomi, give me a hand here." I tore off Cortana's pirate outfit. He had a shirt and slacks on underneath. I whipped off the cord belt from my Thor costume and secured Cortana's hands behind his back. "Help me drag him to the edge of the parking lot. Keep him away from the lights. You and Onion stick with him. I'll swing the Cruiser around."

Naomi grabbed one arm and I took the other. Cortana was mine.

CHAPTER TWENTY-EIGHT

A Land Cruiser is a versatile vehicle. It can go almost anywhere and carry almost anything. Unconscious bodies fit neatly in its rear cargo space.

I lifted a coil of rope from my emergency kit and replaced the costume belt on Cortana's hands and feet. Onion checked our prisoner's eyelids. I stuffed an oily rag into his bleeding mouth.

We jumped aboard. Naomi piled in up front, with Onion filling the middle seat, Thor's hammer in hand, keeping an eye on Cortana. "Now what do we do? Want me to hit him again?"

I shook my head. "We interrogate the son of a bitch. Find someplace out of the way where nobody will see or hear us."

Naomi fidgeted with her zipper. "We can't take him back to your room without being seen."

"No. We'll have to find someplace else. Close." I turned on the ignition and eased the Cruiser to the edge of the parking lot.

Naomi turned to Onion, "You still have that map?"

He pointed between the front seats. "In the console."

She popped the lid and spread the map on her lap. I grabbed her hand when she reached for the overhead accent light.

"Use the flashlight. The less attention we attract, the better."

She pointed to the map. "There's a rest stop on the road to Ojo Caliente—"

"Too far. I know a better place that's less than half that distance."

I swung out of the casino lot and headed south through Española. Four miles out of town, I turned into the entrance to Santa Clara Pueblo and took the tribal road up a mesa to the Puyé ruins. The only place I'd ever killed a man.

We dragged Cortana from the back of the Cruiser and propped him against a low wall of ancient brick. Even with Naomi splashing water on his face every five minutes, he didn't come around.

"How'd you find this place?" She took the rag from Cortana's mouth and opened another bottle of water. She wet the rag and swabbed his forehead.

I wasn't sure how much to tell her. "I had an altercation up here about a year ago. Trying to save a couple of women from a guy just like Cortana." I looked at the sky. Another cloudless night on the mesa, just like that first one.

"A couple of women?"

I looked away. "My daughter and her mother."

"Oh."

"I never thought I'd come back here. But sometimes…"

She looked at the stars. "I'm sure you did the right thing then."

"I killed a man."

Cortana stirred and groaned.

Naomi's eyes widened, glistening in the moon's light. Her mouth snapped shut, her eyes kept staring at me. I didn't like it. Neither did my stomach.

"Look," I said, "this could turn out more than unpleasant. With guys like Cortana, the one thing you cannot show is any weakness or hesitation. I'm going to apologize to you in advance for some of the things I might say or do in the next hour or two."

She stood, zipped up her costume, and backed a couple of steps away.

Cortana's continued groaning grated on my nerves. I grabbed his hair and jerked his head back. "Wake up, scumbag. I got some questions. Whether you live through the night or not depends on your answers."

His eyelid fluttered. It took a minute for it to stop. Then he spat in my face. I pulled my punch and instead wiped my cheek on the sleeve of my costume. "Not used to taking orders, eh?"

"Not from you, gringo."

"Then you better learn fast." I leaned in and jerked his head back again. "You know what I see when I look at you, Cortana? A pathetic little man, a *pequeño hombre patético*. *¿Comprender?* A *little* man who kills a helpless woman, kidnaps a seven-year-old boy, and delivers his own son into a life of abuse. Who gives him up to someone bigger and more powerful who will make more money off your boy than you'll ever see."

He struggled against the ropes but said nothing.

"Understand this, I once killed a man on this exact spot. Right where you're sitting. About a year ago, on a night just like this." I spit on the ground by his feet. "And I can do it again, easy. Onion, get my hunting knife out of the van. And hand me this chooch's gun before you go." I kicked Cortana's ribs and stood above him.

Onion pulled out the Glock 17. He handed it to me and hustled back to the Cruiser. I removed the magazine and checked it. Lots of play in the springs. This gun had killed before. It held fifteen rounds now. Right and ready to kill again.

I walked Naomi out a ways into the darkness, where Cortana couldn't see or hear. "Gimme some of your water." Beads of sweat had formed on my forehead. My mouth felt full of cotton.

She handed me her plastic bottle. I turned my back to Cortana, took a swallow and a couple of deep breaths.

Her gaze burrowed into my face. Her hand grabbed my sleeve. "Gabe, do you know what you're doing?"

"Unfortunately, I do. Maybe you don't want to hang around here. You could wait in the Cruiser."

She stood, frozen. She looked at me, at Cortana, at the Cruiser. Maybe she even looked inside herself.

"Don't worry." I lowered my voice, "I not going to kill Cortana. We need him." I wanted to be more reassuring, but there was nothing else to say. I walked her back to the Cruiser, where Onion brandished my hunting knife in his good hand.

"Here you go." He turned the knife and offered me the handle. I gave him the gun and stomped back to Cortana.

The man's unpatched eye watched me when I crouched beside him. I looked for some fear in it but came up empty. First things first,

I'd have to do something about that.

"Where's the boy?"

"What? You like little boys?" He grinned at me.

I slapped his face with my free hand and wiped blood and sweat on the front of his shirt. "Jay-Jay. What kind of pissant turns on his own son? You put him on a small plane back in La Jara. Where did they take him?"

He didn't speak, but the grin ebbed from his face. He cocked his head like he was listening to soft, faraway music.

I reached out and shook him hard with my left hand. "Why did you kill Estrella?"

Nothing. Until he smiled again. "I no hear you, gringo."

"I can fix that easy." I grabbed his hair and turned the blade of my knife, giving him a clear view of both sides. "Maybe your ears are clogged." I pressed the tip of the knife blade against his left ear canal. He blinked. "Answer my questions."

I felt his body tense in my grasp. I thrust the blade into his ear, then turned it left and right. Cortana thrashed his head and tried to pull away. The knife cut deeper into his ear before I took it out. "The next mark I give you, people will be able to see for the rest of your life." I pressed the tip against his cheek, just under his good eye. "Where's the boy? Why did you kill Estrella?"

I gave him five seconds, then drew the blade along his cheek toward the ear.

"*No mas*! Stop!" Blood coursed down his cheek in a neat line and dripped off his chin, like ice cream off the face of a three-year-old. Cortana choked on each breath, his eye closing with the pain. Bit by bit, he was cracking.

I moved the tip of the blade to a spot below his left eye patch. "Maybe a matching pair of scars, what do you say?" I couldn't believe the words coming out of my own mouth.

"I tell you everything. Please, no more cuts."

I wiped the blade on his shoulder then gave him some time to think. "Okay." I slid over to a large boulder, a couple of paces away. "I'm going to wait for your answers. You have one minute." I turned the knife around in my hand. "If I get up again—"

"I'll talk."

"Then spill. Everything."

"Estrella, she told me how you saved her."

I remembered how busted up she was back then, staggering along with her son in the middle of a desert. "Who beat her up like that?"

"We had a *malentendido*. A misunderstanding?" His eye stared at the knife in my hand. "I shouldn't have done it. But you didn't know her."

"No woman deserves that."

"We talked it over when Estrella came home. We figured you have some money. The kidnapping—involving you with the ransom—it was all her idea. We agreed to split the ten grand between us."

I felt a dull pain in the pit of my stomach. The chain of events never did make complete sense to me. I leaned forward. "Why did you kill her if you were getting half of my ten thousand dollars?"

"I was afraid."

"Bullshit." I walked behind him, crouched, and pulled his head back with the blade pressed against his throat. "What was the real reason?"

"Paulo. Paul Angel. The boss. He found out what Estrella and I were doing. He forbids his *soldados*—soldiers—to do business of their own on the side. He sent one of his men to me."

"Zig? That other guy who was with you?"

"Yeah. Zig say Angel would kill me if I no do what I am told."

"Do what?"

"Kill Estrella. Give Angel all the money…and my son."

CHAPTER TWENTY-NINE

Onion and Naomi ended a private conversation before I reached the Cruiser. Onion continued to fidget with his sling. He offered me Cortana's gun and pointed to our prisoner, twenty-feet away, slumping against a crumbling adobe wall. "What did he have to say?"

I slipped the gun into my jacket pocket. "Says he was ordered to kill Estrella, give Angel the money and the kid. Says Angel threatened to kill him if he didn't."

Naomi leaned across the seat. "You believe him?"

"No. But I want him to think I do. Might make him more cooperative."

"What do we do with him in the meantime?" Onion rubbed his shoulder. A wince of pain crossed his face.

"You okay, Deke?"

"Out of painkillers, that's all. Forget it."

I shot a glance at Cortana. He struggled to wipe the blood from his face with his bound hands. "He's a mess. Can't bring him back to the casino like that. You up for some babysitting the rest of the night?"

Naomi stared at the prisoner. "Which one of us?"

"Whoever's willing to kill Cortana if he gives them any trouble."

Onion reached out his hand. "Gimme the knife."

I did. "We need to find a motel. You can lay low until tomorrow. I'll go back to Casino del Norté, round up Phil and Alto, and swing back to get you in the morning."

"Right." Onion studied both sides of the knife before tucking it into the belt sheath that went with it.

I motioned toward Cortana with my head. "I got a couple more questions for our boy, then we toss him inside the Cruiser and get the hell out of here. Naomi—"

"What?"

"I need you to look real concerned when I bring Cortana back here. Take some paper towels and clean the blood off his cheek. Set this bastard up. Make him think you care."

Her eyes narrowed. "Why?"

"Do it for Jed Stanley."

"With pleasure."

Cortana turned away from me when I approached brandishing his gun. I slid out the clip and checked it nice and slow. I popped the clip back in and walked around behind him, pressing the barrel against his skull.

"You gonna kill me?" His voice wavered.

"Why not?" I looked down at him, the Glock steady in my hands, and assumed an isosceles shooting stance. When Cortana lowered his head, I lowered the gun. "Tell me one thing, Julio. You figure your life's worth more than the life of your son?"

His head bobbed up. "What do you mean?"

"Are you willing to help us save him? Get him back from Angel? I won't waste a bullet on you if you are."

"Sure. Anything. I promise."

"Get up." I tucked his gun back into my belt and waited.

He struggled to rise to his feet. "A hand, *por favor*?"

I backed away. "Not a chance. The minute you become a burden on me is the last minute you live. This way." I fast-walked to the Cruiser, stopping to look back over my shoulder. Cortana stumbled along in my footsteps.

Naomi deserved an Oscar as the Good Cop, gasping when she saw Cortana's blood-stained face. "Hold still." She swabbed his forehead and dabbed under his eye.

I stuck the rag back into Cortana's mouth and lifted him into the back of the Cruiser. "See that he stays quiet."

Onion pulled the knife from its sheath. "Done."

With Cortana secured, I drove down the mesa's access road and pulled back onto the highway toward Española. At the edge of town, a neon sign flashed: *Mountain Rest Resort - $29.95 - Tax Included.* I pulled into its empty lot. The beaten-down buildings were little more than shacks, the kind of motel nobody stays at unless they have to. Perfect.

I left the motor running and opened the front door of the main office cabin. Somebody'd left the light on for me.

A bespectacled old-timer behind the counter turned from a flickering television show after I bellied up to his desk. The clock on the wall behind him said it was five minutes before midnight. "Kinda late to be traveling." He peered over his glasses like he expected an answer.

I took out my wallet and laid a pair of twenty-dollar bills in front of him. "One cabin. One night."

He slipped the bills into an old cash register and handed me a ten-dollar bill and a nickel in change. He fumbled a key off its hook on a pegboard behind him. "Cabin Five. I'll take you there."

I snatched the key and waved him off. "Watch your show. I can find it."

"Checkout at ten a.m." He ripped a couple of tissues from a box on the counter and emptied his nose into them. An old hound at his feet raised its head, then let it slump back to the floor. I stepped quietly out the door.

Each of the cabins had its own name: *Ponderosa, Mountain Ash, Mesquite, Pinon.* Cute. Number five was *Juniper*, one of my allergies. But it had a bed, a chair, a lamp, a dresser and a bathroom. A Gideon Bible sat on the dresser, its title just readable through a layer of dust.

Onion shoved Cortana onto the bed and settled into the chair, clasping my knife in his right hand. I picked up the Bible and gave it to my friend. "Maybe you can read him to sleep. Be ready by eight-thirty. You have your cellphone?"

"Right here." He patted his jacket with the knife.

"Call me if you need painkillers or anything. If he gives you any trouble, slice off one of his ears or something."

"Gotcha."

Naomi and I drove back to the casino in silence. She looked out her side window for most of the drive. The one time she did glance at me, her eyes burned narrow and hard. No time to worry about what she might be thinking. I let it all ride.

We rolled into the casino parking lot, pulling in next to a pair of eighteen-wheelers. The one closest to us was dark, but the other semi still had soft blue lights and pulsating music coming from inside. The driver still had it parked diagonally, still taking up three spaces. Thoughtful.

Naomi kept her distance in the elevator and stalked off with a desultory, "Good night." I said nothing and unlocked the door to my room.

Phil's unconscious body sprawled across my bed. A bag of Cheetos on his chest rose and fell with each snoring breath. Alto sat in the room's lone chair, his stubby legs crossed atop a nearby table. Surrounded by half a dozen empty wrappers, his left hand clutched a half-eaten deli sub, the sole survivor of their late-night nosh-fest. Three empty soda cans lay on the table, a thin trickle of syrup trailing to the edge. Clint Eastwood muttered something to someone on the flat screen TV.

Phil stirred. Alto took a deep swig of a soda and let out a belch. "We charged a few things to room service."

"Great. Now, off to your room, both of you. We leave early, right after breakfast."

Phil sat up and rubbed his eyes. "What happened?"

"Tell you in the morning. Can you make it back to your room?"

His scornful face was my answer. Once they'd gone, I picked up the trash and turned the television off. My cellphone rang.

"Gabe. It's C.J."

"Any word on Matty and his friend?"

"I drove out to Laguna today and asked around. Angelina—"

"You mean *Payoqona*."

"Say what?"

"Angelina is using her tribal name these days. It's *Payoqona*. Payoqona Harper."

"Solid. She still doesn't want any cops involved."

"The boys, C.J., what about the boys?"

"No sign yet. None. But it's been less than forty-eight hours. Your daughter says the money Matty keeps in his bedroom dresser is gone. Maybe they just went off by themselves."

"Maybe. What about the other boy—Richard—anything about him?"

"The kid's dog is missing, if that means anything."

I thought about it. "That's good. Kidnappers wouldn't take a dog along with them."

"Kidnappers? You serious, Champ?"

"Unfortunately, yes. Anyway, thanks for looking into this."

"No problem. I told your daughter you'd be in touch as soon as you could. She didn't look happy."

"I'll try to call her tomorrow."

"That would be good. Anything else I can do?"

"Not right now. If I have to bring in the cops, I'll ask Archuleta to go see her. Might need you to referee."

"Thanks a bunch. Where are you, anyway?"

"On the road. Better that's all you should know right now. I hope to be back in a couple of days. Tell you the whole story over a full rack of ribs."

"Another one of your adventures?"

"Something like that. Talk soon."

CHAPTER THIRTY

Next morning, I stepped outside, resting my overnight bag with Onion's clothes and Thor's costume on the ground by my feet. I reached for my Ray-Bans, then turned up my collar against a cold, north wind. Naomi, Alto, and I waited while Phil wrapped a scarf around his neck and doubled over, coughing out his first few breaths of the frigid air. I rested a hand on his shoulder and bent down for a better look at his face. "You okay to go?"

"Applesauce." He pushed my hand away and shuffled toward his motorcycle.

The semi from the night before—the one with the music and soft blue lights—had gone. A different truck was parked there now, a bright blue Freightliner Cascadian eighteen-wheeler that blocked the path to our vehicles. An orange and red diagonal splash sign on its side read: *EAGLE TRUCKING—Long Haul-Short Haul—Your Satisfaction Is Our Destination.* The driver-side door of the giant rig was half-open, its radio on, its engine off.

Alto reached the truck first and glanced inside. "There's a guy in here." He took the second step up, holding on to a metal door side grip with his right hand. "*Madre de Dios.* Somebody worked him over real good."

"Move inside, let me see." I urged him all the way into the cab and tossed the overnight bag in ahead of me.

The man's brown face was an ugly mess, like that of a prize fighter on the short end of fifteen painful rounds. Angry black and purple skin surrounded his closed left eye. A trail of dried blood led from nose to chin. A forehead gash gleamed red in the sunlight. His pulse was steady, but his breathing labored and irregular.

I struggled to loosen the collar of his flannel work shirt. "Mister? What happened?"

He moaned at my touch. The right eye fluttered, the left remained closed. A professional job.

Naomi brushed my shoulder. "Move over." I shifted aside while she felt the man's forehead.

His eyes blinked. "Who *are* you?" His gravelly voice sounded stronger than I expected, but his face flinched with pain. "Oh…" His head rolled to one side. A ceremonial stone silver Native American wolf fetish hung from a leather strand around the man's neck. Perhaps an indicator of his clan.

The back of the driver's cab had been tricked out like a home away from home—upper storage, a lower bed, a kitchenette, TV and small toilet.

"Gently," I said. "Move him onto the mattress." Alto grabbed the man's feet. Naomi steadied his head while I supported his torso. We shifted him to the bed. He groaned all the way.

Naomi pointed toward the mini-sink. "Get some water and towels."

I turned the left-hand spigot. After a couple of sputters, water flowed into the basin and I let it get hot. I found two hand towels under the sink, soaked them, and handed both to Naomi.

She dabbed at the man's wounds with the touch of a trained nurse, then passed the first towel back. "Rinse and wet this again. See if there's a first-aid kit in any of the drawers."

Alto rummaged around. "Got it." He held up a plastic box. "What do you need?"

She wiped her forehead on her sweater sleeve. "Any antibiotic cream?"

Alto checked the label on a white and yellow tube. "Neosporin? That okay?"

"Great." She grabbed it and squeezed a blob onto the man's forehead wound, then rubbed some into his bloodied nostrils.

"Water."

Alto grabbed a plastic cup and filled it.

Nurse Naomi held it to the man's swollen lips and spoke in a whisper. "Try to drink."

Most of the water dribbled down his chin, but he did manage a couple of swallows. It seemed to revive him. "Who…" He raised his hand and sheltered his closed left eye.

"We were passing by and noticed you," she said. "You need to get to a hospital. Or maybe the casino has a nurse or doctor who can look at you."

"No. Don't do that." The force of his voice startled me. "They're in this together."

"Who? In what together?" I edged closer to him.

"They took Summer, my sister's daughter—she's seventeen."

"Took her? Who are you? Where are you from?" My cellphone rang. I ignored it.

"Miles. Miles Gray Eagle. From Dulce."

Naomi placed a piece of gauze on his forehead. "The Jicarilla Reservation up north?"

Pain cut his next breath short. "Yes," he said, after taking a moment to steady himself. "We've lost three of our young women."

I shared a worried look with Naomi. "Do the cops know?"

He gave a weak nod. "Of course. But our tribal police…they're understaffed. The state cops don't have jurisdiction on the rez. Only the FBI…my brother-in-law and I are hunting them on our own." He stiffened in sudden pain.

"You need to rest." Naomi swabbed his forehead again. She turned her head. "Look around for a blanket."

Alto produced a thin woolen poncho. The man waved it off. "These scum operate at truck stops. Casinos. I finally caught up with some of them here. Last night."

I leaned in. "That big rig we saw—the one with the blue lights and music."

"It's a whorehouse on wheels. We've tracked it all over the northern part of the state. They stop for a night at a place like this, work the women…" The man grimaced, his eyes closed in pain.

I rested a hand on his shoulder. "Take it easy. We've been after them too. For three days. Nailed one of them last night. Guy named Cortana. Julio Cesar Cortana."

His right eye opened all the way. "Cortana? You got Cortana?"

"Yeah. You know him?"

"He's one of the guys we've been looking for. Almost had him last week. He put a bullet in my brother."

"Your brother okay?"

"Chato was in the hospital. He's home now. Healing." He tried to raise himself but fell back. "Will you help me?" He reached for my hand. Naomi's got there first.

"Of course we will. Naomi, can you look after him?" I pointed to the door. "Alto—outside."

Naomi held the water to Miles' lips. Her eyes followed me. "Don't be out there too long. We need to talk too."

Alto and I stood together outside the big rig. Phil sat nearby, straddling his cycle and adjusting his goggles. "What's going on?"

"The driver's beat up. He's after the same people we are." I looked at the truck, then at Phil's cycle, my Cruiser, and Naomi's car. "Too many vehicles. Not enough drivers."

The old man whipped off his goggles. "Maybe I could handle your Cruiser, but that big rig…" He shook his head. "You got any experience driving trucks?"

I checked the length of Miles' eighteen-wheeler. "Some. In the army, but nothing this big."

Phil poked my chest. "You're a professor, right?"

"Used to be."

"Then use your brain for once. If that truck's got a loading ramp inside, we can move my cycle and one of the cars into the back. We can ride together in the back of the cab."

"Brilliant." I extended a hand to the old man.

Phil waved my compliment off. "Horsefeathers."

I took my hand back. "It's worth a try, so long as it's okay with Gray Eagle. And if he's able to travel. We sure can't leave any vehicles here."

Phil squinted. "Gray Eagle?"

"The guy inside. It's his truck." My cellphone pinged this time, a text message. I pulled it from my coat.

Archuleta: *Call me ASAP. Important.*

CHAPTER THIRTY-ONE

"Where the hell are you?" Sam said, in one of his sunny moods.

I winced. "A parking lot in Española."

"Too busy to return your calls?"

I checked my phone log. *Four missed calls.* I shouldn't have turned it off. "So, you been trying to reach me."

"Me? No. The cops."

"Real ones or fake ones?"

"What? Jeez, Gabe, what the hell is going on?"

"Long story. What do you want?"

"The Gallup Police have been trying to reach you for the past twenty-four hours. I received a call from Danny Maestas, an old friend. Head of homicide there. They'd like to know who killed a woman named Estrella Chissie. Any of this sound familiar?"

"Yeah."

"Yeah? All you can say is *yeah*? When Danny couldn't reach you, he remembered our so-called 'association' and phoned me. Tell me you're not on the run again."

"I am running, Sam. Running *after* the killers. The Gallup cops had the chlorine leak disaster on their hands, so Onion and I decided not to wait around. That's not important now—"

"What do you mean it's not important?"

I held the phone away from my ear for a moment's relief. "I thought you might have found something new on that plane."

"Negative."

"Okay. See if you can find out anything about a group called Second Chances. And dig deeper on Paul Angel. Got that?"

It sounded like he was clearing a throat full of nails. "Sure. Let me turn off the vacuum cleaner and I'll get right on it. Gabe, are you *serious*?"

"And I may need you to come up here soon."

"Why don't you ask the cops?"

"I need you to help me sort the real ones from the fake ones. Something big is going on up here. And we're getting close."

"I'm retired, remember?" First a pause, then a groan. "You're not bull-shitting me this time, are you?"

"Not on your life. It's human trafficking, on a large scale. Young women mostly. But kids too. Well organized. A park ranger's been murdered. Cops have been bought or replaced with imposters. I don't know who wants to help me and who wants to kill me. I'm serious."

"Look, Gabe, I know your heart's in thc right place. I'd like it to keep beating, that's all."

A siren's whine spun me around. A police car careened into the parking lot, spitting gravel left and right. The sign on its door read *Sandoval County Police.* The front right fender was badly dented—the same cop car that passed us on its way to the La Jara Airport. *How the hell did he track us all the way here?*

"Gotta run, Sam. Call you right back."

I pocketed my phone. The cop car pulled up next to Phil's cycle. A uniformed pit bull full of bile rushed out, a gun in his right hand. "Stop right there, all of you. Up against that truck. Hands high."

Phil tried to make nice. "What's the matter, Officer?"

"Shut up and do as you're told." He clasped the microphone of his shoulder radio. "Got 'em. Casino del Norté parking lot in Española. How should I proceed?" He kept his eyes on us. "Yeah, there's three of them; one old guy, another one half my size, a third guy who looks like their ringleader. Two cars and an old-as-shit motorcycle…okay, I'll hold them until you get here."

He clicked off the microphone and pointed his gun at the three of us in turn.

I waved my raised hands. "Officer, there's been a mistake."

"That's right. And you made it." He edged closer until I could read his badge.

"What's going on out here?" Naomi jumped down onto the gravel.

At that moment, Phil moaned and fell to the ground, thrashing and coughing, gasping for breath.

The officer dropped his arm when he turned. I shot forward and planted a right cross to the side of his head. The gun fell to the ground. He reached for it, but I doubled up my right fist to his cheek. He crumbled. I pounced, grabbed his head with both of my hands and pounded it back into the gravel. And then again. The man's eyes closed. I grabbed the cuffs off his belt.

Naomi ran over and clutched my arm. "Are you crazy?"

"It's the same cop that bald guy back at the airstrip called to stop us. I'm trying to save our asses. Give me a hand, for God's sake."

Phil bounded up as fast as a ninety-three-year-old can and helped me get the officer cuffed. "Old trick I learned as a POW."

"Thanks." I gagged the cop with one of Miles' towels, cuffed his hands behind his back and dragged him over to his squad car. With Phil and Alto assisting, I pushed him onto the floor of the back seat and cracked the windows. "Here." I handed Phil a second pair of handcuffs from a storage bin between the front seats, then locked the car and slipped the keys into my jacket pocket. I took out my phone and punched in Sam Archuleta on my speed dial. "Sam."

"*Now* what?"

"Check out a cop named Richard Crawford. Sandoval County Sheriff's Department. Find out if he's legit."

"You got a thing against cops named Crawford?"

"Just do it—now. This guy appeared out of nowhere and tried to arrest us."

"Put him on."

"I'm afraid he can't come to the phone."

"Why not?"

"I just beat the crap out of him. Call me back."

CHAPTER THIRTY-TWO

I hung up with Sam's protests rattling in my ears. Almost 9 a.m., Onion had missed breakfast, more phony cops were on their way, and we were half an hour from being ready to leave.

Alto was closest, so I grabbed him. "Help me open the back of this rig." We slid the rear doors apart and I pushed him up and inside the cargo area.

He pointed to his right. "Two ramps here."

"I need both. Fast."

He dragged the first one along the floor. I grabbed it and slid it out until its front end could be lowered to the ground. We did the same with the second, then I spaced them to match the correct distance apart for the Land Cruiser's tires.

With Phil directing, I turned the ignition, lined everything up, and engaged the Crawl Assist, inching the Cruiser up until it was all the way inside, at the front end of the cargo area. Then Alto and Phil adjusted the ramps for the narrower gauge of Phil's Indian cycle.

I jumped down next to Phil. "I can take it from here."

He grabbed my sleeve. "What about the sidecar? It'll never balance on those ramps."

"Right. Alto, look up front. See if Miles has any tools."

"Careful," Phil said. "I've nursed that bike through seventy years. I expect to get another seventy."

"Don't worry. We'll make sure everything's secure." I heaved myself into the cargo area and unhooked some ropes and padding from the inside walls to cushion the rear end of my Cruiser.

Alto dragged a toolbox more than half his size up to Phil's cycle. "Miles says try the heavy adjustable wrench. Use some WD-40 if you need to loosen any bolts."

We removed the sidecar and pushed the cycle up the ramp. I positioned it as close to my Cruiser as I dared, then secured it with rope. Alto and Phil slid the sidecar up next and I tethered everything, stashing the toolbox on the sidecar's floor.

"You guys look after Miles while I handle this rig. Maybe I can convince Naomi to stop playing nurse long enough to drive her own car."

Phil curled an arm around me and leaned in, a father giving advice to his untutored son. "You've forgotten something, Junior."

"What?"

He pointed over my shoulder to the orange and red sign on the side of the semi. "How you going to hide the logo? It's a dead giveaway."

"Good catch." I rushed to the cab. "Miles, is there any way to cover up your *Eagle Trucking* sign?"

He propped himself up and gulped a lungful of air. "It's bolted into the side. You'll need two people to get it unfastened. If you can wait a few minutes—"

"Not a chance. You stay put." Alto and I climbed into the back of the truck and grabbed a DeWalt reversible drill and nut driver set. I undid the bottom bolts and lifted Alto on my shoulders to unscrew the top ones.

The sign thundered down to the ground outside the truck. We lifted it and slid it into the cargo area. Back at the front cab, I looked up at Naomi. "Here's your keys. You'd better drive ahead of us in case we're followed. Go to the Mountain Rest Resort. East side of Highway 30, south of Española. Onion and Cortana are in Cabin Five."

She cleared her throat. "I was there with you last night, remember?"

"Oh. Right."

"What then?"

"You wait. If we aren't there in fifteen minutes, take Onion and Cortana and get the hell out. Head north. Highway 285 to Ojo Caliente Hot Springs. Pull into the parking lot and wait for us. Hopefully, it won't come to that."

Naomi glanced down at Miles. "Rest up. I'll see you soon. Alto will be here if you need anything." She climbed down, settled into her car, and sped off.

"Miles, you got the keys?"

He fumbled in his pocket. "Here…you know what you're doing?"

"I'm doing my best, that's what." I fastened my seat belt. "Everybody hang on." I turned the ignition. The dashboard lit up like a Christmas tree. "What the—?"

"You rushed it. Those are error codes. Prop me up. I'll talk you through it." Alto and Phil grabbed Miles under his shoulders and helped him into the passenger seat. "Turn the key on and off about five times, real quick."

I did what he said.

"Turn all the accessories off, the A/C, everything…good. Now let the clutch out."

Two Camaros screeched into the parking lot and hemmed us in. Their windows were frosted dark. Two pair of young men sprang from the cars. Shaved heads. Tattooed faces. Pointing guns.

CHAPTER THIRTY-THREE

The men opened fire. I ducked behind the steering wheel. "Everybody get down. Miles? Help?"

"Turn the ignition." The semi roared to life. "Put it in gear. Now, gun it. Straight ahead."

Head down, I floored the accelerator. The huge rig lurched forward. The sound of shattering metal rose above the wild roar of our engine. Somebody screamed beneath us.

The front window took a barrage of direct hits, bullets ricocheted; the glass cracked in a couple of places, but held. I ground my way into second gear and dared to peek over the steering wheel. Nothing but daylight in front of us. The side-view mirror reflected the twisted remains of one Camaro. Three of the young guns clustered around the second car, its front door and one of its fenders smashed.

Miles tugged on my arm. "Let me take over. You'll never get us out of here."

"Sure you're up to it?"

"I can handle this better with one eye than you can with two. Move."

I pulled to a stop and slid out of the driver's seat. Miles groaned and slid in behind the wheel.

I checked the passenger's side mirror from my new seat and pulled out my gun. The door on the second Camaro was still hanging by a single hinge, a couple of thugs struggling to realign it. The driver crawled out the other side, popped the hood and then kicked at a tire. The car wouldn't start.

Miles' fingers played the gearshift the way an artist handles a paintbrush. The gunshots fell silent. Our new Apache friend gunned the engine and put some comforting distance between us and our pursuers until traffic forced him to slow down through downtown Española. Three miles later, we pulled to a stop in the parking lot of the Mountain Rest Resort.

"Stay here, all of you." I jumped down and scanned the road behind us before running to Cabin Five and pushing the door open.

Onion had Cortana tied to a chair, hands shackled behind him. The killer hadn't lost his scowl. A New Mexico map lay spread out on the bed. Naomi perched on the edge of a desk by the window.

I pointed my gun at Cortana. "He give you any trouble overnight?"

Onion patted the knife on his belt. "A real sweetheart. Everything ready?"

"Sort of. We're being followed. You got Cortana's cellphone?"

Onion reached into his jumpsuit pocket. "Here you go."

I checked the settings. "Damn."

"What's the matter, Brain?"

"I forgot to look for a GPS app. This thing's been broadcasting his location all night long." I disabled the app, shoved the phone inside my jacket, and glared at our prisoner. "Where's Zig?"

A night without sleep hadn't erased his poker face. "Who?"

I slapped him across the cheek. "Zig. The guy who was with you when you killed Estrella and took the boy."

He stared at me.

I walked behind his chair and pressed the barrel of my gun against the back of his head. Then I raised it and brought it down flush against his skull. He sagged forward.

"I'll ask you one last time. Where's Zig?"

"Okay. Okay. One of your shots got lucky back at Red Rock. Caught Zig in the wrist. He was losing too much blood. Angel sent a couple of *soldados* to look after him."

I pulled his head back by his hair. "Describe them."

Cortana's words came easier. "Never saw them before. Two new guys. Kids. Said they come from El Salvador. *No hables ingles.*"

Onion shifted on the bed. "Where'd they take him?"

"To one of our doctors. Back in Gallup, I think."

I pressed the gun against his head once more. "You have a name for us?"

"No. I swear. I'm no big a deal in Angel's world, not now."

I aimed my gun at his forehead. "Then maybe you're of no use to us either."

Sweat blistered Cortana's face. "I beg you, let me live. I help you… get you closer to Angel than you'll ever get without me."

Onion stuck his face into Cortana's. "How close?"

"I get you into his compound at Midnight. Draw you a map. Get you inside. Whatever you need."

I looked from Onion to Naomi and slipped my gun back into my jacket. "Take him out to the truck. Tie him down in the back of the cab. Keep the cuffs on. We leave in five minutes."

Onion stopped in his tracks. "What truck?"

"A lot has happened in the past twelve hours, my friend." I filled him in on Miles, the fake cop, the two carloads of gunmen we'd left behind, and the info I'd received from Sam. "I'm afraid we're up against something a lot bigger than Cortana and his crimes. Remember what the cops back in Grants said?"

"You mean about all those missing young people statewide?"

"Exactly. We're on a mission here that may be impossible."

"Don't change a thing as far as I'm concerned." He pointed to the bullet wound in his arm. "I'm going to settle this score one way or another." He grabbed the back of Cortana's collar and hustled him toward the door with one hand. "Anything else?"

"Yeah. Your clothes are in my overnight bag behind the driver's seat. Ditch the jumpsuit."

CHAPTER THIRTY-FOUR

I gave the motel room a once-over and hurried back to the truck. Onion was standing outside the passenger door of the Cooper. Naomi stuck her head out of the driver's window. "Ready to lead the way. I'll wait for your signal."

"Will do." I gave Onion a thumbs-up, whether I was trying to convince him or myself, I couldn't say.

Miles sat back behind the wheel of his semi, eyes closed. I hoisted up onto the step and peered around him. Cortana lay in the back of the cabin with his cuffed hands tied to a leg of the lowered bed. Alto perched across from Cortana, out of arm's reach, his Thompson at the ready. Phil rummaged through the small refrigerator. "Got any sandwiches? It's a long drive."

"We'll stop along the way." I crawled into the passenger seat and nudged Miles. "Let's go. Hit the horn twice."

He checked the side mirror, gave Naomi her signal, and followed her car onto the highway. We traveled north through Ohkay Owingeh Pueblo, then northeast on Route 285. The sky was blue, the traffic eased, and we made good time on the two-lane road. Ojo Caliente Hot Springs teased us as we flew past. We all could have used a good soak.

Naomi dialed me on her cellphone. I put it on speaker so Miles could hear. "We're coming to a turn-off," she said. "Shortcut to the Rio Grande Gorge Bridge."

"Where?" I glanced out the window.

"Taos Junction. Follow the signs to Carson."

I looked at Miles. "You get that?"

He nodded. "I know exactly where she means. About five miles ahead."

Phil called from the back of the cabin. "Don't mean to bellyache, but we gonna stop for lunch?"

"Not until we're across the bridge." I checked Cortana. He lay still, his head turned toward the back of the cab. Alto gave me the *okay* sign. I checked the side mirror. Nobody driving behind us, the sun burning above us. I looked across at Miles. "You holding up okay?"

"Don't worry about me." He turned at Taos Junction, then five miles later, swung onto a gravel road along the west side of the river gorge. Cortana's cellphone rang.

I whipped it out of my pocket and checked Caller ID. Somebody named Espinoza. I turned toward the back of the cab. "Wake him up."

Alto shook him a couple of times before Cortana stirred, then groaned, then sat up as far as his shackles allowed.

"Who's Espinoza?" I held up the ringing phone.

He rubbed his good eye on his sleeve. "What?"

"You have a call from somebody named Espinoza. I'm putting it on speaker. Find out what he wants. One false word—one—and Alto will kill you."

"Okay."

I pressed the answer button.

"Julio? It's Espinoza. Where the hell are you? Why is your GPS turned off? You know Angel don't allow that."

Cortana cleared his throat. "Sorry, *mi error*. What's going on?"

"Angel told me to call. He wants everybody to meet tomorrow morning at the compound. Nine o'clock. Everybody. Even you."

He looked at me and I nodded. "I'll be there. What's going on?"

"Nobody knows. There's a rumor he moves the whole operation. Relocates somewhere farther north."

"Count on me."

There was a pause. "Can we? *Amigo*, Angel, he pissed at you. *Muy enojado*."

"What for?"

"He say you freelance too much. You go off on your own, try

to wring money from that gringo. Now he can't keep track of you through your phone. I don't want to be in your shoes. You better be careful, amigo."

"I will. Any word on Zig? He okay?"

"They took him to Gallup. Nobody's heard nothing since."

"Oh." His shoulders slumped. He looked down.

"It's like I say, Julio. Be *muy* careful when you get here."

Cortana hung up the phone and stared at the roof of the cab. I snatched the phone from his hand.

"You did all right," I said. "Need a drink?"

"Yeah."

"Alto, get a bottle of water from the refrigerator. Let him have as much as he wants." I took out my own phone and called Naomi. Onion answered.

"Yeah, Brain, what's up?"

"Drive on ahead. After you cross the bridge, find a place where we can get some food. Make sure it has a big parking lot, so the semi won't stand out so much."

"Will do. How's everything?"

"Cortana just got a phone call. Tell you all about it when we stop."

Miles turned the rig north along Upper Rim Road, two lanes of potholed blacktop along the western ridge of the Canyon del Rio Grande. The lower rapids of the Taos Box ran a thousand feet below and off to our right.

Something whistled past my half-open window with a low-pitched whine. A quarter mile behind us, sand and gravel kicked high into the air. Another bullet cracked the glass of my side mirror.

"They're back." Miles hit the accelerator hard. The truck lurched ahead, black smoke trailing behind from the dual exhausts above our cab.

I kept looking out the window. Another dark Camaro. Couldn't tell if it was one of the ones we'd left for dead at the casino. I unloaded a couple of wild shots in its direction.

"Hang on." Miles swerved left and hit the brakes.

The Camaro couldn't stop. It slammed into us. The truck bucked. Miles groaned as he accelerated in the left-hand lane.

I glanced back. With smoke pouring from its back end, the

Camaro resumed the chase. Weapons stuck out from every window. I ducked back in when more bullets shrieked past.

Miles down-shifted. In the cracked glass of my side mirror, I caught the Camaro accelerating, pulling even with our right rear tires. I turned around and braced my back against the dashboard, then stuck Cortana's Glock out the window and fired blind until half the clip had emptied.

I called to Alto. "Gimme your gun."

He passed me his Thompson. "Fifty rounds in that drum. Full."

I grabbed it with both hands, leaned out the window, and opened fire.

The Camaro's front window caught at least half a dozen rounds, but the glass held. A grenade launcher emerged from the passenger's side front window.

I couldn't allow them another blast. I aimed on the driver and squeezed the trigger. Every round I had left. The window collapsed inward, the driver's head lurched back, then plunged forward against the steering wheel.

The Camaro veered off the blacktop, onto the right-hand shoulder and across the low scrub beyond. The driver never hit the brakes. The car careened across the sand and through the scrub, barely slowing down. It plunged over the cliff and disappeared.

I collapsed against my seat. My hands shook. The Thompson dropped to the floor. I gulped for air, unable to catch my breath. "Water..."

Phil stuck a plastic bottle in my face.

I coughed it down, panting, sweating, my thoughts confused. A sick feeling rose in my stomach. I leaned against the door. The metal felt cool against my forehead.

Miles glanced over. "You know that gun's illegal, don't you?" He turned his gaze back to the road.

I tried to answer but couldn't. I closed my eyes, it was all I could do. I'd just sent four men to their deaths.

CHAPTER THIRTY-FIVE

Miles' truck veered to the right and jostled me back to my senses. We approached a sign announcing *Rio Grande Gorge Bridge – 1965*. The area had a festive feel to it, a mini-carnival in the middle of nowhere full of ice cream trucks, jewelry carts, and tables offering jerky of every type, *ristras* of red chilies, and colorful pottery. Rows of cars lined the highway, with people crowding the bridge railings on the northern side, photographing the scenic view and eight-hundred-foot drop-off. A young boy stood perilously close to the curb, staring into his cellphone. We crawled across the bridge, the beauty outside not quite balancing the ugliness I felt in my gut.

Halfway across, Miles pulled over to the right-hand curb. Two Taos County Sheriff's cars, sirens wailing, lights flashing, sped toward us from the eastern edge of the bridge. I followed them in my side mirror after they raced past. They turned off in the direction we'd come. Somebody'd seen that Camaro plunge into the gorge and called it in.

"Shit." I took another gulp from the water bottle. "Keep going. And hope those cops didn't notice your shot-up windshield."

Miles turned north onto Route 522 through Taos Pueblo land. By now, my hands had stopped shaking quite so much and my head had cleared. A mile up the road, we met Naomi's Cooper parked in front of a roadside stand.

I pointed off to the side. "Pull into that lot behind her."

Miles swung the big rig around back. He set the brake, but kept the engine running.

I looked into the rearview mirror at Alto and Phil. "Okay guys, take five. Pit stop and lunch." I took out my wallet and gave each a ten. "Miles, stay here a minute." I gestured toward Cortana. "Watch him. Have to make a call."

I jumped out of the cab, hurried around the truck, and into the shade. I hit my speed dial. "Sam, it's Gabe."

"Of course. What now?"

"Time to bring in the FBI."

"Whoa there, cowboy. How about a few details first?"

"Paul Angel's called a meeting for tomorrow morning."

"Paolo Samoza."

"What?"

Sam let me twist for a second. "His name's Paolo Samoza. There *is* a file on him. He's from El Salvador. Possible MS-13, though that's unconfirmed. You asked me to look into him, remember?"

"Right. Thanks. He could be moving the whole operation. Sending the captives out. We have to go in now."

"*Where?* You overestimate me, pal. I can't just rub a magic lantern and get you the Feds."

"Sam, we don't have time to waste. They'll all be together. Nine tomorrow morning. It's our only chance."

"Gabe—"

"I just killed four men."

"What? Jeez! Where the hell *are* you?"

"Eastern side of the Rio Grande Gorge Bridge. On our way to Red River. Angel's running his operation out of a compound north of there."

"Go to the local police and wait."

"Can't do that, Sam. You don't understand—"

"I understand what's going to happen to you if—"

"For God's sake, shut up and listen to me. We need help we can trust. You still in touch with that guy from the Albuquerque FBI office? Carlson, or whatever his name is?"

"Haven't talked to him in almost a year."

"Get him up here. Now. Lives depend on it. Not just mine and

Onion's. Young people. A dozen, at least…Sam—"

"Okay. Okay. What do you want me to tell him? You want to meet at nine? Where?"

"I'll call back with the exact location once we're there. Meantime, get the Bureau up to Red River. In force: SWAT team, helicopters, everything."

"Carlson might not buy all that."

"Then go over his head. Listen, I need you to do this more than I've ever needed anything before."

Sam paused. "Okay. Understood. I'll call you back, but don't expect help before morning."

"We'll try to keep Angel, his men and their captives there until then. And Sam—"

"What?"

"If I die before you get here, thanks for everything. I mean that." I hung up and walked back to Miles. "Can you lock Cortana in here safely?"

"How 'bout I just knock him out?"

"No, we need him clear-headed the rest of the way."

"Then I'll secure him and lock the cab. What's up?"

"I need to get everybody together. Plan our next twenty-four hours. Meet you by the food truck."

Miles winced in pain when he grabbed Cortana by the shirt. "Face the wall."

The rest of the gang was sitting at a picnic table next to a food stand that operated out of an old VW bus. Onion and Naomi worked on a couple of Frito pies, Alto and Phil wolfed down butter-laden fry bread. I wasn't hungry.

Onion looked up. "What's happening, Brain?" His words sloshed out through a mouthful of beans.

I sat across from Naomi and waited for Miles to join us before plunging into a summary of my recent phone calls. "So, I figure we spend the night near Red River. Move out in the early morning."

Miles walked up, frowning. "When does the cavalry arrive?"

I tapped the top of the table. "Not sure yet. Our job is to make sure nobody leaves the compound until the Feds get there, whenever that may be. Are we clear?"

Nods and mumbles all around, except for Miles. "What about firepower? I have a shotgun and an old Colt back in the truck, but not much ammo."

"That's something," I said. "I have my Detective Special and Cortana's Glock with half a clip. We have Alto's Thompson." I looked at him. "Ammo?"

"One more load. 50 rounds."

I nodded. "Naomi, ever fire a gun before?"

Her back arched. "There has to be a first time."

"We'll have to see. Onion, you're gonna have to break your promise never to carry again. You get the shotgun."

"For these bastards, I'll make an exception. With this arm in a sling, I'm not much good without a gun."

Naomi reached across the table and grabbed my hand. "Don't leave me out because—"

"I'm not leaving you out. I need somebody to move the young people out of harm's way once we separate them from their captors. They might respond better to you. I mean, look at the rest of us."

She glanced around the table and paused a moment before nodding. "I'll try."

There we sat—six motley but willing sacrificial lambs. The FBI couldn't arrive too soon. "Any questions?" I said.

Phil cleared his throat and raised a hand. "Can we bring some fry bread with us?"

I handed him five bucks from my wallet. "Go."

Miles looked off at the surrounding hills. "My mother made the best fry bread in the world."

"Can I ask you something?" I said. "Every Native guy I know *swears* his mother makes the best fry bread in the world. How is that possible?"

His eyes moistened. "Sacred Mystery."

CHAPTER THIRTY-SIX

Forty miles of bad road stood between us and Red River, our last stop before Angel's compound. Across the street, a clock in a bank parking lot said it was two-thirty-six. A scrolling sign below asked if I'd done all I could to guarantee my secure retirement.

Phil came back with a bag of fry bread and a bottle of water. "I'm made in the shade. Let's go."

"Do you need to use a bathroom first?" I said.

"Nope. If the time comes, there's always the great outdoors."

With that image dancing in our collective heads, Naomi led our way north toward Questa, our turn-off for the highway to Red River. My shirt clung to my back and sopped my neck. New Mexico's November sun can still peel the paint off your car, but then maybe the sweat came from my nerves. I mopped my forehead onto a sleeve. "You have air conditioning on this rig?"

"You're going soft, McKenna." Miles shook his head but reached down and switched it on low.

The breeze helped calm me down, at least until Caller ID announced Curtis Jester was on my phone. "C.J.? What's up?"

"Good news, Champ. Matty and his friend have been found."

I let out a grateful sigh. "Thank God. Where were they?"

"Water Canyon, west of the pueblo. They'd decided to hike to Mount Taylor. Go on a *quest*. Kids…"

"How's Angelina taking this?"

"She was ready to skin Matty alive. I think I calmed her down."

"Tell her I'll stop by in a day or two."

"Gabe, you ought to get her a cellphone. Might make things a lot easier."

"She had one. Gave it up when she went traditional. Don't ask."

"When you coming back here, Champ? You haven't had any ribs in more than a week. You must have the shakes by now."

I held out my fingers. "I do, actually. Should be in town in two, three days. Promise I'll stop by. And thanks so much for stepping in while I've been gone."

"What friends are for."

I hung up, took another deep breath, and tried to relax. Might have even nodded off.

We arrived in Red River at 4:30. I'd kept quiet most of the way, amazed at Miles's ability to shepherd all eighteen wheels along the twists and turns of Highway 38. Thirty miles per hour often felt like sixty as he made our way through Carson National Forest and past an ugly, open-pit mine north of the highway.

Autumn tourists crowded the main drag in Red River. Sale pennants flew from businesses on both sides of the road. The autumn foliage had turned here, the brilliance of yellowed leaves competing with the sun. We drove on.

Naomi turned off the highway and into the parking lot of the Char-Pit & Go-Kart Emporium east of town. Miles followed, swinging the truck behind the building at the back of the parking lot. We all piled out and gathered at a long table in front of the restaurant. Cortana remained tethered to the lowered bed at the back of the cab.

I adjusted my Ray-Bans and turned away from the sun. "Know of any overnight truck stops or RV parks where we can stay tonight?"

Miles answered, "My brother and I use the Alpine." He looked at Naomi. "They also have cabins. Decent place."

I nodded. "Good. We'll stay there. Right now, let's rest and eat. Onion and I will join you in a couple minutes. Right back here."

Onion's jaw dropped. "But I—"

"Your appetite can keep for a bit. We have some business with Cortana. Naomi can get us a couple of burgers, okay?"

She nodded.

"Three," Onion said. "One for Gabe and two for me."

I started toward Miles' truck but turned back when Phil protested. "I want to check out that Emporium. Judas Priest, look at those racers!"

"They're called Go-Karts." I opened my wallet. Sixty bucks left. I handed him a twenty. "Go have some fun. Take Alto with you." For a ninety-three-year-old guy, Phil moved like the wind when properly motivated.

CHAPTER THIRTY-SEVEN

"Wake up." I kicked Cortana in his shoulder. He sat up and shot nails at me with his eye.

Onion closed the glove compartment of Miles' truck. "Here's some paper and the pen you wanted." He parked his bulk in front of the door and stared at the prisoner.

"I'm going to give you one chance to prove we should keep you alive." I slid the paper onto the small table at Cortana's side and handed him the pen. "Draw me a map of Angel's compound. Leave nothing out. I want the approach roads, entrances, everything."

He held out his hands. "I draw better without these cuffs."

"Not a chance. Onion, you still got that knife?"

"Right here." He slid the shining blade out of its sheath.

"Maybe our friend would like his other ear to bleed, too."

"No, no." Cortana bent over and drew a rectangular outline on the page. "I draw you the part above ground first." His hands slid over the paper. "Two entrances. One ten miles up an unpaved road—Sawmill Mountain Road—the other in the back—through these woods. Here." He traced a narrow line around the rectangle. "Only way through is on foot. Angel has guards at both entrances. Four in front. Two in back. Sometimes four."

Onion crouched closer. "Can the path to the rear entrance be seen from the compound?"

"Not now. Leaves are still on the trees."

I looked out at the hills surrounding Red River. "The foliage has yellowed, but most of it's still there. We'll have to take that chance. How close to the compound can you drive?"

Cortana seemed to think on it for a moment. "Quarter mile, maybe. Not in this truck. Too much noise. The road is loose gravel when it's not mud."

"No rain lately," Onion said. "That's something."

"I'm going to send you and Miles around to the back. Alto, Naomi, and I will try the front."

"Brain, that makes no sense. It doubles our chances of being stopped before we get in. We should all go around back. Fewer guards and more cover there."

Onion was right. "Okay. We'll need Miles' heaviest tools, crowbars, knives. Can't use any guns until we get inside."

"*If* we get inside…" Onion pointed to a second, thinner rectangle Cortana had added to the paper. "What the hell is this?"

"The landing strip. Angel, he flies in and out couple of times a week."

Onion winced. "One more thing to worry about."

I shook my head. "Not necessarily. A landing strip also makes it easier for the FBI to come in full force." I stared down at Cortana. "How many soldiers does Angel keep at the compound?"

His smile raised the hair on the back of my neck. "Depends. A dozen. If everybody has to be there, then twenty. All armed. And they will kill you, señor, before you can ask any questions."

Onion turned the knife blade over in his hand. "Gotta keep the element of surprise, Gabe. Take out a few at a time if we can."

I fought the urge to slap the smugness off of Cortana's face. "Turn the paper over and draw us a picture of what's inside the compound."

Cortana flipped the page. "First, you climb the outside stair if you go in the back way. This place, she's an old abandoned mine. Angel hollowed it out last year. One large cavern, like a theater, no? And a walkway all around above it. Thirty feet up." He drew a circle in the center of the page and made a concentric circle above it. "Flat place down below, *escenario*, yes? How you say, stage? Angel talk from there. You stay on the catwalk around the top."

"Where are the controls for the lights?" I looked at Onion. "We need to get as close to them as we can."

"Lights here." He drew a small box on one side of the stage. "Next to door to two smaller rooms, there and there." He marked each room with an X.

I tapped the X's. "What are those for?"

He pointed to the first room. "Angel's office. His computer center. Controls for alarms. The smaller room is for supplies. Guns. Ammo. Some food. Water."

Onion's eyes narrowed. "Where do they keep the young people?"

"This other side." He pointed with the tip of the pencil. "A door that goes down a tunnel. Cages on one side. One or two prisoners to a cage. Depends on how many are being held."

I didn't like what I was hearing. "Any other way in or out of the tunnel?"

He smiled his lizard smile again. "No."

"Alarm system? Tell us more." Onion had broken into his share of buildings over the years.

"Just the guards at the compound entrances—"

"Good," I said. "Any other security devices?"

"Two beam sensor alarm systems, one on the main entrance road and one on the air strip."

"Not so good." I pointed to the paper. "That it? Anything else inside we need to know about?"

"Animals," Onion said. "Angel own any dogs?"

Cortana let out a laugh that startled me. "*Perros*? No. Angel, he's afraid of them."

I took the paper and pen and motioned Onion outside. Before following him, I used the pen to draw a dot in the center of Cortana's forehead.

He tried to back away, but I held him steady. "What are you doing to me?"

"Those maps better be accurate," I said. "If they're not, that dot is where my first bullet goes."

Onion stopped me outside the truck. "What do you think?"

"I think without an element of surprise, all or some of us are gonna get killed."

"What about the FBI? When do you think we can expect them?"

"I don't know." I walked over to a picnic table and sat down. "We'll have to find that out before bringing the others in on our plan." I dialed my cellphone and let it ring. "Sam?"

"Hope you have more info for me. The Bureau wants more details."

"The compound is north and west of Red River. Ten miles up Sawmill Mountain Road. And get this—there's a landing strip on the property. For Angel's plane. Some of the Feds can fly in."

"If they come at all."

"Sam?"

"Carlson's on board, but it's not his call. He's waiting for an okay from FBI and Justice. Whole lot of asses need to get covered in D.C."

"Dammit, what are they thinking? That this is another Waco? You *could* remind Carlson about the last time I asked for his help—"

"Already done that. Carlson's not the problem. Gabe, people are likely to be killed. By law, there'll be an investigation, no matter which way it swings…" I heard a familiar sound on the other end of the line, Sam emptying his lungs of smoke. "Look, s*ome* kind of help will be on its way in the morning, I promise you."

"Thanks for that much. Will you be coming along?"

"Count on it."

I hung up and looked at Onion. I'd seen him happier. "Gabe, you think Alto and Naomi will be able to kill somebody if it comes to that?"

"Alto yes. Not Naomi. And I don't want to put her in that position."

"What do we do with Phil?"

"Been thinking about that," I said. "I don't question his courage. Don't even question his judgment all that much. But suppose we sneak inside and he bursts into one of his coughing fits? We can't risk that."

"He's not gonna like being left out."

"I know. Maybe I can have Phil hang back and stay with Miles' truck. Have him guard Cortana. And I'll give the old guy the map. Have him turn it over to the Feds when they arrive. Then Phil can come up to the compound with them."

Onion looked at the ground and thought for a second. "First thing is to take out the guards at the rear entrance. Get inside undiscovered."

"Right. Then we fan out along the walkway and ring the area below. Hide. Wait to see what Angel tells his soldiers."

"What if somebody spots us?"

"We kill Angel and ask questions later. You willing to go that far?"

Onion rubbed his shoulder. He swallowed hard. "Yeah."

I folded the map and slipped it into my shirt pocket. "Bottom line—we can't start until Angel flies in. And we have to delay him and his operation until Sam arrives with the Feds."

"Hope they can find the place."

"They will. I'll give them another update in the morning. But we've got to stop Angel without losing any of the young people they're holding."

"Maybe we *should* go to the Red River cops first."

"Deke," I said, "after all that's happened so far, do you trust they haven't been bought by Angel too? He's had a whole year to compromise them. I'd rather take my chances with Sam and the Feds."

Onion opened the refrigerator and rummaged around. He gave up and gazed out the window. "I'd like to enjoy a good meal tonight. Just in case..."

CHAPTER THIRTY-EIGHT

Four of us filled up on Char-Burgers and poured over our plans for tomorrow. Nobody choked, something I took as a good omen. The Go-Kart track must have closed at 6 p.m. because that's when Alto and Phil showed up. Alto then ran off to get them some seared meat, but Phil looked pale and wobbly on his way over to our table.

"You okay, man?" I should have known better than to ask him a question that left so much room for bluster. He tried to answer but coughed so hard Naomi popped up and helped him sit on the bench. I slid a bottle of water across to him.

Phil listened to my summary of our plans before deciding to explode. "Judas Priest! What the hell am I supposed to do? Sit on my ass?"

I looked around the table. "Maybe you all could take some food over to Cortana? Make one last pit stop before we hit the road?"

They got my gist and walked as a group toward Miles' semi. When Alto returned with more burgers, I put one on the table for Phil and sent Alto packing along with the others.

Phil tried to glare me down, but a lifetime of hurt simmered in his eyes. "You think I'm too old, don't you? Seventy-seven years ago, they said I was too young. You're both full of beans."

"It's not that at all, Phil. I understand how you feel. You've always wanted to make a difference. What we need from you now are your brains and your judgment. Somebody has to hang back by the truck.

Keep an eye on Cortana. Meet the Feds when they arrive and lead them up to the compound. I know I can count on you to convince them. What do you say?"

His yellowed teeth tore a large chunk from his burger. He took a swig of water, then nodded, barely. "Okay. Okay. You can count on me. Let me see that map."

I unfolded Cortana's drawing and let him take a long look. "I'll make you a copy before tomorrow."

"Think I'm an eight ball? I'll remember this." He thrust the map back at me and took another huge bite of burger. "Where are the fries?"

"We'll get our carbs in the morning. Right now, we need to move out of here." I pointed to the rest of his paper-wrapped burger. "Bring it with you."

Miles had the truck revving. Onion joined Naomi in her car. Alto helped Phil into the back of the cab where they bracketed Cortana. I took the first step into the truck, then caught myself, and hustled over to Naomi. "Follow us. Miles knows the way to the RV camp. Just in case, it's called the Alpine. Couple of miles east of here."

The sun made its slow cascade along the western horizon. Maybe an hour of daylight remained. Traffic was light and within five minutes, Miles braked and pulled across the road into a spacious parking lot that already had its evening lights shining. He pulled around to the rear and set the cab abreast of a recharging station and water line.

Before he turned off the engine, Miles opened his window and called out to Naomi who'd pulled alongside. "The cabins are off to the left, up that hill." He turned to me. "You gonna stay in the truck tonight?"

My back answered for me. "Nope. I need something a bit softer."

"Not a problem. I can manage Cortana by myself." His hand creased the still-angry wound along the right side of his head. "Don't worry about a thing." The man had impressive recuperative powers.

I looked beyond him to the back of the cab. "I'll have Naomi rent three cabins. Phil and Alto, you can share. Onion and I will take the second. Naomi can enjoy some peace and quiet. That okay with you guys?"

Alto and Phil looked at each other. Phil had calmed down some, his face not quite as red as before. "They got TV? Breakfast in the morning?"

Miles gave out a quiet laugh. "Yes, and yes. They start serving at six."

"Perfect." I gave Miles the okay sign and stepped down from the cab. A wind was blowing in from the hills to our north. I zipped up my leather jacket on the way to Naomi's Cooper.

She stepped out and stood with her arms wrapped around her for warmth. I took out my credit card and offered it to her. "Put that thing away," she said. "You've paid for everything so far. Tonight's on me."

Phil walked up and threw another arm around her shoulder. "That's mighty kind of you, my dear," he said, oblivious to her cringe. Then he turned to me. "Son, can I borrow some money? I'd like to treat everyone to breakfast."

My first reaction was to search for a cash machine. Then I thought, *maybe better wait until tomorrow night.* "Sure." I took out my wallet and gave him my last two twenties.

The guy behind the business office counter looked over his half-glasses when we walked in, checking us out one at a time. I guess we passed muster. He broke out a smile and a booming voice. "Welcome to the Alpine! How many cabins?"

Naomi plunked down her credit card. "Three…close together if you have them."

The clerk checked his registry. "I can do two together. One will have to be down at the end of the row, if that's okay. Units five, six, and eleven."

"Perfect." She checked the room cards. Her hand reached out toward Phil. "Here you go, eleven." She looked back to the clerk. "Breakfast at six?"

His eyebrows rose. "That's right. You been here before?"

"Nah," she said. "Lucky guess."

We mumbled our collective thanks and walked out of the office and out into the early evening. The sound of crickets unsettled me. Spooky thing, facing the night that could be your last.

I called after Alto and Phil, who'd gone ahead of the rest of us. "Wake-up call at five-forty-five tomorrow. Don't stay up too late."

Phil stopped. "Mind your own beeswax."

Naomi glanced at me and let out a sigh. "What's the use? Don't worry about me oversleeping. Probably be awake all night."

"Would you like to help me take care of a little business? Onion needs to rest his arm and I have a couple of small items that need attention. We'll need your car."

She didn't have to think about it. "Sure. Anything."

I looked at Onion for approval. "That okay with you?"

He rubbed his shoulder and nodded. "I could use some time off."

I let a hand settle on Naomi's shoulder. "Meet me back here in five minutes."

Onion and I moved into unit six. Miles was right. The cabin was clean, the linens fresh. I tossed my few things onto a small table by the rear window. Onion tossed himself onto the first bed.

"I'll be back within the hour, hopefully."

Onion looked up and cocked his head. "Where you going, Gabe?"

"To take out an insurance policy on Cortana."

CHAPTER THIRTY-NINE

I stopped at Miles' truck and banged on the driver's door. "Open up. I need the key to the back."

Gray Eagle rolled the window down. "Hang on a minute." He disappeared into the darkness of the cab. Ten seconds later, his hand stuck through the window, keys dangling from his forefinger. "What for?"

"Need to get something from my Cruiser. Back in a minute."

I moved behind the semi, opened the padlock, and slid the rear door until I could slip inside. I snapped on my flashlight and snaked along to the front of the cargo area. My night vision goggles were in the Cruiser's rear cargo area. I snagged them, then closed and locked the truck. Miles looked down from the driver's window.

"How's Cortana?" I showed him the goggles.

"Not a peep. Didn't eat anything."

"Fasting is good for the soul. Thanks for the keys. See you when the sun comes up."

I knocked on Naomi's door and turned the knob. She'd left it open. I popped my head in. "Ready?"

"In a minute." She finished combing her hair and joined me outside, testing the lock behind her. "Okay. Where to?"

"Junebug Campground. We passed by it about five miles east of Red River this afternoon."

"That tells me where. Now tell me why."

"A couple of loose ends I need to tie up on Cortana before tomorrow. Don't trust the guy."

"I don't either. But why the campground?"

"Remember the old fairy tale about Hansel and Gretel?" She nodded. "Well, I'm going to lay down a trail of electric breadcrumbs. Just in case our prisoner decides to double-cross us when the chips are down."

"Electric breadcrumbs. Okay…"

"We need to get moving first, then I'll explain." We settled into Naomi's car and she started the engine. I slipped a hand into my jacket pocket and took out Cortana's cellphone. "They're tracking his cellphone. Even now. So, we're gonna use this to sow some confusion."

"You've got *me* confused. That's a start."

"Espinoza—the guy Angel has keeping tabs on Cortana—knows he's close-by the compound. But he must be wondering why our boy isn't coming all the way home, why he's hanging back this late at night."

"So?"

"So, I'm going to make it look like Cortana's collaborating with the FBI. Plant some text messages on his phone. Maybe a Google map of directions to a rendezvous with the Feds. Then we'll let Angel's guys find the phone."

"Is the FBI in on this?"

"No. But you are. Your cellphone, anyway."

She gave her head a slight shake. "Come again?"

"We'll make it look like your number belongs to somebody at the Bureau. And we send a few texts back and forth. Make it look like Cortana and the Feds have been in contact."

"But won't you be tipping off Angel to the real thing?"

"Angel has to suspect his operation is in the law's crosshairs already. That's why he's moving out. We'll make it look like the raid is going to happen the day after tomorrow instead of tomorrow. Disinformation." I looked at her for some sign of approval. It wasn't there.

"Not going to work."

"I agree, Angel's too smart to fall for it. But we don't have to fool *him*, just the guy he has monitoring Cortana. Let Espinoza convince Angel for us. Take out your cellphone." I opened Cortana's phone and read off his number and address.

Naomi punched them in. "So, I pretend to be some guy from the FBI, right?"

"You got it. Bring up your text messaging."

"Done."

"Okay. Send the following message to Cortana's phone: *On for Thursday. 4 p.m. Carlson.*"

She punched in the message. "Next?"

"Now I send one from Cortana's phone: *Check. Meet at Raton. Friday morning. JC.*"

"That it?"

"For now. I have one more phone message to leave, but we need to let some time lapse in between." I took Cortana's wallet from my jacket. It held three-hundred dollars, all in twenties. I handed them to Naomi. "Here. Cortana's paying for our rooms."

"Gladly. Now, I assume we're not going to sit here all night?"

"Go west on Route 38 for a couple of miles. Turn into the Junebug campsite."

"*Oui, mon Capitaine.*" Not sure why, but I caught myself smiling at her sarcasm. Her tires spun in the gravel parking lot, squealing once we hit the roadway. I spent the ten-minute drive going over the plan in my head. I had no margin for error.

Junebug Campground didn't look like much when we'd passed it on our way into Red River. Now, in the darkness, it looked like even less. A handful of picnic tables under clumps of birch, overflowing refuse barrels, empty parking spaces—but it was perfect for what I had to do.

Naomi slowed to a halt. "Where do you want me to park?"

"Stay right here for a minute." I opened Cortana's cellphone and called up Google Maps. I asked it to plot the route from Red River to Raton, a town on the main route to Denver, sixty miles to the northeast. I saved the map under the heading, *"FBI rendezvous."* Corny, still it might fool Angel's watchdogs.

I climbed out of the car and placed the wallet on the ground beside the closest picnic table. Then I checked the call log on Cortana's phone and punched in the number Espinoza had used when he called us back at the Rio Grande bridge.

Three rings. Then Espinoza. "Hello?"

"Espin—" I hung up. He called back seconds later. I let it ring and go to voicemail, then I placed it on the ground a couple of feet from the wallet and climbed back into the car. "Drive to the far edge of the campground. Someplace that can't be seen from here. Pull in behind some bushes or rocks. If anyone's been electronically following Cortana, they should show within an hour or so."

Naomi took her hands from the steering wheel and turned toward me. "Where do you get your ideas?"

"From the sidewalks of New York, my dear. Playing a hunch. You ever do that?"

"Sure," she said. "When I decided to tag along with you and Onion." She drove a hundred yards or so down a narrow gravel path to the far end of the campground, parked behind a rock outcropping, and turned off the engine and the headlights. "Now what?"

"Now I put on these." I slipped the night vision goggles over my head and tightened the straps.

Naomi studied me for a moment, then shrugged. "I didn't figure you asked me here for a make-out session."

CHAPTER FORTY

I touched Naomi's forearm. "Wait here. No radio. Be back in ninety minutes at the most."

With the goggle straps digging into my skull, I slunk into the darkness, coming within a hundred feet of where I'd left Cortana's wallet and cellphone. Somebody had recently tried to steal a picnic table, giving up when its chain wouldn't budge. They'd flipped it on its side, snug against a pair of white birches. I crawled behind it and sat there, peering through a slit in the table top.

Ten minutes passed. Then twenty. I slipped off the goggles and rubbed my eyes awake. Half an hour. An ambulance screamed by on the highway. Ten more minutes of nothing.

A car pulled into the park. The driver dimmed his headlights and came to a stop no more than twenty feet from Cortana's phone. Two men climbed out of the car, each wearing white t-shirts, jeans, and do-rags. One brandished a handgun, the other carried what appeared to be an M-16.

They stood back-to-back with their weapons raised, scanning the area with flashlights. One man took out a cellphone and stepped away from the car toward the bait I'd left. "*Venga por aquí.*"

Step-by-step, the two men approached the phone. Another ambulance raced by on the highway—*what the hell?* The second man stumbled but caught himself on one knee. "*Míra esto.*" He stood, clutching Cortana's wallet in his free hand.

The two converged and examined the wallet. A minute later, they turned back to the ground, scouring it once more with their flashlights. I adjusted my goggles.

"Aquí." The first man bent down and lifted Cortana's phone. He opened it, punched at the screen with his finger, and spoke to his companion with ever-increasing agitation. I slept too much back in Spanish class, couldn't tell what he was saying, but from his tone the dude was clearly upset. He pocketed Cortana's phone on the way back to their car. Lights back on, they sped off east toward Red River.

My long shot was even money now.

Naomi startled awake when I opened the passenger door and plopped in next to her. "What happened?"

"I exercised my God-given talent for misdirection."

"They take the bait?"

"Maybe. I hope so. They found the wallet, the phone, checked them both, and took off in a hurry."

"What do we do now? Can I start up the car? It's getting cold out here."

"Let's wait ten minutes. Make sure they don't come back."

We sat and waited. The wind picked up. Raindrops splattered against the windshield, a few at first, then a heavy barrage that lasted thirty seconds before stopping in an instant. Another New Mexico rainstorm. Then silence. I listened to Naomi breathe.

"What are you thinking about, Gabe?"

I felt my cheeks burn. "You…I want you to stay alive tomorrow."

"You too, okay?" She didn't turn or even move, as far as I could see. Just kept staring out the front window. Yet another siren shrieked its way east toward Red River.

I stared straight ahead. "You know, tomorrow could be a truly terrible day."

She didn't respond right away. "It could also be what we were born to do."

I turned to her. She seemed more shadow than substance in the dark. We inched closer until our lips met. No hands, no bodies, just lips. An odd sort of kiss. Warmer than any kiss I could remember. It lingered.

She caught herself before I did. "We should get back."

I didn't move. Then I tilted my head and stared at her. "I didn't think you cared."

She smiled for a bittersweet instant. "You and me, Gabe—we're too much alike to ever get together." Now *she* turned and stared.

I slumped back in my seat. "Maybe that's it." I let out a breath that turned into a small, gray cloud inside her car. "I hope I don't sleep tonight."

Her head jolted back at my words. "Why not?"

"Every night I spend chasing these guys, my dreams get darker. I'm turning into what I hate."

She laid her soft right hand on my forearm. "You're a good man, Gabe. Whatever happens tomorrow, thank you."

"Thank you? For what?" I searched her face for an answer. It felt like looking for Waldo. All I saw were her tears in the faint light.

"You got me out of my head and into something important. I was so wrapped up in my own problems, I couldn't see anybody else's. Gabe, if we do make it through this, I'm going to quit digging around in the past and do something constructive with the rest of my life."

I gave her a smile from my heart. "Let's go."

She turned the ignition. Ten minutes later we pulled into the Alpine Motor Lodge.

CHAPTER FORTY-ONE

By six-thirty the next morning, the condemned had eaten a hearty breakfast. Naomi picked at her scrambled eggs, but the rest of us held nothing back. Phil stuffed a couple of donuts into his pocket after paying our tab. Together we drank enough coffee to fill a casket.

Once outside, I took a New Mexico road atlas from Miles' glove compartment and we matched it to Cortana's hand-drawn pages. I pointed to the atlas. "You familiar with the roads once we get out of town?"

Miles gave me a thumbs-up. "We turn onto Mallette Road and go north where it becomes Route 597. Couple miles later, it changes again to Sawmill Mountain Road."

I traced the route with my finger. "Lot of switchbacks. Can this rig go all the way?"

"Unlikely. I'll take us as far as I can. At some point, we'll have to pull off and take out your Cruiser. Get in close as we can with that."

"No. The last stretch we'll have to go on foot. Can't risk being seen before we reach the compound itself." I folded the maps, putting the atlas back in storage, keeping Cortana's pages in my shirt pocket.

Miles popped the hood of his truck and ran a final check. I stood next to him and called Sam to let him in on the details.

Archuleta cleared his throat. "You might want to hold off for a while, Gabe."

"What's the matter?"

"We're still waiting for authorization from the Bureau."

"Oh, for crying out loud—"

"Carlson's on board. The SWAT team is ready. Helicopters. We'll be on our way soon as we get the word."

"This can't wait, Sam. We're starting out now. We'll take up positions and pause as long as possible. But if it looks like Angel is moving before you arrive, we'll stop him ourselves if we have to. Can't you at least have Carlson move his men up to Red River?"

"I'll ask. From there, we'll converge as soon as we get the okay. Carlson can notify local law enforcement too."

"Tell him to be careful. Deal only with personnel he knows, okay?"

"Right. See you soon."

"I hope so, Sam." We hung up.

Miles looked off to the west. "Can I borrow your phone to make a call, Gabe? I'd like to talk to my family one more time."

"Sure." I handed him my cell. He walked around to the far side of his truck, out of earshot.

"All aboard." Onion walked up with Naomi and opened the passenger door of Miles' truck. Alto and I helped Phil climb in. Naomi went next. Onion stepped into the foothold and grabbed the back of the seat with his good hand. I pushed him in the rest of the way.

Miles returned a couple of minutes later and started his rig without saying a word to anyone.

Before we left, I told everyone about my latest call to Sam. "If anybody thinks we should call this off, anybody wants to back out, let me know now. No questions asked."

Cortana raised his head. "Can you leave me behind? I'd rather live."

I pointed. "Somebody shut him up."

Alto aimed his Thompson at our prisoner's face. "*Silencio.*"

I checked my watch. Six-forty-five.

The Alpine was on the south side of Route 38, Red River's Main Street. Before Miles could pull out, a chorus of sirens screamed from three police cars racing east, the direction we were headed. An ambulance and a second EMT vehicle followed. The roar of an approaching fire engine kept us at the side of the road.

"What the hell?" I looked after the vehicles. "Where's everybody going?"

"Hold on." Miles put a hand on my arm. A second fire engine roared past. He winced when he craned his neck to look back to the west. Yet another siren grew. A third fire truck passed by.

Phil's voice sounded from the back of the cab. "Bad news for somebody." Nobody else spoke.

Miles checked his side mirror and turned east. "Let's go."

The firc must have been outside of town. We drove all the way to Mallette Road and north onto Route 597 without any sign of an emergency. The sun broke through the cloud cover and offered the first bright note of the day. Mallette Creek flowed alongside us as we drove, reflecting the morning rays. No sign of any private aircraft. Just birds flying south.

We hit the turn-off for Sawmill Mountain Road at seven-fifteen. Miles down-shifted again and swung left. The semi chugged along twenty minutes of gravel road and switchbacks. No guard rails. I stared straight ahead or up at the sky.

Still no sign of the emergency vehicles. Whatever all the commotion had been about, it wasn't happening here. Not yet.

The mountain road took a sudden dip and swerved to the right. Miles rode the brake. The opposite side of the road opened into a wide turnaround. A narrow, unmarked gravel road led off to the west, sloping up the hillside. Dense forest growth overhung both sides of this trail, making it look like the center aisle of a green cathedral.

"Hold on," I checked Cortana's map. "This might be the road to Angel's compound." I called back to Onion. "Bring him up here."

Cortana fell to one knee when Onion pulled him off the cab's bed. "Take it easy. I don't give you no trouble, señor."

"Look outside," I said. "Is this the road we take?"

"Sí."

I waved for him to be pulled away and heard him thud against the rear wall of the cab. Even with one good arm, Onion appeared ready for action.

I looked over at Miles. "Pull into the turnaround and shut her down. Make sure we have enough space to get our vehicles out of the back."

Miles swung into the turnaround and left plenty of space behind us. I opened my side door, jumped down, and walked away from the cab to take a better look around. A steady buzz sounded overhead, off in the distance at first, then louder. A private plane was headed our way.

I ran out into the middle of the road to get a less obstructed view. Ten seconds later, the aircraft flew directly overhead. A white Cessna, just like Angel's. I couldn't read the N-number on its side. It soon passed from sight beyond the trees, but the deepening sound of its engine told me it was descending and banking. I checked the map again. It showed the landing site north of the compound. We were less than a mile away.

CHAPTER FORTY-TWO

"Everybody out."

Miles, Onion, Naomi, and Alto gathered in front of the truck. I walked past them, balanced on the first step up, and checked on Phil.

"You want to stay inside with Cortana?"

"Danged if I'm going to be that fella's babysitter. Get my cycle out of the back."

I raised a hand in protest. "You won't need it."

"Don't tell me. What if something happens and I have to get word to the rest of you? What if the FBI wants to use it? What if—"

"Okay, okay. We'll take it down. But stay at your post until the Feds arrive, promise?"

"You better give me the map. The Feds might need it."

"Sorry, Phil. You told me last night you wouldn't need it, so I didn't make a copy. I've got to use this map when we get close to the compound. No time to argue." The sound of the airplane stopped. Zero Hour.

Miles and I opened the cargo area and set up the ramps. We lowered Phil's cycle to the ground and pushed it off to the side. I climbed back up and started the Cruiser. With Alto on one side and Onion on the other for guidance, we backed out of the truck and down the ramps.

I looked around. Too many vehicles in plain sight. "Let's put the cycle and Cruiser where they can't be seen." With Alto's help, we secreted them under the canopy of a clump of Aspens on the north side of the gravel road. The overhang would keep them out of sight by any aircraft as well.

Miles crawled into the cab and handed out his shotgun, a handgun, a hunting knife, and two crowbars. He shut the cab door, gave Phil the keys to the truck and to his motorcycle, and joined us at the head of the trail. We'd gotten closer with the truck than I'd expected. Trying to get in closer with my Cruiser would be taking an unnecessary risk.

I gave Onion the shotgun, keeping my .38 and one of the crowbars. Naomi got the pistol we'd taken from Cortana. She handled the gun like it was about to explode. I showed her the safety and how to slide it off. Alto checked his Thompson, then slung it over his shoulder.

"We'll go single-file along the road until just before we get in sight of the compound," I said. "Then we'll slip off into the trees and head for the rear entrance. Any questions?" We'd rehearsed our plan well. Nobody said a word. "Alto and I will take the lead, Miles and Onion bring up the rear. Naomi, you—"

"Stay in the middle and watch both sides, I know. Let's get on with this."

We headed up the trail. A hundred yards later, I was sucking wind. Nine thousand feet above sea level will do that to you. I listened for the plane, just to be sure. Nothing. It must have landed. No wind, no birds, no sound but the thumping in my chest. The crowbar felt heavier with every step I took.

"Stop." Naomi spoke in a tense whisper. "Did you hear that?"

We halted. Off in the distance, someone had yelled. I didn't catch what he said, might have been in Spanish. We froze for an eternal ten seconds, then resumed our approach.

Birch trees stood thick on each side of the road. A pair of crows called to each other from somewhere in their branches. A low, electric hum reached my ears and increased in volume as we walked on. I slowed the pace, hoping we'd see Angel's men before they discovered our presence.

Cortana's map showed the compound to the right of the trail, with the airstrip still farther off in the same direction, a ways down the side of the mountain. I figured it was right down the hill from where we were standing.

"Nice and easy now," I whispered. "Into the woods. And quiet as you go."

Alto stepped off the trail first. Within five seconds he'd passed from my sight. Good. Thicker cover here than I'd expected. We followed him off the road and worked our way through young birch, golden aspen, and green pine. Signs of a fire on this mountain some years before lay all around us—charred tree trunks skewed at an angle, young saplings crowding each other, little undergrowth anywhere.

The farther we edged along the mountainside, the slower we moved. Closer meant more danger. A single sound could betray us.

Alto stopped ten feet ahead of me and crouched behind a young pine. He turned to the rest of us, a finger raised to his lips. I worked my way to his side. We'd come to the edge of the trees.

A cleared section of hillside extended for hundreds of yards. Ancient, half-finished log cabins dotted a barren slope. This had to be the former site of Midnight, the short-lived mining camp from the late nineteenth century that Naomi first told us about. The ruins had the eerie appearance of a work-in-progress, as if the building of the cabins had just been interrupted and could resume at any moment.

Naomi tugged at my sleeve. "Gabe, something's different here now." She pointed off to our left. "See that gravel road? That wasn't there last year. And this clearing's been enlarged, maybe for large trucks or something."

"Interesting. I wonder if Cortana's map is still accurate."

"And that closest cabin, it's been enlarged, or rebuilt, or something. I remember it as more of a ruin."

The nearest cabin stood out from the others. Unlike the partial buildings, this one appeared complete. At least fifty concrete steps led to its entrance. A metal roof rested atop four log walls. The windows in its closest wall were fully framed in, even the glass was intact. The front door looked solid on its hinges. Stranger still, the cabin had been built right against the side of the mountain. Its interior had to be underground.

Cortana was right about one thing—two armed men sat side-by-side at the bottom of the front steps. White t-shirts, jeans, do-rags on their heads, AK-47s cradled in their arms. We had no way to approach the entrance without being seen.

Naomi crept to my side. "I'm ready."

I gripped her hand. "Don't get too close to them. Remember, you're a hiker, that's all. You see them, become concerned, turn, and run back here. Got it?"

"Of course I got it. This was my plan, remember?"

"Sorry. Give Miles and me enough time to position ourselves. And be sure you reenter the forest at this exact spot. Can't have anything happen to you."

"Don't go soft on me now. Ready?" After I nodded, she handed me Cortana's pistol and walked out into the sunlight, a lone woman out for an autumn mountain hike.

I passed the gun back to Miles when he came up. We hid behind a pair of old, gnarled bristlecone pines at the forest edge, each holding a crowbar.

Naomi played nonchalant like a pro. She gazed at the sky, picked a sprig of autumn sapphire sage from the hillside, sniffed it, and then stopped, feigning alarm when she spotted the guards. She dropped the flower and froze, like a doe in their headlights.

They called to her in Spanish. She waited until they moved in her direction. Then she shrieked, turned, and ran back to the forest just slow enough for the two men to gain on her. She ran past Miles and me, into the forest and out of sight.

Miles and I drew back our crowbars and waited. Our luck held. The two guards ran close together and side-by-side. I estimated the height of the guard closest to me and raised my metal weapon, estimating the level of his face.

Miles swung out first, cracking one guard squarely in the nose. The one closer to me turned toward him. My blow landed on the side of his head. Both of them collapsed at our feet.

"Hurry." I motioned back to Onion and Alto. They brought ropes and cloth to blindfold the men and bind their hands and feet. It could have been overkill—the guy I hit didn't seem to be breathing. I bent down, slapped his cheeks and pounded his chest.

"Leave him," Miles said. "We gotta move. Now."

We rolled the guards under one of the pines, gathered our weapons, and ran across the open hillside to the cabin entrance. The door was unlocked.

CHAPTER FORTY-THREE

"Gather around," I said to the others. "Block out as much daylight as you can." They crowded in close. I tried to see inside and we all listened.

A man's voice snapped off commands somewhere below us. Too far away for us to make out the words, it sounded like he spoke first in Spanish, then repeated himself in broken English.

I whispered, "He must be speaking to a large group." My fingers clutched at the door latch and pulled it out a cautious couple of inches.

"*Tenemos que irnos de aquí Hoy*." He paused. "We must leave here—now."

Angel hadn't swallowed my bait about the FBI arriving tomorrow. I slid the door open and edged my way inside.

The side of the mountain had been hollowed or more likely blasted out, leaving a cavernous auditorium-like space at least a hundred feet across. High-intensity floodlights lit the entire room. They hung from beneath a narrow walkway that ringed the open space below. My breath quickened. I flattened myself against the rear wall. My comrades followed, crouching as low as they could. We waited, ready to fan out along the catwalk, hidden from the people below, protected from their view by the glare of the lights just beneath us.

A man I took to be Paul Angel stood in the center of a staging area. More than a dozen armed men ringed him—some standing, some kneeling. Behind them and to the left, two rows of young people stood in sullen silence. Most of them young women, dirty and beaten-down, late teens, maybe early twenties, it was hard to tell given their appearance. A diminutive female guard paced in front of them with a switch in her hand and a scowl on her face. We'd met before, when she introduced herself in Estrella Chissie's living room. That night, she'd called herself Luna.

Angel turned to Espinoza. "Did you start the fires?"

Espinoza nodded. "We lit up all four ski lodges in the area. One last night. Three this morning. Fire departments and the law're gonna have their hands full."

Angel smiled and patted him on the shoulder. "Round up the captives." He turned to the rest. "We clear *los esclavos* out first. Get them ready to go."

"Move." Luna barked at the bedraggled young people and pointed to a door off to the left. They shuffled out of the cavern and down the corridor Cortana told us contained their holding cells. That put them out of harm's way, for now. Good.

Without a word, I motioned in both directions along the catwalk. Miles and Onion slid off to my right, Alto and Naomi to my left. I gave them enough time to reach their positions. We had Angel and his men surrounded. In another place and time, I might have allowed myself to smile.

One of Angel's men pointed after the young captives. "Where are we taking them, sir? Are we closing this place down? Setting up somewhere else?"

Angel strutted back and forth in front of his soldiers, a modern *Il Duce*. "The youngest ones will join another group we have in Denver. From there, we move them out to various cities. Older ones we sell off. More money in *fresh* produce, eh?"

Some of the soldiers laughed out loud, all of them at least smiled. My stomach turned.

Angel wasn't finished. "You don't need to know anything else. As for future operations, you'll be notified where to reassemble. We're setting up a new facility. It should be ready next month." Then Angel switched to Spanish, repeating the message, as best as I could tell.

I looked across the cavern for Miles' signal. The light was too dim to see. I stared harder into the darkness. Then—the tiny flicker of a match.

I stood and took a deep breath, ready to call down and order Angel to surrender. But a crash sounded below, at the front door. A uniformed police officer and Julio Cesar Cortana burst into the cavern, his hands free, his voice strong. "Angel! Get out now! *Los federales* are on their way!"

Damn. It was Crawford, the fake cop I'd beaten up back in Espanola. I took a fighting stance with my .38 and aimed at Cortana.

"Five of them are here now! Up there!" Cortana pointed toward my spot on the catwalk and then waved his arm in a circle.

A series of shots rang out from Miles' position across the way. Cortana slumped to the ground next to Angel. Crawford fell next to him. Their bodies twitched in a sick dance and then lay still.

The gates of Hell broke loose. Angel's men formed a protective ring around him—half standing, half taking a knee. They swept the catwalk with automatic fire. I hit the floor. The wall behind me exploded, bits of stone raining down on my head. I held my fire, waiting for a lull in the barrage. When it came, I raised my arm and emptied my .38 wildly toward Angel. Gun smoke billowed throughout the cavern. I couldn't look up to see if I'd hit anyone. Angel's men kept up coordinated volleys in my direction, half of them shooting while the other half reloaded.

A voice cried out in pain a quarter of the way around the catwalk to my right. Onion's position.

I took the chance of my voice drawing added fire. "Deke! You okay?"

He didn't respond. I kept my .38 in hand and crawled along the catwalk in my friend's direction. Somebody down below must have been able to see the top of my head. Automatic fire fractured the wall above me once more while I moved. I stopped, pressed myself hard against the floor, and gasped for air.

The firing refocused to my right and left. I raised my head just enough to see ahead of me. Onion lay face-down twenty feet away. He wasn't moving. I reached into my jacket pocket and reloaded. After a couple of deep breaths, I raised to a crouch and scurried ahead, diving to the ground when I reached Onion's side. I pressed him down hard when another barrage tore into the wall above us.

"Deke! Can you hear me?"

"Yeah, I hear you. Goddamn it, Gabe, they winged me in my good shoulder. The shotgun's behind me."

"Lay still." I reached across his body and slid Miles' Winchester into my grasp. The magazine was full—four shells. Onion hadn't gotten off a single shot. I rolled onto my back and then up on an elbow, peering down through the smoke. A group of Angel's soldiers were charging up the incline toward me.

I tried to shield Onion as much as I could, laying across his body and bracing my elbow against his chest. I played possum, twisting my head off to the side and stretching my legs out behind me. I lay there waiting, with my finger on the trigger guard.

The first of Angel's gunmen reached the catwalk and stopped. The next three piled up close behind him. The fraction of a second it took them to assess the situation was all I had. I emptied all four shells into them, tossed the shotgun away and grabbed my .38. Gun extended, I inched toward their mounded bodies, two of them still moving, still groaning.

Onion spoke in a gravelly whisper. "Gabe?" The sight of Estrella being shot down in front of her son flashed across my mind. I fired away at the two moving soldiers until all four bodies lay still.

The catwalk shook beneath me. A rumble grew to a roar. A crashing sound gave way to a cacophony of shrieking voices—a Native-sounding war cry of whoops and hollers. Phantom figures entered the cavern through the main entrance, letting loose a rain of fire on Angel's cornered forces below.

The cavern transformed into a dream chamber, a charnel house of confusion and death. I stood. The spirit-like warriors let loose a fearsome volley of screams and bullets. Angel's remaining men fell back. Most dropped their weapons and raised their hands.

A clouded figure spoke into a cellphone, then darted from the staging area and disappeared into the gunpowder haze. I caught a clearer glimpse when he moved through a break in the smoke. Paul Angel headed for another side entrance Cortana had failed to mark on his map.

Alto ran to intercept Angel, but the taller man bowled him out of the way and rushed toward the side door. "Señor Gabe—Angel is getting away!"

I fumbled my .38 but caught it before it left my hand. Too late to shoot.

Onion perked up enough to talk. "Go for him. I'll be okay. I think the bleeding's stopped. Don't let that bastard get away."

I shot a glance down at the stage. Angel was bobbing and weaving his way outside. "Stay down, Deke." I sprinted to my left along the catwalk past Naomi.

She looked unharmed. "Gabe?"

"It's Angel—" I didn't look back. Once through the entrance, I scurried after him into the light of day.

A hundred feet ahead of me, Angel disappeared over a ridge. I stumbled after him, my lungs full of smoke and thin air, my head buzzing. A dull ache grew in my legs. It felt like I was running through deep mud. I'd never be able to catch him.

An airplane motor roared from somewhere below the crest of the hill. I reached the top of the ridge but stumbled, face-first into the sand. I shook my head to clear my eyes and my brain.

Angel's Cessna motored down a runway that bisected the cleared meadow. He stumbled across the grass to meet it, one arm clutching his shoulder. The pilot opened the side door and Angel swung into the plane without a backward glance. I emptied my gun at them, overwhelmed by a surge of impotent rage.

Off to my right, a buzzing noise turned my head. Something flashed out from the trees, hurtling toward the plane. My jaw dropped.

Phil's cycle barreled out of the woods at full-throttle. It careened down the hillside, bouncing twice into the air, landing hard each time. But the old man never lost control, hurtling toward the airstrip, closing ground on the Cessna.

"Remember Pearl Harbor!"

Dear God.

The plane powered up for take-off, but Friganza never slowed, holding his cycle on an intercept angle. I should have called out. Instead, I lay frozen on the ground, watching it all play out in dreamlike slow-motion.

Angel's plane picked up speed. Phil's cycle kept up. The Cessna lifted a foot off the ground, then two feet. The pilot leveled the wings.

Phil hit the Cessna broadside, his body thudding against the metal fuselage and dropping to the ground. His cycle sliced ahead, through the Cessna's landing gear, breaking off one of the plane's wheels. It spun to the ground beyond the fuselage, with its two-cycle engine smoking to a stop.

The Cessna shuddered and pitched to the right, the tip of a wing catching the ground. The plane's momentum spun its body into the air, pinwheeling it down the runway. The aircraft flipped over and burst into flames. A second later, its gas tank exploded into a fireball. A shock wave hit me before I felt the heat.

I dragged myself down the hill. By the time I reached him, Phil lay on his back, eyes open, chest struggling for breath.

"Hang on, Phil. Help is on the way." I cradled his head in my arms.

"We did it, kid." His head turned toward me, but his eyes stared far away. "Rattled his cage, didn't I?"

"What happened back at Miles' truck? How did Cortana get—"

"A cop car came along. Dented fender, like the one back at the casino...figured it might be the same guy you beat up...the guy working for the cartel."

"It was." I mopped his forehead with my sleeve.

"I hid behind your Land Cruiser...no way to stop him...he freed Cortana." He gasped for breath. "They took off..."

"And you got on your cycle and came after them." I looked at the crumpled remains of the Indian Chief.

Phil coughed, and his chest surged, his body thrashing for a moment. Then a deep, final breath escaped from his lungs and he went limp in my arms.

I choked back tears and closed his eyes. For a split-second I saw the face of a young naval recruit rotting on a Japanese POW ship, searching the sky for hope. When I opened my eyes, his face relaxed, its lines melting away as I held him. Phil had made his difference at last.

I picked him up in my arms and headed back for the compound.

CHAPTER FORTY-FOUR

Naomi called from the top of the ridge. "Gabe, Onion's been shot!"

"I know."

She pointed to the body in my arms. "Is that—?"

"It's Phil."

She ran down the hill. My back ached. I waited for her and rested Phil on the ground. She felt his wrists and neck for a pulse, then tore open his shirt and tried CPR.

I knelt and put an arm around her shoulders. "It's no use. He's gone."

Tears poured from her eyes and flooded her cheeks. "What happened?"

I told her about Angel attempting to escape. "Phil burst out of the woods on his cycle and crashed into Angel's plane, like a *Kamikaze*. How he got his bike through all those trees, I'll never know."

"He stopped Angel when the rest of us couldn't."

"Let me carry him back to the compound. Then I'll go get the Cruiser. We can put Phil in the back. I have some blankets…"

"Gabe?"

"What?"

"Onion needs help right away."

"I know."

"I saw you leave him up there and figured the worst. I got to him as fast as I could."

"I got the guys who shot him and checked on him first."

"Alto and I stopped the bleeding. The bullet went through Onion's arm. He nearly passed out. Doesn't like the sight of blood, does he?"

I sighed and thought for a second. "He's seen too much of it in his life."

Naomi pointed back toward the compound. "And who were all those guys who burst in right in the middle of everything? Where'd they come from?"

"You saw them too? I thought I was dreaming. We'll ask Miles about them after we take care of Phil's body. You want to stay here?"

She nodded. "We shouldn't leave him alone."

I hauled myself back through the woods and down the gravel road to the Cruiser. This time, my return trip to Angel's compound was full of sadness rather than fear.

Alto met me outside the front entrance. He trooped over to the rear seat window and peered inside. "Where's Phil? Why didn't you pick him up?"

"I'm going to get him right now. Climb in."

He crawled aboard and shut the door. His shirt was torn. A long cut on his cheek had left a trail of blood that disappeared beneath the collar. "Who were all those guys who showed up all of a sudden?"

"That, my friend, is the question of the hour. They sure weren't the FBI." I glanced at him. "Where's your Thompson?"

"Ran out of bullets. She was too hot to carry. I left her inside." He rubbed his hands together. "Boy, is Phil going to be surprised. Too bad he missed out on all the action."

"No, Alto. Phil ended up smack dab in the middle of it." I cleared a catch in my throat. "He's dead."

"Oh." Alto didn't look at me and he didn't say anything more. I drove around the side of Angel's compound, off the road, up to the ridge beyond, and to Naomi. Alto opened his door and ran over to Phil. He knelt on the meadow grass and made a sign of the cross. The little man with the big heart prayed in silence until it came time to wrap the body. Again, without a word, he helped us with the blankets.

When the three of us lifted Phil into the back of the Cruiser, a sudden burst of wind rose. A large, yellowed aspen at the top of the ridge tottered before its trunk split and the tree creaked to the ground. Alto left us and walked off by himself.

I turned to Naomi once she settled into the Cruiser. "We have to hurry. Onion's been laying up there on the catwalk too long. He may swear he's okay, but let's not take chances."

Naomi rummaged through her jacket before smacking her hand against the dashboard. "Damn, I left my phone back in my car. Let me use yours."

"Miles still has it. Once we're back to the compound, I'll get it from him and call for help." I floored the Cruiser through the gravel and sand up to the compound's front entrance.

Before we'd even pulled to a full stop, Naomi jumped out and ran through the main entrance. I checked Phil's body, then turned to follow her.

The Sandoval County cop car with the dented fender sat off to the side of the main door, where Crawford and Cortana had left it. Both front doors were still open, its motor still running. I ran past it and through the entrance.

The sour, acrid smell of gun smoke hit me once again, but the cavern was now quiet enough that you could hear every voice.

I followed Naomi up the incline to where Onion had fallen. His eyes were closed, but his breathing steady and strong. She knelt and examined his shoulder one more time. "He's lucky. Looks like the bullet missed the humerus bone." She pressed down hard enough that Onion groaned. "It's okay. I'm making sure the bleeding stopped." She turned to me. "Get that damn phone and call for an ambulance."

"Like she said." Onion opened an eye long enough to give me a wink. "And if you pass any burgers…" His way of assuring me he wasn't in danger.

I found Miles in the middle of the staging area, on the same spot Angel once stood, talking low with another man I'd never seen before. I moved along the catwalk, trying for a better look at the man's face, but I was too high up, too far away.

The two men shook hands before the stranger and at least ten other feathered, leather-and-buckskin clad shadowy men headed toward the rear entrance. I ran down from the catwalk, hoping to thank them. By the time I reached the door, they were well outside.

"Hey," I waved a hand, hoping one of them would turn around. "Wait a minute…"

They ignored me. Maybe I wasn't speaking their language, who knows? They disappeared into the trees. I never saw them again.

I walked back inside. Miles circled the surviving members of Angel's goon squad. Six of them sat on the ground, hand-cuffed, blindfolded with strips of cloth tied behind their heads. The woman who called herself Luna sat cuffed beside them, her eyes unshielded. She could have killed someone with her glare.

Miles waved me over, his face beaming by the time I arrived, his bruised eye now open. "It's done."

I looked at his prisoners. "Where'd you get all those cuffs?"

He pointed at Luna. "That woman had a drawer full. It was a pleasure taking them from her."

"I need my phone back. Onion's down, but he'll pull through. I'm calling an ambulance. He needs to be seen." He dug my phone from his pocket and handed it to me. I dialed 911. The line crackled before a damn recording clicked on: *All of our personnel are out on call. Please leave a message at the tone. Your request will be handled soon.*

"I don't believe this." I shook the phone and dialed again. Same message.

"Try Main Street Medical Center back in Red River." Miles extended his hand. "Give me your keys, I'll drive him there. You stay here in case the FBI arrives. Everybody else okay?"

"No," I said. "Phil's dead. He crashed his cycle into Angel's plane before it could take off. Didn't survive the impact."

He looked away a moment and sighed. "He gave his life for people he never knew."

"Phil is a hero. The world needs to know." I started to go tend to the young people, but hesitated. I needed one question answered first. "Miles…who were all those guys that showed up in the nick of time? What the hell happened here?"

"You do not understand."

"I guess not." I looked at the ground, kicked some sand, then peered back at him with suspicious eyes. "Friends of yours, were they?"

His face betrayed no emotion. "You can say that. My brothers, my cousins. My ancestors."

"You've lost me."

"Believe this, Professor—each time a young one is harmed, a warrior spirit awakens. That way, no evil goes unpunished. Balance is restored. Our people survive."

I chewed on his words but found it all too much to swallow. "Okay…let's go get Onion."

Miles' face softened. "Thanks for letting me use your phone, my friend."

A young twentyish woman stumbled toward us and then—after a glance of recognition—ran to Miles, who dropped to a knee. She hesitated and studied him for a moment before slowly entering his arms. They clutched one another in silence, both crying. Miles soon pulled back and wiped her tears before looking up at me. "My niece. Summer."

She shot a frightened glance at me, then looked away, burying her face in Miles' shirt. He gripped the back of her head and maintained his sheltering embrace.

Summer's tunic slipped off one shoulder. Maybe it was a couple sizes too big, maybe she'd lost a lot of weight during her ordeal. A fresh, garish tattoo marred the back of her neck. Its image showed the index and fifth fingers extending from a clenched human fist. Perhaps someone had branded her, I didn't want to know. Her left cheek—the only one I could see—showed two harsh bruises and an open cut.

Miles looked up at me. I must have had a puzzled look on my face. "My friends got her out of her cell. You'll need to free the rest and look after them." He handed me a heavy set of bronze keys. "For the cells."

"Okay."

"I'm taking Summer with me back to Dulce. She's spent too much time here. We'll drop Naomi and Onion at the medical center and get back as fast as we can." Miles looked at the young woman and took her by the hand. "Come along."

"One problem with that, Miles."

"What?"

"Phil's body is still in the back of my Cruiser. Can't have you driving around with him like that. I need to leave him here for the FBI. I want to make sure he gets cremated and has a proper military funeral."

Miles pointed to his niece.

I got the message. "His body is shrouded in blankets. It'll only take a minute."

"Okay." Miles turned to the young woman. "You wait here. I'll be right back."

Once at the Land Cruiser, Miles and I slipped Phil's body from the cargo area. We set him down in the shade of an aspen where he wouldn't be disturbed.

"Thanks." I shook Miles' hand and gave him the keys to my vehicle. "I'll go get Onion. You get your niece settled."

Back in the cavern, Naomi and I helped Onion out the door and into the back seat of the Cruiser. Naomi mopped Onion's forehead with her sleeve. "Can you sit up okay?"

Onion let out a breath and leaned his head against the side window. "How far do we have to go?"

Naomi crawled into the back seat behind Miles. "Main Street in Red River. Thirty minutes?"

Miles looked at Onion through the rearview mirror. "At most." He pointed to Summer in the front passenger seat. "My niece. I'm taking her home."

She waved a hand at Onion and Naomi but didn't turn around to face them.

I poked my head through the open rear window. "I can come along if you want, Deke."

"Nah. You take care of business here. I'll be fine."

I walked around to the driver's side and shook Miles' hand. "Keep the car with you. I'll get a ride to town once I've cleared things with the Feds. We'll get you back to your truck as soon as we can." I tapped the roof above him and stood there until they disappeared down the gravel road.

Time for me to find Jay-Jay.

CHAPTER FORTY-FIVE

Luna Cortana hunched on the ground with the rest of the prisoners. I reached down and jangled the keys in her face. "The next time you hear this sound, you'll be on the wrong side of a jail cell door." She spat at me but missed.

I left her there and walked through the door to the left of the main entrance. I continued down the corridor, unlocking each cell along my way, freeing each of the young captives. Twenty-two cells, twenty-one young women. Like Miles' niece, all were survivors of abuse I didn't want to think about. I pointed each of them up the hall to the stage area and gave each the same encouragement.

"You're safe now. We'll get you home as soon as we can."

Hard to believe human eyes could look so empty on this side of death. Many appeared ill-fed, some carried bruises on their faces, a few limped up the corridor. Many of the young women's faces had been caked with make-up, some overly so. All wore juvenile clothing that made them appear even younger than they were. Must have made them more desirable to their abusers.

All down the corridor, a sick feeling deepened in my stomach and an anger shook me and wouldn't let go. Was I walking through the second or third circle of hell?

And there was no sign of Jay-Jay.

At the end of the corridor, twenty feet past the last cell, a heavy wooden door had been secured with a padlock. I fumbled through the keys on Luna's chain once more. The sixth key I tried was a bit larger than the others. It fit. I turned the key and pulled on the door.

Jay-Jay sat on a cot in the far corner. Another other young man crouched against the wall to my right. He appeared to be about twelve or thirteen. Neither boy looked up.

I had to bend down when I entered his cubicle, the enclosure being less than my six feet in height. "Jay-Jay? Remember me?"

He must have heard me, but my words didn't connect.

"Are you okay, son?"

His gaze never left the ground. "I'm fine."

I knelt down and took a better look at the boy who'd watched his father gun down his mother, the same father who now lay dead less than a hundred yards away.

If Jay-Jay was thinking anything or feeling anything, I couldn't in all honesty say. His face told me nothing. Empty, like all the others. The second boy stood up. He was crying.

"Come on." I stood up part way and backed out of his cell. Jay-Jay wouldn't budge from the cot. "Come with me. Please." I pointed up the hallway.

The older boy brushed past me and ran up the corridor. Jay-Jay at last moved from his bed to the cell door and hesitated. He stared along the empty corridor. Seemingly satisfied, his cautious steps put him back on the road to freedom and recovery.

I took care not to touch him all the way out of his underground prison. I kept a step behind until he joined the other young people huddled in silence in the main room, at the bottom of the slope.

The presence of Angel's soldiers, even though shackled and blindfolded, appeared to intimidate the former captives. I tried my best to assure them. "My name is Gabriel McKenna. My friends and I came here to free you from those who were doing you harm. You're all safe now. In a little while, we'll begin returning you to your homes and families. In the meantime, we're going to put your captors into your old cells." Their faces showed little emotion. "Let me repeat. You are all safe."

Alto stood in front of the abused group, watching and listening. He turned to check on our prisoners. "What do we do now, Señor Gabe?"

"Got any more ammunition for your Thompson?"

"Not here. Maybe back at the truck."

I took out my .38, reloaded, and handed him the gun. "Follow me, and if any one of these guys bolt, shoot him. I want their victims to see us lock every last one of them up."

"Good idea."

I grabbed the nearest survivor among Angel's gunmen and pulled him to his feet. "Shut up and don't try anything if you want to live." I was a head taller than the prisoner, but he was a lot younger, so I took no chances. I pushed him down the jail corridor to the last cell. He struggled against me when I shoved him inside, hooking his foot on the cell door.

I made a fist with my right hand and buried it in his stomach. He groaned and slumped to the floor. I pushed his legs inside the cell with my foot, slammed and locked the door.

"Get used to the feeling, asshole. You'll be an old man before you breathe free air again." I left him blindfolded and in cuffs. I did the same with the rest of Angel's men who'd survived the battle. Eleven in all.

That left Luna Cortana. I stared at her, trying to figure how much hatred it must take for a woman to arrange the murder of her sister-in-law and sell her nephew into slavery. I pulled her up by her cuffs. She hollered in pain and I smiled for the first time that day.

"Shut up. Come with me." I dragged her into the jail corridor. "Sit down." I gave her a helpful shove, undid one of her cuffs, and attached it to a bar on the first cell. I turned away and marched back to Alto.

"We can't leave these young people here, señor," he said. "They need more help than we got."

"I agree. But we can't move them until the Feds get here and see what's been done to them. Maybe we can give them something to eat, for now." I handed him the key ring and pointed toward the cells. "First door on the left is where Cortana said they stored the guns and ammo. See what's there. And don't go too close to that woman."

"Want your gun back?"

"Good idea. You might need both of your hands." I tucked my gun in my belt and accompanied him to the storeroom.

Alto unlocked the door and stood on a chair to turn on a light. "Not much in here. Some energy bars. Boxes of fruit juice. That okay?"

Within five minutes, all the young people had at least something to eat and drink. None of them said a word, so I figured it was still my turn.

"There's more food if you want it. Just ask Alto here. You have to stay here until the cops arrive. They may want to ask you some questions. Please answer the best you can. I promise we'll see you get returned to your families as soon as possible."

But what about Jay-Jay? What could I do with him?

I phoned the Education Center at Laguna Pueblo. No answer. So, I called my friend Curtis Jester back in Albuquerque. "C.J.? It's Gabe."

"Good to hear your voice, Champ. Beats reading your obituary."

"I'll give you an *Amen* on that."

"Am I going to read about this one in the papers?"

"I hope they keep it out of the papers. Better for my health. Listen—I need a big favor."

"Anything. You know that."

"Can you clear some time to drive out to Laguna and deliver another message to Angelina? I called her office, nobody's there."

C.J. covered the phone and spoke to someone on the other end of the line. Getting clearance from his wife Charmaine for anything was a delicate proposition. He returned a minute later. "Okay, Gabe. We're looking at a slow evening tonight. I got a young guy working here now. Got some initiative and all. But I'll have to be back when we close at ten. That okay?"

"Great." I gave him a brief rundown, from the killing of Estrella Chissie earlier in the week to the Feds not showing up today. "I need you to go to Laguna and ask Angelina if she can take care of one abused boy until I figure out a long-term solution."

"I'll do better than that," C.J. said.

"Oh?"

"I'll give her that extra cellphone you foisted on me last year. Still have the charger around some place."

"She doesn't like phones."

"Can't do smoke signals from here. I'll tell her to keep it for the kid's sake. And so you can keep in touch. I'll turn on the charm if I have to."

"What woman could resist?"

"Only one. And I married her."

"Tell Angelina I'll be there tomorrow to talk with Matty. Day after, at the latest." My phone beeped. "Got another call on the line—"

"Bye, Champ."

It was Naomi, calling from Red River's medical center. "Onion's being moved down to Santa Fe. Crispus St. Vincent Hospital."

"Is it bad?"

"No. Just precautionary. The facilities here are limited. They've had casualties coming in from all those fires at the ski centers."

"Damn that Angel."

"I'm going to go with him, if that's okay. Miles will drive back to the compound. Should be a couple of hours."

"Have him wait for me at the hospital. I'll see Phil's remains are cared for first, then I'll meet up with you there. Naomi—"

"Thanks for everything?"

"Something like that."

CHAPTER FORTY-SIX

The U.S. Cavalry arrived at 2:15 p.m. when four FBI helicopters appeared in the distance, then descended on Angel's narrow airstrip. I imagined martial strains from *The Ride of the Valkyries* as the choppers broke over the trees and settled on all four sides of the still-smoldering Cessna.

At the same time, two armored vehicles bounced their way up the gravel trail to the front entrance of the compound. A dozen more cars followed them. SWAT teams blew out from the armored vehicles, a K-9 team on their heels. Agents spread out, armed and ready. The term *brute force* popped into my head.

Before meeting them at the door, I called behind in a loud whisper. "Alto, go hide your tommy-gun." I slid my .38 from my belt to my jacket pocket and zipped it inside.

Walter Carlson and Sam Archuleta walked together through the crowd. I plastered a sheepish smile on my face and waved to attract their attention. Their grim expressions didn't change.

"The situation is under control," I said.

"You think so, do you?" Carlson's face could curdle sweet cream. He'd never liked me much. Now, he had several new reasons to like me even less. He glared at Sam. "You deal with him. I'll be back."

Sam watched him walk into the compound before he spoke to me. "You couldn't have waited?"

"No, Sam. We couldn't. Don't you think we'd have rather turned this over to the Bureau?" I pointed to a nearby yellow aspen. "I have one dead friend laying under that tree and Onion on his way to the hospital in Santa Fe with another bullet wound. The Feds should thank us. We did their dirty work all day."

"Where's Cortana?"

"Inside on the floor. Dead."

He ran a hand through what was left of his hair. "Where's Angel?"

"He's somewhere in the burned-out hull of his Cessna, down at the airstrip. I'm sure the FBI fly boys have found him by now."

Sam looked heavenward. "Mother of God—where are all his armed men?"

I have to admit I enjoy tweaking Sam at times like this. I took a deep breath and let it ooze from my lungs, giving him some time to twirl. "About half of them are laying dead next to Cortana. We arranged their bodies nice and neat, the way Carlson likes things. The rest are locked in a series of cells down the corridor from the main cavern. Where they were keeping their captives."

Sam forgot he had a cigarette dangling from his mouth. He took out another one and stuck it between his lips. The lit cigarette fell to the ground. He struck a match to the new one without noticing. "Any casualties among the victims?"

"Physically, no. Psychologically? I'd be amazed if they don't all need long-term help. Maybe I do too."

"You could have gotten the lot of them killed, you know."

I'd had enough. "Damn it, Sam. I kept you informed. I gave you warnings in advance. I told you every minute counted. If we hadn't gone after Angel when we did, those poor young people would be halfway to Denver by now. Tomorrow they'd be scattered around the country, lost forever. Angel was shutting this place down and relocating—something I suspect the Bureau already knew."

"What do you mean?"

"Come off it, man. You know how the Feds would play this—they'd wait for Angel to blow this place and track him to his new base of operations. Then they'd hang back and 'observe' his operation for a couple of months. Dot every 'i' and cross every 't' before moving in on him. All the while, innocent young women would be abused. They even had two young boys."

Sam backed away a full step. "Okay. Okay."

I couldn't stop. "So, while they diddled in Washington, we took them out. And it was terrible, okay?" I felt my legs tremble beneath me. I gasped for a deep breath. "We did what had to be done."

"Gabe, I'm trying to be a friend. You'd better be ready to explain things in detail. The Bureau is going to take this place apart, gather every piece of evidence—"

"They treat their friends worse than their enemies."

"Not fair, and you know that."

"No. Actually, I don't. Fuck off, Sam. Leave me alone." I took a step toward Phil's body.

Sam caught my sleeve and held me back. "I'll help you in any way I can. I can deal with Carlson better than you. Tell me everything that happened." He scanned the compound. FBI operatives carted a shrouded dead body out the front entrance. Another followed. And then another. I didn't know where they were taking all the bodies. I didn't care.

I stopped watching. "What is it you want to know, Sam?"

"I'd like to know what the hell happened here. Everything. How did the—what? Five? Six of you—"

"Six."

"How did the six of you manage to take out Angel and all his soldiers? It doesn't add up."

"Let's find a place to sit down." I wandered toward Phil again and sat down next to his shrouded body. Sam crouched at my side.

I took a gulp of air and saw it all over again, all that had gone down since our arrival. I saw Miles' warriors again appear in the midst of the battle. I remembered every horrible second when I blew away four men with Miles' shotgun. And I watched Phil's eyes go blank in death. When I came back to the moment, I told some of it to Sam. I left Miles' warriors out.

"Sam, it's amazing what you can achieve with enough despair, desperation, and recklessness."

He blew a tobacco cloud into the air. "You've proven that before."

I put a hand on his shoulder. "Let's go inside and face Carlson."

Before Sam could answer, my phone rang. It was Miles. "I dropped Onion and Naomi at a hospital in Santa Fe. Be back in less than—"

"I know all about that. Naomi called." I wanted to avoid the complication of having the Feds question Miles at all and perhaps involving his people. "You stay right there with them. I'll take care of everything here. I'll catch a ride down later and pick up my Cruiser."

"But my truck."

"Let it be for now. It's safe." I motioned to Sam. "Can I have a minute here?"

He took the cue and moved off a few paces.

I lowered my voice. "Miles, if you come back here, it's going to complicate things. Your people—or whoever they are—were never here, okay? If we have to come clean later, we will. But not until I call in my lawyer, got it?"

"Got it. Thanks. I'll stay right here."

Sam was crushing out a cigarette when I walked back to him. I pointed toward the open space outside the compound's front entrance. "Might as well go and face the Crew Cuts. You're probably going to enjoy this."

CHAPTER FORTY-SEVEN

Somebody from the Bureau had a folding table and two chairs set up on the grass in front of the compound. Carlson had his jacket off and his shirt sleeves rolled up. Not good. "Sit." He pointed to the chair closest to me.

"You talk to your dog like that?" Even with my jaw thrust forward all the way, I couldn't match his.

"Relax, McKenna. I'm not looking for any trouble."

"Thanks." I shifted around on a wooden chair. It wobbled, just like my legs. "What *are* you looking for?"

He sat across from me, planted his elbows on the table, and hunched forward. "Some way to understand what happened here. That would be a good start."

"That all?" I leaned back, folding my arms along the way.

"Not by a long shot. Look, I'm sorry we couldn't get here faster. Even twenty-five years after the Waco mess, the wheels turn slowly in D.C. The Bureau has a long memory for some things. At least none of the young people died here. I'll give you credit for that."

"Big of you."

Carlson's phone rang. "What? Okay, we'll be there in a couple of minutes." He looked at me. "Let's go."

"Where?"

"Down to the airstrip. EMT's found your boy Angel."

Five minutes later, Carlson, Sam Archuleta and I stood side-by-side watching a team of blue-clad EMTs stagger away from the burning wreckage of Paul Angel's plane. A man's charred body lay on their stretcher. Most of his clothes had burned away. His browned, bloody feet stuck out from the remnants of boots and one of his arms dangled off the edge of the stretcher. I couldn't tell if he was breathing. Then he coughed in my direction.

Paul Angel was alive. *Damn it to hell.*

I took a step toward him. Sam Archuleta moved between us, holding me back with a straight arm to my chest. "Hang on, Gabe."

At the sound of my name, Angel's eyes struggled open. He grunted, raising his head a few inches. "McKenna?" His guttural voice sounded more animal than human. "Start making plans for your funeral."

I felt a reddening in my face. "Everybody dies, Angel. But I'll live long enough to spit on your grave." I pushed against Sam's arm. He didn't budge.

Carlson grabbed me from behind. "That's enough." He motioned to the medics. "Get that man out of here. Keep him isolated. He talks to no one. I'll meet you later at the medical center."

The team moved Angel into a waiting EMT AmbuBus. A couple of minutes later, its siren announced their departure for Red River. By then, Carlson, Sam and I were halfway back to the FBI interrogation table outside the complex.

While we walked, I squeezed my arms over my gut to keep my stomach from heaving. "I can't believe he survived that explosion."

Carlson gasped for air even more than I did. "He may or may not make it. If he does, we're going to need you as a witness."

I waved my hand back and forth. "No way. I won't go down that road. I know all about how you protect your witnesses. And I'm not going to hide."

"You *do* want to live, don't you?"

I looked down at my shoes. I clenched my teeth. I did everything except give him an answer.

Sam laid a hand on my shoulder. "Gabe, even if Angel dies, his people have you marked. Your friends might want to make themselves scarce too."

"He's right." Carlson sat back down once we reached the table and sucked wind for a good ten seconds. "Here's the best I can do for you—"

I remained standing. "I won't run."

"It won't be forever, trust me." Carlson looked up at Sam before continuing. "Sam and I have been in law enforcement all our lives. We've seen what can happen to witnesses after the fact. McKenna, you may not like to hear this, but you need us."

I thought of Angelina, and Matty, and all my friends. I even thought of my cat. Maybe I *should* get away. Just for a little while. I took a seat. "What do you want me to do?"

It was Carlson's turn to lean back. I caught a split second of warmth in his eyes. "Tell us everything that happened here. Every detail. Begin at the beginning."

"Do I need to call my lawyer first?"

"No. No. You don't get it. The Bureau *wants* to keep you out of this. Of course, we'll need all the facts for our file. Then we can develop a plausible narrative that leaves all of you out. Nobody outside the Bureau will know you were even here…as long as you agree to testify against Angel."

My eyes opened wide. I swallowed hard. "You're going to fudge your report."

"Professor, I'm sure today was traumatic for you and your friends. But this is just another battle in a war we've been fighting for years. Angel has a boss. His boss has bosses. This compound is—or was—part of an international network of human trafficking, child trafficking, sex trafficking, drugs—and all the scum who run it." He pointed toward the cavern. "You may not realize it, but this here is a significant victory. You have our gratitude and we'll do all we can to protect the lot of you. But our war goes on."

I rubbed my chin and nodded. "Well…okay."

For the next hour, I dished every detail I could recall. The night of Estrella's killing seemed far away now, but those kinds of things stick in your mind. I gave Carlson every step of our journey, all the way to the Armageddon we'd just survived. I left Miles' friends out of the story but included everything else. I told him about Phil Friganza and his heroics. And how I wanted to see him get a burial with full military honors.

"You'll have to take that up with his branch of service."

"He was US Navy. Second World War. Pacific theater. He was a POW."

"You want a burial at sea?"

"He deserves no less."

Carlson wrote in his notepad. "We'll see what can be done, Professor. My cousin works at the Navy Liaison Unit in Honolulu. Trepler Medical Center. You'll need a death certificate, of course. And some other forms. Give me his full name and I'll put in a call."

"Thanks, Carlson. You're okay. Let me do you a favor."

"What would that be?"

"Be careful before you trust local law enforcement."

Carlson's default hard look returned to his face.

"Over the last few days, my friends and I have encountered imposters. Guys pretending to be cops who weren't." I looked at Sam. "Like the guy I told you about a couple of days ago."

"Is this true?" Carlson shot his own look at Sam.

Sam pulled at his collar. "Tell you about it later."

"And in case you're wondering, the fires at the local ski lodges yesterday and today were ordered by Angel. A diversion for his departure. Maybe the Red River cops are clean, I couldn't tell you. The rest of them—vet them before you trust them, okay?"

Carlson grunted. That was as far as he'd go.

I raised a finger. "One last thing. Miles Gray Eagle has been looking for his kidnapped niece. So have others from his tribe. Leave all of them out of this. There's enough apprehension on his rez as it is. They feel hopeless, like the government and state police didn't care about their missing loved ones."

Carlson spoke slowly, stretching out his words. "*That* is not true."

"Well, that's how they feel, and I don't blame them one bit. Let their families go without making statements. Leave it at that. Or I clam up right now."

Sam cleared his throat and turned away from me, a reaction I'd seen many times before.

"And don't nitpick us on the finer points of the law," I said. "We did what had to be done. We saved twenty young women and a couple young boys and made a dent in a national tragedy."

"Spare me the sermon, Professor." Carlson ran his hand along the flat top of his crewcut.

"And I got two suggestions for you."

"What would those be?" Carlson asked. Every question an accusation. At least he took out his notebook.

"Look into an organization called Second Chances. They're behind some of this, at least. But be careful. They seem to have connections."

"That's one." He jotted something down.

"And I like Angel for the murder of Jed Stanley, the forest ranger found down near Taos Junction."

"Okay, we'll look into all of that."

"Can I go now?"

"Nice try. McKenna, we'd like to keep this clean and simple. But you and your friends will need to make statements. Their involvement should end there. I'll try to make it happen. Fair enough?"

"If you do all I ask, I'll go underground for you. At least until after you get my testimony—maybe a while longer." I didn't know where my sudden cooperative attitude was coming from.

After another half hour of answering Carlson's questions, I ended with a promise and two requests. "I'll give you a formal statement as soon as possible. Back in Albuquerque. With my lawyer present."

"Oh, *that* guy? What's his name?"

"Erskine Pelfrey. The third."

"Okay." Carlson's face looked suddenly older than when he'd arrived.

I turned to my friend. "Sam?"

"What?"

I slipped my .38 from inside my jacket and handed it to him, butt first. "Next time I ask for this back…tell me to go to hell."

"Done," he said. "Anything else?"

"Yeah. I'd like to take temporary custody of one of the children."

Carlson looked over at the wretched group of young people who had been moved out of the cavern and were now sitting nearby. "Which one?"

"Jay-Jay Chissie." I pointed to him. "That boy over there. It was his kidnapping that started this for me. On the night his mother was murdered, I promised her I'd bring him back safe." I cleared a catch in my throat. "The least I can do now is see he's properly cared for."

Carlson sighed and thought for a bit. "I'll have him questioned first. If he agrees—can you stick around for an hour or two?"

"Yeah. I do want to get down to Santa Fe to check on Onion, but I'll need a ride."

Carlson blinked once and stared at me. "Who?"

"Deke Gagnon. My friend from New York. He's been shot. The two of us opened a PI business in Albuquerque and—"

Sam interrupted. "I'll give you a ride to Santa Fe."

"Thanks."

"It'll give me enough time to convince you and Onion to retire."

"That shouldn't be too hard. Onion's beat up awful bad."

He checked me up and down. "Gotta say, Gabe, you look pretty okay after such a violent ordeal."

Good old Sam. He never gets it. The real scars are on the inside.

CHAPTER FORTY-EIGHT

Sam pulled into Christus Saint Vincent parking lot on St. Michael's Drive in Santa Fe. We'd hardly spoken during the drive down from Red River. My right arm trembled all the way. Two hours wasn't enough time to cope with the day's carnage. On the other hand, it might have been sufficient time to develop nicotine addiction from the tobacco residue inside his car.

I pointed to Jay-Jay, asleep in the back seat. "Can you stay here and keep an eye on him? I shouldn't be more than half an hour."

Sam nodded and rolled his window down a couple of inches.

The woman at the hospital's front desk checked her computer. Onion was out of emergency and into a private room. Naomi must have opened her wallet. I stepped off the elevator and nearly bumped into Miles motoring down the hall with a cup of coffee in each hand.

I regained my balance. "Sorry. How's Onion?"

"They worked on him in emergency for the better part of an hour, but he's out now. Needs to stay overnight. Should go home in the morning." He held up the two cups. "Need some?"

"Thanks, not right now. No complications then?"

"They found some infection in his earlier bullet wound. Cleaned it out, gave him an anti-biotic. He'll be fine. But the poor guy has two slings now."

We walked together down the hallway. "Naomi okay?"

"Hard to tell. She's playing nursemaid and all. She's kind of intense, you know?"

"Got some good news for you. The Feds are willing to keep you all out of the *official* account of what happened today."

"That *is* good."

"But they do want statements for their file. You okay with that? They don't need to talk with your friends. Just you."

"My friends won't speak to them. No way."

"I figured. Anyhow, let me check on Onion and Naomi. Then I'll drive you back to your truck. Can you give Alto a lift? He's somewhere back at the compound."

Miles gave me what passes for his smile. "Not a problem."

"Your niece in with Onion?"

"My brother came and took her back to Dulce."

"Oops. Carlson—the Cheese from the Bureau—wants to question all the captives before releasing them."

Miles stiffened. "Not going to happen."

I tried to imagine Carlson choking on that. "If you say so. Of course, he might not notice she was ever there. If he asks, I'll cover. No harm."

Onion's door was shut. I knocked, turned the knob, and stuck my head inside. "Somebody order coffee?" I looked at Naomi and flashed a smile. "You still putting up with this guy?"

Onion sat propped up on a mountain of pillows. "Brain, what's going on?"

I brought him and Naomi up to date on my session with Carlson. Naomi clasped her hands in silent prayer when I mentioned our being kept out of the news. Onion let out a huge breath.

I pointed to his slings. "That's bad. How you going to hold on to a burger like that?"

"I'll find a way. Besides, my old wound should be fine soon as the antibiotics kick in."

Naomi interrupted. "I'll look after him."

My eyebrows made a short trip up to my hairline and back. "Well, Deke, I guess you're in good hands."

Onion turned a shade of red and swallowed hard. "Gabe, I've been thinking—"

"Look out world."

"I'm going to retire from the PI business."

I pointed toward the window. "Sam Archuleta is down waiting in his car. He has the same idea."

Onion's eyes moistened. A poignant expression came over his face. "He's right, you know."

"Yeah. I know."

"One more thing. I'm moving back to the Big Apple." He tried to lift his arms a couple of inches and winced. "This state is too freaking dangerous."

Naomi turned toward me. "I'm going too."

My head jerked back. "You?" I pointed at the bed. "And *him*?" The next thing I was going to say, whatever it was, got stuck somewhere inside.

"Certainly not." Naomi gripped both sides of her head and shook it from side to side. Onion's face now burned a bright crimson.

I held out a hand. "I just thought—"

Naomi took out her cellphone and held it up. "I got a text message from an old friend. A classmate of mine. There's a history position opening up at Dumbarton College. I'm going to apply."

"No way," I said. "That might be my old job we're talking about. Pre-Columbian North American History?"

"Yes."

"Full-time position?"

She shook her head. "Adjunct instructor."

"Welcome to Twenty-First Century Academia."

She drew closer to me. "Will you give me a reference?"

I held her hands and looked in her eyes. "Naomi, if I did that, you'd never get the job. But I might be able to tell you what not to say and whom to avoid. Give me a call before your interview."

She kissed my cheek. "Thanks, Gabe."

I looked at Onion. "When can you leave?"

"My doctor said tomorrow, so long as there aren't any complications. Naomi offered to drive me back." He looked down for a minute. "What about my sublet? I don't want to stiff Angelina. When I took over her apartment, I promised—"

"This is October—no, November now." I did some quick calendar math in my head. "There should only be two months left on her lease.

Fuggedaboudit."

"Thanks, Brain. Next time you get back to the Big Apple, we all get together, okay?"

"In a New York minute. Listen. Seriously. The Feds are saying we all need to be careful in the days and months ahead. Angel was part of a huge criminal enterprise that doesn't like to be crossed. New York may be all the way across the country but be careful. I'm going to disappear for a while myself."

A nurse came to the door. She handed Onion a card. "Tonight's menu. Supper will be in two hours. I'll come by to take your order as soon as I can."

He gave the card a quick read. It fell from his hands. "No burgers?"

"No burgers," the nurse said. "We do have some wonderful consommé."

Onion hunched over, like he was choking back a sob. "I want out."

CHAPTER FORTY-NINE

Miles walked me down to the parking lot. "Your Cruiser's over there." He pointed off to the right and handed me the keys.

"I've got to get one of the children from Sam first. I promised to look after him."

"Oh? That younger boy?"

"Yeah. I'm taking him down to my daughter's place on Laguna Pueblo."

Miles' face refused to reveal the surprise he must have been feeling. "Your daughter is Laguna?"

"It's complicated, but yeah. I have an eight-year-old grandson lives there too. I thought maybe the two boys…"

"You're a good man, Professor McKenna."

"Try to be."

Jay-Jay was awake when we reached Sam's car. He'd opened his window all the way. Kid had smarts.

Sam popped out on the driver's side. "Ready to go?"

"Sam, this is Miles Gray Eagle. He helped us."

The two shook hands after an awkward pause. Sam looked across the roof of the car at me. "I have to get down to Albuquerque. The bodies will be arriving at the medical investigator's office. I told Carlson I'd be there when they arrive."

"Do me a favor," I said. "Look after Phil Friganza's body. Carlson promised me Phil would get a burial with military honors and I intend to see he does. If anybody asks, I'll pay for the whole Burial at Sea package. You got that?"

Sam gave me the okay sign. "You and me and Carlson need to get together to work out the details of your 'retirement'. When will you be back in town?"

I checked my watch. It was going on four-fifteen. "Day after tomorrow. Early." I bent down and looked into the back of Sam's car. "Jay-Jay? You ready to come with me? I have a family you can stay with for now. Nice people."

He rubbed his eyes and stepped out and stood by my side.

"So long, Gabe…Miles, nice to meet you. Good-bye, Jay-Jay." Sam turned to head back to his car.

"Sam, wait a minute." I walked around to the back of my Cruiser.

"What is it now?"

I took out the Rolodex and flight log I'd loaned myself back at the La Jara airstrip. "Here."

"What *is* this stuff?" Archuleta's voice held all the excitement a man feels when new telephone books are delivered to his door.

"You're the cop, check it out. You might find names, dates, flight logs, and contact info on Angel and the cartel. Early Christmas present."

He turned without a word of thanks, trudged back to his car, and spun out of the parking lot.

I looked around. Jay-Jay was standing by the Cruiser. "You hungry? What's your favorite food?"

His eyes showed a faint glimmer. "Pizza."

"You're going to get along just fine with another young boy I know." I motioned to Miles. "Hop in. Let's go."

Jay-Jay, Miles, and I found a Pizza Hut on Cerrillos Road and ended up boxing most of the second pie for the road. The sun was setting by the time we hit 285 North back to Red River. The drive was easy. Nobody tried to run us off the road.

Miles' truck sat in darkness. No sign anything unusual had occurred. I edged behind the truck and had to hit the brakes fast. The wreckage of Phil's Indian Chief cycle lay on the ground. A shadowy figure hopped down from the cab.

Alto held his submachine gun in his right hand. "What took so long, Señor Gabe?"

"It's a long way to Santa Fe." I pointed toward Phil's cycle. "How'd that get back up here?"

"I asked the *Federales* if I could take it. I can fix it, but it will take some time."

Miles walked over to the heap of metal and bent down. "Getting parts for this is gonna be a bitch."

"Don't matter to me. I wanna keep Phil's memory alive. Miles, can you drop me off at his old filling station on your way back to the rez? It's ten milcs west of Pueblo Pintado."

Miles took out a handkerchief and mopped his forehead. "That's kinda out of my way...but okay." He pointed at the Thompson. "You ride shotgun with that thing?"

The three of us grunted the battered 1946 Indian Chief into the back of Miles' truck. It felt so much heavier than before.

I stopped Alto before he climbed up into the cab and extended my hand. "Thank you, my friend. Couldn't have done what we did without your help."

The gleam in his eyes cut through the dusk. "Thank you for the Go-Kart rides. I'll stay and rest up at Phil's place for a while. He's got some great stuff in there. You stop by if you come that way again?"

"I surely will. Miles, I think I owe you a crowbar. Don't remember where I left yours."

"I have others."

They climbed into the truck. Miles fired up the engine. They soon disappeared in a cloud of dust along the gravel road back toward Red River.

If I live to be a hundred, I'll never forget those guys.

I dialed the number of C.J.'s extra cellphone, in case Angelina had accepted his gift. To my amazement, the darn thing rang.

"Hello?" Her voice sounded thin. Troubled.

"Angelina? That you?"

"Dad? Where the hell are you? Everything okay?"

"North of Red River, and things are better than they've been in a while. How's Matty?"

"Still grounded. You need to talk to him."

"I will, soon as I get there. Did C.J. tell you about the young boy I have with me?"

"Oh, dear, he certainly did. What horrible things to happen to a child…"

I cleared my throat. "Thought maybe you might be able to help me place him with a Laguna family. He has no one left."

"Bring him here. I'll see what I can do."

"That's my Payoqona."

"Maybe Matty can help him adjust…maybe this boy can be a better friend to Matty than some of the crowd he's running with now."

I didn't like the sound of that. "Time for a man-to-man?"

"Past time. When will you be here?"

"It's a good five-hour drive in this darkness."

"Why not stay the night somewhere and start out in the morning?"

"No. Jay-Jay and I want to get far away from here as fast as we can. Is 2 a.m. too late?"

"Of course not. If I tell Matty you're on your way, he won't sleep. So, you'll see him in the morning. Be quiet when you arrive. I'll set up the couch for the young man to use."

"He'll sleep most of the way there."

"I'll be waiting at the window." I heard the relief in Angelina's voice and smiled to myself.

CHAPTER FIFTY

I stopped for gas at an all-night filling station in Taos. Jay-Jay ate a couple of slices of the pizza and drank some water. I braced myself for a middle-of-the-night run down the Low Road to Española. Funny how cliffs that look so warm and inviting during the day appear so ominous in the moonlight.

To get to Laguna, I had to drive to Albuquerque and catch I-40 west to the pueblo. Angelina and Matty live near Paguate, a village on the northern edge of the tribal land. Traveling at night meant I didn't have to look at the Jackpile Mine and all the blight left behind by uranium miners.

My right forearm continued to tremble, but I convinced myself it was less wobbly than before. I had no trouble staying awake, despite the late hour. At a quarter-to-two, I pulled into Angelina's driveway and eased the Cruiser underneath her carport. Jay-Jay had fallen asleep somewhere around Albuquerque.

The porch light came on before my feet touched the gravel drive. Angelina walked onto the front patio. We embraced.

"It's so good to see you, Dad."

"Been too long." I held her out at arm's length. "How are you?"

"I'm doing pretty well." Her smile reached her eyes. "Except for that grandson of yours."

"Of *mine*? This sounds serious. First chance I get, I'll take him out to the woodshed."

"Where's the young boy—Jay, is that his name?"

"Jay-Jay. He's asleep in the back seat. He's been through so much."

"His father died, didn't he?"

"Less than a week after he watched his father murder his mother."

Angelina drew back. "Oh, dear God."

"Let's get him inside. Then we can talk." I walked back to the Cruiser and cradled Jay-Jay in my arms from the back seat, up the front step, and into the house. I put him down on the couch and Angelina covered him with a blanket.

"I made another bed on the floor with the cushions." She pointed across the room.

"My bed." I stretched.

"Sure your back can stand it? I could sleep there."

"A night or two won't kill me."

Angelina bent down and checked Jay-Jay. "Oh. He looks Native. You never told me that."

"On his mother's side. One of the reasons I brought him here. I know he'll get better care on the pueblo."

"You're learning."

I tapped a finger against my chest. "Your old man has learned more than a thing or two this past week." I looked around the cozy living room and got reacquainted with her home. "You're doing quite well here, aren't you? I'm so proud."

She looked at me with sudden concern. "What's wrong with your arm? Are you hurt?"

"I'm afraid it's nerves. Can you put on some coffee? I won't be able to sleep…there's so much to tell you."

"Of course. Is there anything in the car you need to bring in?"

I laughed. "Do dirty clothes count?"

"I'll take the day off and do laundry in the morning. You can sleep all day, if you want to." She filled a kettle with water and set it on the stove, then added a couple of spoons of fresh coffee to a French Press. "Hungry? I have some fry bread."

"Why not? Payoqona, I heard you make the best fry bread in the world."

"We all do."

By the time the first rays of sun filtered through the front window, I'd told Angelina the entire saga. How Onion and I botched Jay-Jay's ransom and found ourselves pitted against a multi-national human trafficking ring. I told her about Phil, Alto, Naomi, and Miles Gray Eagle. I left out that I'd caused the deaths of nine men in the past thirty-six hours.

She reached across the kitchen table and clasped my free hand. "What happens now, Dad?"

What I had to say hurt deeply even before I found the words. "I have to go away for a while."

Angelina looked down at the checked tablecloth. Then she reached for a napkin and dabbed her eyes. She remained buried until I eased the napkin away from her face.

"I'm so sorry, honey. It won't be forever. I'll find some way to stay in touch. But the FBI wants to make sure I'm safe. To testify. I'll keep in touch through Sam Archuleta."

She spoke through her tears. "You could hide here. Who would know?"

"I can't do that. It would place you and Matty in danger."

She leaned against the back of her chair. "Why do you do these things? Why are you always sticking your neck out? It's a wonder someone hasn't killed you already."

"I ask myself those questions every day."

Her voice rose. "I don't want to lose you *again*. I want Matty to have a grandfather."

"Shhh." I put a finger to my lips. "Don't wake the boys. I don't have any choice in this. I promise you, I will stay in touch…until I get my life back."

"I don't want Matty to know. Tell him you're going away on business or something."

I squeezed her hand. "I will."

Angelina allowed Matty to stay home from school the next day. He and Jay-Jay circled one another like wary cats. Their first bonding experience was splitting the leftover pizza for breakfast. Later, while washing the dishes, I noticed the two boys playing catch outside. I'd made the right decision.

Angelina saw them, too. "Do you think I should take him in with us? We do have a tribal foster care program."

"As a single mom, could you handle two of them?"

"You know, Dad, sometimes I forget how old-fashioned you are."

Ouch. "If you decide that's what you want to do, you have my support, of course. But I think you might want to go slow. See how Jay-Jay adapts to pueblo life. See if Matty adjusts well to having another boy in his house. Those are two boys who've seen a lifetime of trouble already."

"*You're* telling *me* to take it slow?" She hugged me and stroked my cheek. "You look so tired. How about I take the boys out somewhere and let you get some sleep?"

A loud knocking on the front door woke me. The living room clock said it was quarter-to-two. I rolled off the cushions and hoisted myself to my feet. "Just a minute." A few more grunts propelled me toward the noise.

"It's us, Grandpa! Guess what?"

I opened the door, shading my eyes from the brilliant sunshine. "What?"

"Mom bought Jay-Jay a baseball glove. We can play catch anytime we want."

"What a mom."

The two boys scooted past me into the room. Angelina moved more slowly. She had grocery bags in both arms. I lifted one and closed the door behind us.

"Glass of milk before you go out to play." Angelina laid down her groceries and took a couple of glasses from the kitchen cupboard.

Matty bounced into the room. "Cookies?"

"No cookies. You'll spoil your appetite. I'm doing one of Grandpa's favorite Native dishes tonight."

Oh-oh, I thought to myself. "Jay-Jay, let me see that glove."

He still had trouble looking at me directly. He stopped a couple of feet away and handed the glove to me with his outstretched arm.

I pounded my fist into the leather. "Nice. Good pocket." I returned his glove.

"Come on, Jay-Jay." Matty put his empty glass of milk in the sink and raced to the back door. His glove and ball lay on the floor just inside. He scooped them up and was out the door before I could say, "Have fun."

Jay-Jay's glass remained half full. "That's all I want." He held the glass out to Angelina.

"I'll put it in the refrigerator. You can finish it with dinner." The back door closed behind him. Angelina and I were alone again.

"So…what is this favorite meal of mine you're cooking?"

"Juniper lamb and chile stew."

She was right. "Excellent."

"And—" Her eyes twinkled. "Something special for dessert. Easter pudding. I made extra on St. Joseph's feast and froze it."

I smiled inwardly. When we'd buried her mother three months before, Angelina had insisted on a traditional-only ceremony. Nothing Catholic. Maybe she'd loosened up a bit since then. "Sounds good. What's in it?"

"You'll be amazed."

"I'm sure I will."

Dinner was the best meal I'd had in weeks. When the Easter pudding was gone, I turned to Matty. "We need to talk, okay?"

He gave his mother a quick glance and stared down at his plate, like he knew what was coming. "Can Jay-Jay be with us?"

"Nope. Just you and me. Man-to-man. Let's go outside." I looked at a quizzical Jay-Jay. "Maybe you could help Matty's mom with the dishes?"

He stood up and brought his plate and glass to the kitchen.

"Let's go, Matty." I pointed to the door.

"Do I *hafta*?"

"You *hafta*."

The warmth of the day lingered. I walked over to my Cruiser and opened the driver's side door. "Get in and slide over."

Matty pressed himself against the passenger door, staring out the window.

"Your mother asked me to speak to you. You know what this is about, don't you?"

"Yeah. I know."

I spoke in a slow, gentle voice. "Why did you go away like that? Without asking your mom for permission?"

"The other guys—"

"Don't tell me about the other guys, Matty. You're old enough to make your own choices, aren't you?"

"But they wanted us to go on an adventure. They said no sissies allowed. If I had to tell Mom, they wouldn't let me go with them."

"I see…how old are these other guys?"

"Chino is twelve. Ronnie and Hawk are eleven."

I had the picture now. "Must have been tough."

He didn't say anything. His tears said it all.

"Hey, no need for that." I looked out the window at a darkening sky. A large bird swooped down into a nearby cottonwood. "You know, I ran away once. I was just about your age too."

He sniffled at me. "What happened?"

"I came back home after a couple of hours."

"Why?"

I let out a quiet chuckle. "It was dinnertime and I was hungry."

Matty burst into laughter.

"Yeah, I know. Pretty stupid, eh?" I gave him a light shoulder punch. I paused and took a deep breath. "One thing about it wasn't so funny."

His nose wrinkled up. "What?"

"I made my mother cry." I gave the words enough time to work. "You see, I didn't realize how my running away would frighten her. She loved me. Sometimes she kind of smothered me, you know?"

He nodded.

"But she wanted the best for me, even when I didn't realize it… Matty, please don't ever do it again."

"I promise."

"Tell me something. Where were you and your pals going?"

"To Mount Taylor. It's a sacred mountain. We were on an adventure."

"A spirit of adventure is a good thing to have. But next time, ask your mom, okay? And maybe someday you and I will climb that mountain together."

A warm smile covered his face. I tousled his hair. We went back inside and watched some TV show I'd never seen before.

Next morning, the four of us sat around the kitchen table. Both boys had their gloves next to their plates.

Angelina would be taking Jay-Jay to Laguna Social Services on her way to work. Matty would be taking the bus to school. I would be leaving, not sure when or if I'd ever return.

I looked at Angelina and held up a finger. "Matty. Jay-Jay. There's something I have to tell you both…I have to go away for a while."

Matty looked up from his cereal. "Why? Why can't you stay longer?"

"I'd like to. But I have some business that's going to keep me away for some time."

"What kind of business, Grandpa?"

Angelina wasn't going to be any help on this, her face told me as much. I cleared my throat. "Um, let's just say it's secret business. Kind of government business."

Jay-Jay's face lit up at last. "Are you a spy?"

"No, not a spy. I'm going to help put some criminals away. So they can't do bad things ever again."

Matty turned to his new friend. "He does this kind of stuff all the time. It's totally cool." His gaze turned to his mother. "Can we go out and play catch before the bus comes?"

"Do you have your books and lunch together?"

"In my bag."

"Okay. Just stay out of the street."

The two boys ran out the front door. They didn't understand. Angelina remained at the table. She understood too well.

CHAPTER FIFTY-ONE

"Refill?" I pointed to Sam's empty glass.

"Sure."

I creaked up from my desk and walked to the small refrigerator in the corner of my library. Lifting out a couple of ginger ales, I returned to my seat, popped the cans open, and slid one over to Sam.

Walter Carlson of the FBI sat across from me. At my insistence, Erskine Pelfrey III, my lawyer, sat to my right. Since my coming to Albuquerque, Erskine had proven himself to be competent, trustworthy, and even courageous. Not many men wear seersucker in November.

For the next half hour, we covered all the necessary steps for my "temporary disappearance" under the Witness Security Program. Paul Angel had explicitly threatened my life in the presence of FBI operatives. And even if he died, the man was still connected to an international cartel I'd crossed. Carlson and Sam did their jobs, convincing me that—left on my own—I would be in mortal danger.

To tell you the truth, I needed a break. The past two years had cost me, body and soul. But I wanted any disappearance or relocation to be on my terms, and now, as the Bureau's main witness against Angel and his operations, I had some leverage.

Carlson assured me Treasury Department personnel would oversee the sale of my house and the Land Cruiser. My Hudson would go into storage and C.J. would hold the keys. The Feds would move my possessions to a new out-of-state residence—details to follow—and I'd be given a new identity with all the trimmings: passport, social security number, bank account, driver's license, telephone, and a contact person through whom I would communicate with the Bureau. I asked Sam if he would be that person. He agreed. Carlson said they'd take care of transferring my teacher's retirement account to my new identity. If I chose, I could cash it out and manage the money on my own, free of Dumbarton College. I agreed.

I requested the Feds' approval to maintain communication with Pelfrey, keeping him on retainer as my legal representative. Carlson choked on this. I threatened to pull out of the deal. He caved.

"How much time do I have before I disappear?"

Carlson drummed his fingers on the top of my desk. "We're talking hours, maybe a couple of days, tops."

"I'm not asking that. Pelfrey can handle all that for me. How long does Gabe McKenna have?"

Carlson rested his elbows on my desk and pointed a finger at me. "You're in danger right now. We have to assume Angel's bosses know what happened. They'll also know his preliminary hearing is less than a month away. They could be planning to get to you right now. Can you be ready tomorrow?"

"No."

Carlson leaned back and looked across at Sam. He crossed his arms.

"I need at least forty-eight hours. I have to see that Phil's ashes—"

"We can handle it."

"You promised me I could do it. And I made a promise to Phil."

"McKenna, you are one hard ass."

"I thought we had a deal."

He let out a sigh. "I'll have Friganza's death and cremation certificates sent here tomorrow morning from Vital Check. And the DD Form 214. You'll also have your designation as Person Authorized to Direct Disposition. We'll pay for everything. Satisfied?"

"Yes. Then I'll accompany his ashes to the burial and return here the following day."

Carlson exploded from his chair. "What?"

"I like to see things through to their end." I looked at Sam and pointed at Carlson. "Can't you do something about him?"

"Forty-eight hours. Not a second more. Let's go, Archuleta." Without a handshake, Carlson turned and stormed out my front door. Sam rolled his eyes and tagged along.

"Well, Professor, you certainly pressed his buttons." Erskine forced a smile and offered to share it with me. I passed.

"Erskine, there are no more than a handful of people I still trust, and Carlson isn't one of them. Sure I can't get you a drink?"

"No thank you." He snapped his briefcase shut.

"Not so fast. I have one thing I need you to do."

"Certainly."

"Before I meet with Carlson forty-eight hours from now, I want you to gather my friends here. I need to say some good-byes. I don't know how long I'll be gone…and of course, there's the possibility this deal is going to end badly. Got your notebook?"

Pelfrey fumbled around in his oversized briefcase. "Right here."

"Take down these names—Rebecca Turner and her husband, APD Officer Darrell Jackson. Curtis Jester and his wife Charmaine. Sam Archuleta. And yourself, of course. You have their numbers already."

"That's it? What about that friend of yours from New York?"

"Deke Gagnon? He'll be halfway back to the Big Apple by then. I've already said good-bye to him, Angelina, and Matty."

"Very well."

I walked over and shook his hand. "Thanks, Erskine. You've been a great help to me on so many occasions."

He snapped his briefcase closed for good. I walked him to the door and turned out the front porch light.

I spent an hour on the *www.navy.mil* website, checking out all the details for burial at sea. I had to ship Phil's ashes Priority Mail Express Service to Honolulu, where they would embark from a designated naval vessel at Pearl Harbor and be buried somewhere at sea with a group of other veterans' remains.

The fine print told me no family members or friends could accompany the vessel. So, I'd have to stay in harbor. As Phil might have said, *horsefeathers* to that.

I'd hoped to scatter his ashes myself. Guess this would have to do, but it left me with a sadness I couldn't shake.

During the past week, through all its horrors, I hadn't had a single drink. Now, as I faced the end of this ordeal, I noticed myself reaching down and opening the bottom drawer of the library desk. No sense leaving a half-empty bottle behind.

I woke up, my head plastered to the desktop. Sunlight streamed through the library bay window and stung my eyes. My head weighed as much as my car. I tossed the empty whiskey bottle into the wastebasket.

The front bell rang. I lumbered out of the library and peeked through the tempered glass of the door. Fed-Ex. The materials Carlson promised.

"Good morning, sir." She was muscular, ruddy-cheeked, and too flat-out perky for the way I felt. "If you could sign at the bottom." She held some electronic device. I signed, and she was on her way with a smile intact.

I returned to the library desk, sat down, and tore open the package. A death certificate. A cremation certificate. A bureaucratic form I didn't want to read. Three pieces of paper to tell the world another hero's life had ended.

No booze left, black coffee would have to do. I set the drip machine on the desk by the mini-fridge and waited.

The coffee woke me up, mouth first, head to follow. I turned on cable, BBC World News. Why? Because some vestige of me is still high-brow, I guess. And there figured to be less of that incessant 24/7 U.S. political crap. I got lucky, or maybe Phil was pulling some strings.

A proper young lass with an attractive accent and no facial expression whatsoever brought me to the edge of my chair:

A bit of world history ends this week. The last naval vessel to serve in World War II will be decommissioned by the Philippine Navy. The former USS Slattery, *a destroyer escort that saw service in the Pacific and for the past seventy-one years has been a part of the Philippine fleet, will take its final cruise around Manila Bay. Renamed* The Lanceta *when it transferred to the Philippine Navy two years after the war, the Buckley-class ship was commissioned in 1943. It will be mothballed in Manila and turned into a World War II naval museum. The two surviving members of its original crew will be aboard when she makes her final voyage.*

I put my coffee cup down and checked the banking app on my cellphone. One phone call to the Naval Liaison Unit in Honolulu cancelled the shipment of Phil's remains to Pearl Harbor. A second call to Fed-Ex redirected his ashes to their shipping center in Manila. A final call to Flight Hub put me on a plane to the Philippines leaving from LAX that afternoon.

Manila's sun was bright, just like Albuquerque's, but it dripped water all over my shirt. I booked into a hotel at the airport, placed a call to Philippine Naval Headquarters on Roxas Boulevard, and asked a special favor. To my amazement, they agreed. When I called the local Fed-Ex, the woman who answered said "my package" would arrive by six the following morning. I went out and enjoyed some garlicky *adobo* with a side of chicken rice porridge. For the first time in a while, it felt good to be Gabe McKenna, if only for one final night.

The next morning, I cradled Phil inside his biodegradable box and caught a cab to the shipyard. At nine o'clock sharp, Phil and I disembarked on the final voyage of the final ship of the war he never got to fight. In the center of Manila Bay, the captain ordered the crew to stand at attention. The last two surviving sailors from the *USS Slattery* saluted when I scattered Phil Friganza's ashes on the water. Another part of the Greatest Generation floated away.

CHAPTER FIFTY-TWO

My connecting flight out of Los Angeles got me into Albuquerque at ten-thirty the following morning. I had time enough to shower, change, and get some of my things together before my friends arrived. Erskine's phone message said they'd be at my house by noon.

I'd changed my mind about the Hudson. As far as I knew, neither Angel nor any of his cartel members had ever seen me in it. I loved that car and decided to bring it with me, wherever I ended up. Whatever else I was taking could be packed in a few hours. The rest I'd leave for Carlson and his crew.

C.J. and Charmaine arrived first. They looked subdued, like they suspected something was up, but I kept to small talk until the rest of the gang arrived.

"Let's go into the library. This won't take long."

Rebecca Turner sat at the desk she'd used as my secretary. I helped Charmaine into my leather chair behind my big desk. Sam, Erskine, and Rebecca's husband Darrell took the other seats. I remained standing.

I slipped my hands into my pockets, to steady myself and conceal the slight tremor still afflicting my right arm. Trying my best to smile, I took a long, appreciative look around the room at each of my friends.

"You must be wondering why I asked you to come here. Well, for the past week, Onion and I have been fighting to destroy a human trafficking ring here in New Mexico. We didn't start out to do that—

Sam, C.J., you remember the call I got during our poker game last week? Anyway…one thing led to another and we found ourselves pitted against some hardened killers."

Rebecca put a hand to her mouth. "*Another* cartel?"

"Same one, I think. You'll be glad to know we stopped them. You won't hear anything about it on the news. The Feds are hushing it up. We freed a couple dozen young people, but at a cost. Onion took two bullets and is now on his way back to New York. He'll be okay, but I'm a marked man…with a hit out on me." I stopped, unable to go on.

Sam picked up the ball. "The Feds and I have convinced Gabe he needs to disappear for a while. He's going to testify against the cartel and will need protection."

"Witness protection?" C.J. shook his head. "Shit."

I took a deep breath and cleared my throat. "It's not easy for me to go into hiding. Against my nature. But I have Angelina to think about. Matty. And you, my friends. So, I'll be away for a bit."

C.J. rested a hand on his wife's shoulder. "How long?"

"I don't know. It depends on a lot of things out of my control—the pace of the legal proceedings, the Bureau's success in rounding up more of the cartel, their evaluation of my safety…"

Sam bailed me out again. "If you need to reach Gabe, for any reason, you're to get in touch with me. I'm his official contact until further notice. You all have my cell number. Any questions?"

"What about *this* place?" Rebecca's hand swept the room. "The house, your cars, the furniture, all that?"

"The Bureau has a team that takes care of everything. If there's something here you'd like to have, let me know before you leave."

Darrell Jackson raised his hand. "Is there anything APD can do for you?"

"Check with Sam on that." I looked over at Archuleta.

He shrugged. "I'll let you know."

My cat wandered into the room and hopped up on the windowsill. Rebecca walked over and cradled him. "What about Otis?"

I nodded like I expected the question from her. "I was hoping you might be able to take care of him. You knew him before I did, after all."

"Of course." She stroked his back and pulled him up to her cheek.

"Like I said, this isn't easy for me. I'm going to miss you all. But I *will* be back. And we *will* get into trouble all over again." A moment of quiet, uncomfortable laughter followed.

I walked around the room, embracing each of my friends. We emptied the last few ginger ales from the library refrigerator. Sam smoked a couple of cigarettes. C.J. told me his Cadillac hearse had been giving him trouble, so I handed him the keys and title to my Land Cruiser. Rebecca asked to take home her desk and all its memories. I offered Erskine Pelfrey his choice of my clothes, but he declined.

That night at dinner, a double order of baby back ribs arrived from C.J.'s restaurant.

CHAPTER FIFTY-THREE

One month later.

My name is Harold Rasmussen. I live in a modest, one-story home in Cochise, Arizona, a community of fifteen-hundred people set forty miles west of the New Mexico-Arizona state line. I'm a retired life insurance salesman from White Plains, New York; widowed, no kids. At least, that's what they tell me.

When I moved here, my old furniture was included in the listing of my North Valley home. The Feds said I wouldn't need it anymore. Said they'd provide a fully furnished place for me. So now I'm stuck with Danish Modern, a taste in décor I've yet to acquire. But I still have my beloved books and a couple of boxes left to me by my Great Aunt Nellie. Some old papers in one of them belonged to my ancestor James A. McKenna. Maybe someday I'll sift through those crates and see what's in there.

Nowadays though, I'm too weary, reluctant to even go outside. It's too hot, everything too uncertain. During the past month, I've driven to the grocery store twice and the liquor store three times. I'm limiting myself to one drink per night. Okay, maybe the glasses *have* gotten bigger each week. I'm much better now at fooling people, including myself.

Each day begins around nine. I exercise. Shower. Eat a bowl of cereal. Turner Classic Movies distract me until lunchtime. I try to read in the early afternoon—often online, mostly early Southwestern history, my first love. I take a nap before dinner. My evenings consist of more old movies. I'll watch baseball when the new season begins next April.

I have a whole lot of time on my hands and little to do, except think. I've done a lot of that. In the two years since I left New York and moved to Albuquerque, I've witnessed more than two dozen killings, ten of them by my own hand. I now realize when you get involved with evil, you run a risk of becoming infected. Evil claims a part of you and you can't wash it off. Every day I wonder: *What have I become?*

I left New York to escape the pain of life without my late, beloved wife Holly. I fell in love with Nai'ya Alonso-Riley, then lost her to a fatal car crash. I became father to her daughter Angelina and a grandfather to Matty. Now, they're no longer in my life as well. I got back in touch with some old friends and made some new ones, now they're all absent friends.

I'm not complaining, it's just…what the hell, of course I am. I'm a man without a past and no discernible future. Life in the Witness Security Program doesn't have much to recommend it. Except it beats being dead.

The phone in my kitchen rang for the first time since I'd moved in. It was seven o'clock. I took my dinner dish to the sink and answered the call.

Sam Archuleta told me my house had sold. The equity would be transferred to my new bank within a day.

"How you doing, Gabe?"

"I'm alive."

There was a pause. "Sorry for the delay in Angel's trial. Expensive lawyers have a knack for drawing out prosecutions."

"When do I testify?"

"Soon."

"Right."

"Any messages for family and friends?"

"Call Angelina. Tell her I'm well. Give my love to her and Matty. Call C.J. and thank him again for that barbecue. Call Rebecca and make sure Otis is okay. Call Onion in New York. Make sure he's recovered from his wounds. Call Erskine Pelfrey and tell him to buy some winter clothes."

"I'm gonna run out of quarters."

"I'm going out of my mind, Sam."

"I hear you. I'll call Christmas Day."

"Thanks. By the way, how are things in Gallup these days?"

"Better. Twenty-three deaths all told. But they've cleaned things up and are returning to normal at last."

"Guess Onion and I did the right thing after all. Bye."

"Take care, Gabe."

I leaned against the back of my recliner. The sun said its daily good-bye on the other side of the drawn curtains. The room darkened, like a theater when the house lights go down. My left hand held the whiskey, my right hand cradled the remote. TCM came on with *Dark Passage*. Okay. I'd spend a couple of hours with Bogie and Bacall, getting even farther away from it all.

The doorbell rang.

I swallowed hard, then emptied my glass and set it on the table next to my chair. Another ring and then a gentle knock. I stood, inched my way to the door, gripped the knob, and turned it.

Her hair was different now, gentle silver waves that kissed both shoulders. Her eyes were the same, her smile as hard to believe as ever. Her name used to be Simone St. Cyr. I wondered what it was tonight.

"Hello, Gabe. May I come in?"

She purred past me with all her curves. Curves that grabbed my eyeballs and promised me a better world.

I'm not sure how she found me. I'm not sure why I let her in. I was sure of only one thing then—I would hate myself in the morning.

AUTHOR NOTE

Midnight Blues is fiction. The problem of human trafficking is, unfortunately, tragically real. If you wish to know more about this scourge, or if you would like to know what you can do to help, here is a list of sources for additional information and a list of agencies engaged in combating the problem:

National Indigenous Women's Resource Center
515 Lame Deer Avenue
P.O. Box 99
Lame Deer, Montana 59043
USA

New Mexico Organized Against Human Trafficking (NM-OATH)
2117 Sudderth Drive #1
Ruidoso, New Mexico 88345
USA

Freedom House
P.O. Box 52044
Albuquerque, New Mexico 87181
USA

National Human Trafficking Hotline
1 (888) 373-7888

National Human Trafficking Resource Center
SMS: 233733 (Text "HELP" or "INFO")
Hours: 24 hours, 7 days a week
Languages: English, Spanish and 200 more languages
Website: traffickingresourcecenter.org

A portion of profits from *Midnight Blues* will be donated to the cause of eradicating human trafficking in the United States.

ABOUT THE AUTHOR

Robert D. Kidera's debut novel, "Red Gold," received the Tony Hillerman Award for Best Fiction of 2015, and won Best Mystery of 2015, and Best eBook at the New Mexico/Arizona Book Awards.

"Red Gold" is the first novel in the *Gabe McKenna Mystery* series from Suspense Publishing. Its sequel, "Get Lost," won Best Mystery and Best eBook in the 2016 New Mexico/Arizona Book Awards competition. The third Gabe McKenna novel, "Cut.Print.Kill." debuted in September of 2017 and has been nominated for Best Mystery and Best eBook of 2018. "Midnight Blues" is the fourth Gabe McKenna novel.

The *Gabe McKenna Mysteries* are available as audiobooks from Audible, Inc.

After an early fling in the motion picture industry and a long and successful career in academia, Mr. Kidera retired in 2010. With his desire to play major league baseball no longer a realistic dream, he chose to fulfill his other lifelong ambition and became an author. He is a member of SouthWest Writers, Sisters in Crime, Rocky Mountain Fiction Writers, Western Writers of America, and the International Thriller Writers organizations. The author lives in Albuquerque, New Mexico with his wife Annette and Woody the cats. He has two daughters, a grandson, and granddaughter.

Mr. Kidera loves hearing from his readers and keeping them informed of his upcoming books. You can reach him at the following web locations:

Author web site: www.robertkiderabooks.com

Facebook page: https://www.facebook.com/bob.kidera.3

Amazon author page: https://www.amazon.com/Robert-D-Kidera/e/B00IP23642 (reader reviews most welcome)

Twitter page: https://twitter.com/RKidera

"RED GOLD"

A GABE MCKENNA MYSTERY (BOOK 1)

"Author Robert D. Kidera owes me big time. His debut novel in the promised *McKenna Mystery* series, 'Red Gold,' kept me up all night. Who can resist a good old-fashioned treasure hunt? 'Red Gold' is a thriller packed with deceit and danger but also compassion. McKenna is a damaged hero, but also one to root for."

—Vincent Zandri, *New York Times* and *USA Today* Bestselling Author of "Everything Burns," "The Remains," and "The Shroud Key"

"If you're going through hell, keep going…"

Shaken by the death of his beloved wife and wrestling with powerful personal demons, Professor Gabriel McKenna leaves New York City for New Mexico to claim an inheritance from mysterious distant relatives. He finds something other than a Land of Enchantment.

Unseen enemies threaten his life. Old friends turn up and rally to his side. Together they plunge into a lethal struggle for a 19th Century treasure, the fabled Lost Adams gold. McKenna enters a world of violence, passion, sexual abuse, deceit, and death that cause him to question his core beliefs and values, and even his sense of self.

Desperate to find a way home, McKenna must first unearth the secret of an old family manuscript and risk his life against overpowering odds. He must rekindle his long-dead fighting spirit and discover new reasons to live and love.

http://a.co/exYvyyo

"GET LOST"

A GABE MCKENNA MYSTERY (BOOK 2)

"Robert Kidera is an absolute master of mystery! He grabs you with irresistible intrigue and fresh, seductive writing and refuses to let go while he pummels you with twist after delicious twist. I highly recommend this book and this writer!"

—*New York Times* Bestselling Author **Darynda Jones**

What do you do when the dead come back and your loved ones disappear?

All Gabe McKenna wanted was a new floor for his barn. What he got was seven corpses, all long dead. Seven rich men, missing from New York.

One of his closest childhood friends is gunned down in an Albuquerque casino. After escaping two attempts on his own life and with time running out, McKenna must uncover the connection and prevent his loved ones from joining the growing ranks of the dead.

From New Mexico to New York to a lonely cliff once home to an ancient people, McKenna struggles against a bloodthirsty criminal enterprise for whom money matters more than any man's life.

http://a.co/fATFENX

"CUT.PRINT.KILL."

A GABE MCKENNA MYSTERY (BOOK 3)

"Robert Kidera is a rising star in the mystery genre. His latest offering, 'Cut.Print.Kill,' is an epic story propelled by a dynamic cast of characters and a roller coaster ride of action and tension. Don't miss this third book in Kidera's *Gabe McKenna* series."
—**Joseph Badal**, Tony Hillerman Award-Winner and Amazon #1 Best-Selling Author

There's always room for one more lie…

Reeling from family betrayal and tragedy, Gabe McKenna charts a new course as historical consultant on a motion picture filming in New Mexico. Before you can say "Action!", he is entangled in a web of illusion and deceit, where death plays a starring role. With the help of The Onion, a private investigator and long-time friend from New York, Gabe peels away layer after layer of dishonesty, battles brutal drug cartels, is accused of murder, and must unmask a mysterious, seductive woman to reveal the truth in a world full of lies.

http://a.co/d/i16JDgk

Made in the USA
San Bernardino, CA
27 September 2018